THE TRAILER PARK RULES

A novel

Michelle Teheux

The characters and events portrayed in this book are fictitious. Any similarity to real persons, living or dead, is coincidental and not intended by the author.

ISBN: 9798320045184

Library of Congress Control Number: 2018675309
Printed in the United States of America

To my husband, Harrie.

No writer ever had a more supportive spouse!

I love you.

All wealthy families are alike; each poor family is poor in its own way.

LEO TOLSTOY, IF HE HAD WRITTEN ABOUT A TRAILER PARK

Posted on a bulletin board in the trailer park rental office:

The Loire Mobile Home Park Rules

Welcome to the Loire Mobile Home Park, the premier mobile home park in Loire, IL since 1957! We are proud to offer 75 quality mobile homes in a country setting, each with full sewer, water, garbage and cable (billed separately).

Rent is due on the first of each month. ***NO EXCEPTIONS WILL BE MADE.*** *Late payments or returned checks will be charged a $50 late fee and you* ***MAY BE SUBJECT TO EVICTION.***

For your convenience, a coin-operated laundry room is available directly south of the rental office. ***NO SMOKING IN THE LAUNDRY ROOM!***

Keep your lot neatly mowed AT ALL TIMES. If you do not mow your lot, we will mow it for you and a $50 landscaping fee will be charged. Any flower beds etc. must be kept neat and free of weeds or a $50 landscaping fee will be charged.

NO CLOTHESLINES ARE PERMITTED. TOYS MAY NOT BE LEFT OUTDOORS. *Wading pools* ***MUST BE EMPTIED DAILY*** *as they are a mosquito hazard. Repeated failures to keep your lot neat* ***MAY LEAD TO EVICTION.***

NO PETS *are allowed in this community. This includes pets you're "just watching" for a friend.* ***NO EXCEPTIONS WILL BE MADE.*** *If you are caught harboring an animal of any kind, you will be charged a $50 fee and you* ***MAY BE SUBJECT TO EVICTION.***

Please be courteous to your neighbors and maintain quiet ***AT ALL TIMES.*** *Loud parties and music etc.* ***MAY RESULT IN EVICTION.***

MANAGEMENT RESERVES THE RIGHT TO IMPOSE NEW RULES AS NEEDED AT ANY TIME.

The Loire Mobile Home Park is a friendly place to live. WELCOME!

Charles Darby
Owner, Darby Properties

CHAPTER 1

Jonesy

The bowling alley had been on fire for some time before anybody noticed, and flames were shooting through the curved roof when Jonesy got there. That would be considered a bad thing by everyone in town except Jonesy: Nothing photographed like a good fire.

A lot of times, he'd get there after firefighters had already beaten back the flames. Especially if the fire broke out late at night, there was every chance he'd arrive too late to capture great photos.

Not this time. He pulled out his camera as the flames brightened his face.

He'd covered the Loire City Council meeting earlier that evening. After he finished writing the story, he stayed late to meet the quotas that wasted hours of his life every week. He always put off doing the required videos, photo galleries and social media posts as long as he could, but he knew the regional editor would have his ass if he didn't post them tonight. The paper had already had a round of layoffs six months ago. If he wanted to delay his own eventual layoff, he understood, he had to meet the quotas.

The paper's website was glitchy as hell and it took him several tries to get his videos — a boring snippet from the council meeting, an even more boring bit from a Loire Chamber of Commerce ribbon-cutting ceremony — properly edited and posted. But he finally got everything done while eating his dinner, a bag of chips and some beef jerky from the vending machine.

Exhausted and looking forward to a drink and a smoke and some sleep, he shut down his computer. He was getting too old to work these kinds of hours, running on junk food, spite toward the system and a fast-fading belief in journalism as his calling.

But driving home, he had to pull over to let two fire engines pass. Part of him toyed with the idea of pretending he hadn't seen them and just driving home — he had already put in a long day, much of which would be unpaid. Chances were good the fire would be much ado about nothing anyway.

But he was old school, so he'd turned around and followed the fire trucks to the scene of the fire. Just in case. With any luck, it would be nothing and he could go to bed. Instead, he saw the flames from a block away.

Instantly, excitement replaced his exhaustion

and disillusionment. He started shooting while the fire crew was still setting up the scene.

"Jonesy." The fire chief nodded at him as he walked by.

"Hey, Chief. Fancy meeting you here." They'd just seen each other at the council meeting a few hours ago. Jonesy would talk to him more later.

Jonesy knew how to stay out of the crew's way while getting his pictures, and they all recognized and ignored him. They did their job and he did his. They hurried to extinguish the flames while Jonesy hurried to preserve them, if only digitally.

The newspaper owned an old digital camera Jonesy carried everywhere but his own cheap phone actually took better pictures. The only reason Jonesy used the paper's obsolete camera at all was to conserve his personal data plan, which he routinely exceeded and for which the paper refused to reimburse him.

As soon as he knew he had his bread and butter fire shots — flames shooting through the roof, firefighter silhouettes seen against the brightness of the flames, a closeup of a firefighter aiming a spray of water, a shot of the department's most expensive aerial truck streaming water from above — he stopped shooting long enough to post a few pictures to the paper's social media.

Next, he texted one to his editor, just to give him a heads up, although the bastard was probably sound asleep at this hour. Jonesy hoped the text woke him up.

The paper had finished printing hours ago, so it was far too late to make the morning edition. When Jonesy was younger, that would have meant he could get what he needed and go to bed, with plenty of time to craft a story in the morning.

Not now. The paper's website was a hungry beast that demanded to be fed 24/7. He got his pictures and then shot several videos. Fire videos always got lots of clicks, and that was all upper management cared about anymore.

If clicks actually brought in any revenue, it's not like any of it trickled down to the reporters. Although, now that he thought about it, the reporters did get a $25 bonus for Christmas last year. His bonus came to something like $19 and change after taxes.

Finally, images secured, he used his phone to look up the county property tax records to learn the property's assessed valuation and owner. Charles Darby. Jonesy vaguely knew him as a local slumlord. Only then did he ask the fire chief a few questions.

"Have a cause yet?"

"Too early to tell. We'll see what the fire marshal finds in the morning," the chief said. "It's a total loss, but I'm pretty sure you can see that." He swept his arm dismissively at the ruined bowling alley.

"Maybe you can add this into the story about the need for a budget increase. This makes my point, right? Check it out. It's like the city manager doesn't value the guys who are out here looking after the city while he's sleeping. You can't expect people to bust their asses all night for nothing, right?"

Jonesy didn't bother telling the chief that was exactly what he himself was doing.

At the city council meeting both men had attended a few hours ago, the chief had requested more funding for equipment and salaries, money the city manager maintained could not be found. The firefighters received a cost of living increase every year, but the chief thought they deserved more.

Jonesy agreed with him. He could see fighting a big fire like this was a strain on the department and he had plenty of sympathy for anybody who regularly lost sleep doing his job. There was always money in the city budget for the city manager's annual raise even when there wasn't much there for anything else, he'd noticed.

Similarly, the CEO of the company he worked for pulled down millions even as many of the newsroom employees depended on things like their parents, a better-paid spouse, food stamps, or, in one case Jonesy knew of, a dominatrix side hustle to make it.

That was the way of it everywhere, wasn't it? But he kept his opinions out of his stories.

Anyway, that story was done and now he needed quotes for this one.

"How does the size of this fire compare to others this year?" He knew this was the biggest fire in Loire for at least a couple of years, but he wanted to hear the chief say it.

"Pretty big," the chief said. Jonesy sometimes wondered if he went out of his way to be as unquotable as possible.

The department had called in everything it had for this one; it obviously was the biggest fire they'd had all year, by far, so would it have killed the chief to just say that? Jonesy had the uncomfortable feeling that the chief had already read his city council story online and was irritated that Jonesy hadn't championed his effort to increase the fire department's budget.

Jonesy asked more questions, waiting for the chief to say something memorable he might be able to jazz things up with. The chief was done talking tonight though, so Jonesy scanned the scene, looking for someone else to interview. But there were few gawkers this time of night, and Darby wasn't present, so he gave it up. That could wait for the next day's follow-up.

He was writing the story in his head as he drove back to the office, let himself in and booted his computer back up. It only took him a few minutes to write the story. It was brief; he'd flesh it out in the morning, when he might have more information about the damage estimate and cause. Or maybe he'd track down some sad bowlers who'd talk about all the good times they'd had there.

Fire strikes Loire Lanes was the hed. Jonesy liked puns and he'd thought of this one as soon as he'd pulled up to the scene. "By Gilbert Jones" was the byline. He used his actual name for his byline and for signing legal documents, but never for anything else.

"A major Loire landmark was not spared by a fire that broke out around 1 a.m. Tuesday morning" was his lede. He prided himself in using the old newspaper lingo, although the younger reporters tended to say "headline" and "lead." You could always tell who was and who wasn't in any club by whether they knew their slang.

Jonesy had taken a year of conversational French in college, so during his interview he'd pronounced "Loire" properly, as little more than a soft breath of vowels. The French love to lard their words with unused letters they never bother to pronounce.

But the editor interviewing him had corrected him immediately. "We pronounce it 'Lori' here, like the name," he'd said.

Jonesy never got over feeling conflicted about that, and when he met an outsider, he'd say he worked in Loire, pronouncing it correctly, and then explaining the pronunciation the locals used.

After posting his story, three videos and about thirty photos to the paper's website, he shut down his computer again. Now he had way more videos and photo galleries than he was required to post each week, but if he hadn't been here posting the throw-away stuff, he never would have known about the fire in time to get the good shots.

He hated how important the online quotas were now — not to his editor, Carl, or to the readers, but to Dani, the chipper little twenty-something regional editor installed by the hedge fund that had bought the paper several years back.

It didn't matter if you were working on a stellar piece of investigative journalism that the wire services and TV stations would all pick up. It wouldn't have mattered if he'd just won a goddamned Pulitzer Prize — God forbid you not post the required shitty videos every week.

He'd seen the writing on the wall about newspapers a long time ago and had started applying first at business magazines and later for business organizations that needed copy churned out for their websites. But he learned fairly quickly that having years of experience as a reporter at small newspapers did not impress anybody except other newspaper reporters.

So he pressed on, doing what he knew how to do. Sometimes he thought about jumping ship and just tending bar or something. He knew some former journalists had gone on to make good money doing communications in the corporate world, but he had no idea how they'd done it. He had applied for all those jobs and had never gotten a nibble.

He knew far more ex-journalists who were delivering pizzas or working at nursing homes. Sooner or later, he knew, he'd be forced into doing the same. But for now, by working sometimes as many as sixty hours per week and posting tons of pointless content to social media, he was able to hang onto his job.

He was paid for exactly forty hours per week. The company was very strict about not allowing any overtime, but was equally strict about requiring at least six stories per week, four social media posts per day, three videos per week and three photo galleries per week. There was no way to get it all done in forty hours, and it was seldom that anybody in the newsroom worked less than fifty.

Complaints to Dani did not end well. "Use your time more wisely," she'd chirped. "Think about whether journalism is the right career for you."

How the hell had she gotten that job? She had no meaningful experience. She'd never worked as a reporter. Her degree was in human resources. How did a dozen seasoned editors end up answering to somebody like her?

"You're thinking like a dinosaur, Gilbert," Dani had said the last time Jonesy had offered some pushback. "You want to think like a digital native. Videos bring in the clicks. Have you been tracking your analytics? Compare the numbers for any one of Bob's football videos with that lame video of the city comptroller you posted last week. You need to do better."

"That video did a pretty damned good job of explaining why property taxes are going up this year. Did you watch it? The city hasn't properly funded its pension obligations for at least thirty years, and now that they have to catch up, ninety-five percent of all property taxes goes straight to police and fire pensions. There's literally nothing left to run the city, unless they increase taxes."

"I watched the first fifteen seconds. It was boring, Gilbert. Look at the analytics. Your videos are too long. Your last one got like thirty views. Bob's football videos are short and snappy and get thousands of views. You need to pick more interesting topics and you need to incorporate more B-roll. And for God's sake, add some punchy background music."

Jonesy had stopped arguing then, because it was pointless. His city council videos were never going to get the same number of views as Bob's sports videos, and he knew that even Dani understood that. She would eventually eliminate the city reporter position altogether. That used to be the meatiest beat in the newsroom. Now it was a target for the bean counters.

He took off his smeared glasses to rub his eyes, which were red and watering from both the smoke and his nineteen-hour day. He'd be paid for eight. The chief cared about his crew's working conditions and so did Jonesy's editor, but Dani and the hedge funders did not.

Then he raked his fingers through his graying brown hair, touching the spot on top where it felt noticeably thinner than it used to. It was nearly four in the morning now, and he'd have to be back at eight. Time to get some rest.

He kept the windows of his car up and blasted the air conditioning and his music until he rolled into the trailer park. Then he turned off the radio so he wouldn't disturb anybody, although his neighbor Darren, the guy in the first trailer on his street, was still up and playing old heavy metal that Jonesy could hear just fine through his car windows. Jonesy got along with everybody, and he and Darren shared a taste for vintage metal, but Jonesy had quickly learned Darren could drink him under the table. Darren didn't have to get up early to work, but Jonesy did, so most of their interactions now were limited to a passing wave.

Jonesy felt too wired to go right to bed when he got home. Instead, he sat on his front steps smoking a cigarette and drinking the last of his off-brand whiskey mixed with the last of a two-liter bottle of store-brand cola.

His refrigerator's ice maker had been broken

when he moved in a year ago and he had forgotten to make any ice, so when he added the room-temperature booze to the flat cola, the whole drink was warm.

Every sip tasted of disappointment. The unfulfilling drink was a perfect metaphor for his journalism career. This wasn't the satisfying culmination to his day he'd been looking forward to.

But the night's last cigarette was good, replacing the particular reek of a burning building's smoke with the more familiar tobacco stink. He would have to wash his clothes before he could wear them again, which was too bad because his work wardrobe was small and he hated spending time in the trailer park's damp, mildewy laundry room.

The cigarette was gone before the drink was, though he'd tried to get them to come out even. Darren's lights and music at last went off, just as the lights came on in his next-door neighbor's kitchen. Jonesy had considered himself the hardest-working guy in the trailer park, but Jimmy Jackson gave him a run for his money. Here it was — he glanced at his phone — four-thirty in the morning, and Jimmy was already heading to his factory job.

Jonesy always meant to get to know his neighbors better, especially Jimmy, who could work like a sonofabitch. But as with Darren, his interactions with Jimmy seemed to be limited to friendly waves. At least one of them always seemed to be on his way to work.

"Good morning," Jimmy said, waving as he walked to his car.

"Good night," Jonesy called back. And then he went back inside and put his dirty glass in the sink. He headed down the hallway to his bedroom but then turned back. If he didn't make the damned ice now, he wouldn't have any tomorrow.

He filled both plastic ice cube trays with water and carefully returned them to the freezer. Then he stripped off his smoky clothes and showered before going to bed, because if he didn't, his sheets would smell like that until he got around to washing them. Anyway, it would mean he could skip showering in the morning. He was going to feel like death when his alarm went off at seven-thirty.

He briefly toyed with the temptation of emailing his editor to explain he would come in a couple hours late because he'd been at the fire, but he knew that would never fly.

Or, he could call in sick. He had plenty of sick days; he'd never used a single one. When he'd had the flu, he'd come in. When he'd had a bad toothache, he'd come in. When everybody in the whole newsroom had had the same crud last winter, they'd all come in.

Coming in sick was part of the newsroom culture, and he didn't have the stomach to be the one to deviate from it. If he didn't come in, everybody else would suffer for it, and nobody wanted to be that guy.

So he'd go to work on time, but he'd try to slip out after eight hours if possible and then go to bed just as soon as he got home.

His last thought before he went to sleep was how much he was looking forward to the following night's sleep.

CHAPTER 2

Kaitlin

Kaitlin wasn't a morning person, but she was in the shower every morning at six.

By seven, she was all done up, light brown curls cascading past her shoulders and mascara focusing attention on her wide-set green eyes.

She wasn't a naturally neat person, but there were never dirty dishes in the sink in the morning. The throw pillows on the davenport were placed just so. The bed was made but neatly turned back. She didn't have to be at the convenience store until much later. She'd told them when she took the job there that she couldn't work early mornings because she had to babysit for her cousin. This was a lie, but it had the desired effect and she was only scheduled for afternoons and evenings.

She had a whole story she rolled out whenever she needed to. Her cousin did have a kid, but Kaitlin had never been asked to take care of him.

Her cousin was stuck up and took the kid to a daycare center that charged $300 per week.

"I'll do it for $250," she'd offered. That had been a few years ago, before she had figured out how to make money. But Teri had said she wanted somebody licensed. As if anybody needed a license to change diapers.

She heard the car roll up and checked her appearance in the mirror over the sofa before Nathan let himself in with his key.

"Hey, honey," she said, and gave him a big smile. Nathan smiled back, already removing his shoes and placing them neatly at the edge of the mat. She pretended she was delighted to see him, wrapped her arms around his neck and kissed him.

Then she took his hand and led him to her bedroom, where she let the silky robe fall to the floor.

She and Nathan had this down to a science. He didn't want to be late for work, and she wanted to make sure he was happy when he left, so the foreplay was minimal and all about him. She didn't mind having sex with him, but she didn't especially enjoy it, either. Still, she knew better than to let him know that. They kissed when he arrived, but after that it was all business.

It's not that there was really anything wrong with Nathan. For a guy past 50, he didn't look half bad. He still had most of his hair and he was only a little overweight. But the guys she was actually attracted to were, like Kaitlin herself, less than half his age.

She usually gave him a brief blowjob right off the bat, and that generally got him most of the way there. Then he'd enter her and she'd moan and let out little cries of pleasure until he was done. When he wanted her on top, she sometimes actually did reach orgasm, but his favorite position was doggy-style, and that never got her off.

He didn't know the difference, though, and she wasn't about to tell him she found any part of this less than satisfying.

The way Kaitlin looked at it, she could get real satisfaction elsewhere if she really wanted to. But he paid her $800 cash every month to pretend to be satisfied, and that money more than covered her rent and utilities. And frankly, it was easier than watching a kid all day.

Sometimes, like when her phone screen cracked, or she had to pay her DUI lawyer, she'd ask if he could help her out, and he usually would. On those occasions, she didn't even take him into the bedroom. He would open his pants and sit on the sofa, and she'd kneel in front of him and finish him that way. That was the deal.

The $800 did not cover him coming in her mouth. That was extra.

He always left happy, usually in less than half an hour. He took a brief shower right before he left, using the same exact soap his wife bought for him at home, so no unfamiliar scents would give him away.

This was also why he forbade her to wear any perfume, ever, and why he also supplied her with his wife's favored laundry detergent and fabric softeners for the sheets and towels. Kaitlin thought that was pretty smart. He had thought of everything.

As to how he explained the half an hour of extra time, she never asked. His wife probably thought he went to work early, or maybe she thought he went to the gym, or maybe she didn't care.

And didn't his wife ever notice the missing $800? Didn't she ever ask him why they didn't have more money? If Kaitlin were a wife, she'd want to know where every penny of her husband's money went. She wouldn't tolerate it going to some other chick.

Nathan and Kaitlin had met at the strip club across the river where she had been dancing for a few years.

She'd been ready for a change. Everybody said dancers could make a lot of money and sometimes you could. Sometimes you couldn't. The first thing that surprised her was that the club didn't pay her a dime; *she* paid *them*. You had to pay the house fee of $50, more on the weekends, and you had to tip the DJ.

Sometimes she made a lot, but on some slow days she didn't even make enough to pay the house fee. And keeping the hair on her head perfectly highlighted and her hoo-ha waxed and her nails done? Buying the high heels and the tiny outfits?

All that added up. Being a dancer was expensive.

But one day Nathan came in, and the two of them had hit it off. He was a good tipper and treated her well.

Sapphire, who was in her 40s and had been doing this on and off for almost twenty-five years, clued her in.

"That's a man who is shopping for a sugar baby," Sapphire had told her. "Play your cards right and you'll be sitting pretty."

"How does that even work?" Kaitlin had asked.

"You'll have to have sex with him, but you'll only have one dude to pretend to like instead of a roomful of them. Besides, dancing don't pay like it used to. It's getting harder to make the big bucks if you won't give a few blowjobs in the VIP room."

Kaitlin had steadfastly refused to do that. Sapphire had no such qualms, and most of the girls would do it at least occasionally, especially if they had squandered their tips all month and had rent coming due.

"You make sure you get him to agree to the money you want before you have sex with him. Don't you do it even once until you get what you want. You still got all your bargaining power right now while he's horny. Get as much as you can. What kind of job does he have?"

"I don't know."

"Well, talk to him. Flirt with him. See what he does for a living. What does he spend his money on? Find out what kind of car he drives. See how much he can afford and if he's gonna take you on trips. I had one until a few years ago that used to take me to Jamaica every winter."

"Why didn't you keep seeing him?"

"Oh, he finally died. He was old. Couldn't hardly get it up anyways the last six months. But he still liked to try. This one is a lot younger and he's not that bad looking. This could be a good thing for you."

It was a slow Tuesday night when Kaitlin and Nathan made their deal. She had given two lap dances earlier in the evening. That was forty bucks in her little tip box, still not enough to pay her expenses for the night. It wasn't her turn to go on stage yet, and she was trying to look bright and approachable while feeling bored and irritated. Nothing was more exhausting.

When Nathan walked in, she knew her night was saved. He would probably pay for time in the VIP room, and he'd have real conversations with her in between dances. And other than the first night they'd met, he'd never pressed her for oral sex or anything else. Just dances and talking.

"Hey, it's my favorite guy," she said, truly happy to see him.

"And it's my favorite dancer," he answered back. "Ann?"

"Nope, not Ann. Karma." It was a thing they did. He would try to get her to tell him her real name.

"Barb."

"What am I, 50?"

He looked her up and down, slowly and thoroughly. "Not 50. Not even 20, am I right, Cathy?"

She had just turned 21, but knew better than to talk about her age. "Not Cathy. And how do I even know your real name is Nathan? Maybe that's just your club name."

He smiled. "Maybe my real name is Xavier. And maybe your real name is Donna."

"Not Donna. Guess again, Xavier."

"E is a hard one. Evelyn?"

Kaitlin had laughed. "Whoever heard of someone my age named Evelyn?"

"I have a new theory," Nathan said. "Your stage name is Karma. So I'm going to guess your real name also starts with a K. Kelly?"

"Ha, no." He put his hand on her bare knee and she looked at it and gave him an encouraging smile.

"Karen?"

"Nope. I'm going to charge you for guessing," she said, joking but maybe not joking.

He pulled some money from his wallet and formed it into a perfectly stacked rectangle on the table between them.

"Here's the game. Every time I guess, and I'm wrong, I take back the top bill. It's a single on the top, but look." He flipped over the stack. "There's a hundred-dollar bill on the bottom. Maybe there are a lot of them. Maybe there is only one. Who knows? But when I guess your name, you get to keep whatever's left of the stack. And once I know your name, we'll have a real discussion about giving you a monthly allowance so you don't have to work here anymore. You can just let me visit you every morning. How does that sound?

It sounded good. He guessed Kirsten, Kylie, Kimberly, Khloe and Kayla. He'd already taken back three ones, a twenty and a fifty. "Kate?"

"Um."

"It's Kate?"

"Almost."

The next bill showing was a hundred-dollar bill, and she had a feeling the rest of them were, too. She leaned against him, making sure he could feel her breasts pressing into him, and whispered breathily into his ear. "It's Kaitlin."

"Well, Kaitlin, the rest is yours." He handed the stack of money to her, and she slipped it into her tip box, noting that there were at least several hundred-dollar bills in the stack. She'd count them later.

"I would like to make an arrangement with you. I'd like to see you for about half an hour every day before work. Do you understand what I'm looking for?"

"I think so."

"How does $800 per month sound?"

That would pay for her rent and utilities and then some. She remembered Sapphire telling her not to take the first offer.

"Well, I mean, that won't cover everything."

"No, it won't. I'm not Elon Musk, Kaitlin. But I think you'll find you'll be happier if you have at least a part-time job in the afternoons. That way, nobody has any reason to suspect where your money is coming from. It can be your secret. It *needs* to be your secret. Just be available to me from around 7 to 7:30 in the morning. Every weekday morning. I'll be gone in time to get to work by 8, and the rest of the day is yours. What do you say?"

She knew Sapphire would tell her to ask for more, but what if she asked for more and he lost interest? There were lots of other girls in here who would jump at the chance.

"OK." He wasn't bad looking, and he was nice. If she was going to do this, she'd rather have it be someone like Nathan, not a gross old wrinkly man, even if the gross old man might pay more.

"You know I need you to be discreet, and I'll explain all the rules about that later. But there's just one more thing. You have to kiss me every time I see you."

That was a big no-no, and Kaitlin knew it.

You didn't kiss customers. You might do a lot of things in the VIP room, but you sure as hell never kissed.

"You want me to kiss you?" It was puzzling.

"Whores don't kiss their clients. You're not a whore, right? Now kiss me."

And Kaitlin did, and it hadn't been that bad. Plus, now she could think of this as having a rich boyfriend. There was nothing wrong with having a rich boyfriend.

Now all she had to do was look pretty and spend half an hour with Nathan every weekday morning. She didn't need to maintain such an expensive grooming regimen, either. She could paint her own nails and shave her own bikini area, and she could be a little more lax on the hair appointments. It wasn't a bad way to make a living. He never tried to see her on the weekends or after work. It was just a morning gig, and she felt lucky to have it.

She used the word "boyfriend" when she referred to him, which was almost never. She didn't talk about him at all if she could help it.

When Nathan left every morning, she immediately cleaned herself out. That was what she called it. Her bathroom had one of those cheap plastic hand-held shower heads and she aimed the sprayer right between her legs to clean the one part of her that actually needed it, since the rest of her was still good from her pre-dawn shower.

Then she got back into bed, crawling over the sex part of the bed and onto the uncontaminated area next to the wall. She was careful to fall asleep lying flat on her back so her hair and makeup would still look good when she'd get up for real. That, in her mind, was when her day actually began.

When she woke up, she'd walk next door and hang out with Shirley for a while. Shirley could often be counted on for a ride to the convenience store where Kaitlin worked. Shirley thought she was better than everybody else, but she wasn't.

She still had a Lincoln, but it was old as shit, as was Shirley.

The store was less than a mile away and Kaitlin could and often did walk to work. She'd applied for that job specifically because of its location after she lost her license. But Nathan had been good about helping her pay her attorney's fees, and she'd get her license back eventually. In the meantime, she banked the money she'd otherwise spend on a car and cultivated her friendship with Shirley.

Kaitlin scooped up a fresh pack of Winstons from a drawer and her own Virginia Slims and headed next door.

"Hey, Shirley. I brought you a pack," Kaitlin said.

Shirley was impeccably dressed in a pair of white slacks, a silky button-up green blouse and matching emerald earrings. She had all that stuff from the old days. Her silvery hair always looked nice, for an old lady, because she had it done every single week. Your average stripper had her hair done less often than Shirley did.

"Want a cup?" Shirley asked now, holding up her own cup of coffee before topping it off with more coffee, and then adding more cream and sugar to get it the exact shade she preferred.

"Sure," Kaitlin said. She preferred energy drinks but drank coffee when Shirley offered it, just to be sociable. Going along with another person's preferences was a thing you did if you needed something someone else had.

Kaitlin never put sugar or creamer into it; the coffee was equally unenjoyable either way, so why bother? Shirley handed her a cup of coffee in a souvenir mug from the Ozarks. She had a set of fancy cups she never used. Kaitlin had seen them in the cabinet. But they always drank out of mismatched mugs that had cute sayings or business logos on them.

The two women went outside to smoke. Shirley had the best outdoor furniture in the trailer park. She had had it in her backyard when she had a house, Kaitlin knew. She knew because Shirley talked about that a lot. Kaitlin felt if she were to be dropped into Shirley's old house, she'd have no trouble finding her way around.

It was a wrought iron table with curly grape vine embellishments and four matching chairs, but two chairs would have been enough. Nobody ever visited Shirley except Kaitlin.

"Nancy told me somebody's moving into that trailer on the corner tomorrow," Shirley told her. Nancy was the bitch who ran the trailer park.

"Oh yeah?" Kaitlin took a sip of her coffee. It wasn't anything like the stuff they sold at work. Shirley didn't seem to know that coffee could have flavors now.

"Nancy says it's a single mom and her daughter. I can't imagine trying to raise a child here."

Kaitlin had lived in far worse places, but she just nodded. "I'm not having kids at all."

"You'll change your mind someday," Shirley said. "If you and your boyfriend get married, he might want kids. You never know."

Kaitlin always avoided talking about Nathan and took a long drink of coffee to avoid answering.

"Although it doesn't look like my boys are ever going to make me a grandmother."

Kaitlin had never met Shirley's sons, but pictures of them growing up were all over Shirley's living room walls.

"The people across the street have two kids but I've never talked to them," Kaitlin said. "I just know them from the Christmas card."

There were seven trailers on the cul de sac. As you turned in, there was the trailer that had been empty for a while, and then there was the black family. The Jacksons. Every one of them had a name that started with a J, and all of them except the dad had a weird spelling. Jimmy and Janiece, and their little girls, Jordynn and Jazzmyn.

They knew the spellings because Janiece had dropped off a Christmas card at every trailer on the street last year. It was kind of nice of her, but she should have known it wasn't that kind of a neighborhood.

Next to the Jacksons was Gilbert Jones. He went by Jonesy. He was a reporter; she had seen his name in the newspaper Shirley read in the morning. They'd traded waves but had never spoken, and she'd never seen him come into either the convenience store or the club.

And then at the very end of the street was Nancy Meyer. She was the one who decided who got to rent and who didn't. Whose references were good enough and whose weren't. Who would be given a little more time to come up with rent and who would be kicked out. You couldn't trust her. And if you thought Shirley could put on some airs (and she could), you hadn't seen anything until you saw Nancy.

But Kaitlin knew how to treat Nancy. It was something she had learned in the club. She was as friendly and talkative to Nancy as she would be to a man with money in his hand. Except it was even more important to win over Nancy than to win over any man. Nancy ate it up.

Last week, Kaitlin noticed Nancy had a new ugly-ass handbag, and she'd complimented her on it. When Nancy got a terrible haircut recently, she told her it was cute and she should take a selfie and use it for her profile picture online. It was too easy.

Shirley lived right next door to Nancy and seemed to like her, so Kaitlin never let on to Shirley what she really thought of Nancy. It was best to pretend to be part of a friendly little club.

Next to Shirley was Kaitlin's trailer and then at the end was Darren Lewis. He was a creepy guy probably no older than Nathan but he looked like he'd had a hard life. He always seemed to have an ugly woman around. Nancy had cited him numerous times for playing his old-dude music too loud, but he kept doing it.

There were dozens of other trailers besides the ones on the cul de sac, but Kaitlin only knew the people on her own street, and most of them she didn't know well. In her case, it was really just Shirley and Nancy. And it wasn't that she had anything against the black folks, either. But what would be the point? She needed to be nice to Nancy so she didn't get kicked out and she needed to be nice to Shirley to get rides to work, but she couldn't see the upside to hanging out with the rest of them.

As they finished their first cigarettes, Kaitlin felt it was a good time to ask for a ride.

"I gotta work at one," she said.

"Need a ride?" Shirley asked.

"Wouldn't mind one," Kaitlin said. "Thanks."

This was why she occasionally gave Shirley a free pack of smokes. It was her way of paying. Nothing came for free, and Kaitlin was well aware of that.

The morning passed pleasantly, but Kaitlin's stomach was rumbling. She hadn't eaten anything yet. Whenever possible, she would wait until she got to work and scrounge for hot dogs left too long on the rollers, or sandwiches that were past their sell-by date.

Strictly speaking, none of that food was supposed to be eaten, but they all did it and if you were a good worker, that sort of thing was overlooked. What wouldn't be overlooked was stealing cigarettes, but she was careful to make a big show of always paying for her Virginia Slims. Why would she be stealing Winstons?

She knew where the security cameras were and how to get away with it, and she never stole more than one pack a week. Shirley, of course, didn't know she stole them or she'd never accept them.

"You ready to go?" Kaitlin asked. It was early, but she was hungry.

"Let me just get my keys," Shirley said. She went inside, got her purse, locked her front door and unlocked her car.

Shirley's ancient Lincoln Town Car was a trip. Shirley kept it very nice. It was old but luxurious and Kaitlin enjoyed riding in it. Once in a while, Shirley offered her a ride to the grocery store, which was cool, but Kaitlin never asked. That would be overstepping, she felt. And anyway, she could get most everything at the convenience store. It only took a few minutes to get there by car.

"Thanks!" Kaitlin called out, and she went into work.

"You're early," Naomi said. That was her supervisor.

"Yeah, I had a ride," Kaitlin said, tying on her smock. She didn't mention that she was hoping to score lunch.

"You can pick up trash first. Since you're early."

That dashed her hopes for a free lunch. Naomi was probably onto her. Picking up trash from the lot was the worst. Well, after cleaning the men's room. It sucked, running around the parking lot and behind the building, picking up food wrappers, cigarette butts and all the miscellaneous crap people threw around.

Yeah, Naomi knew exactly why she was here early. But Kaitlin didn't complain, just got a trash bag and went outside to do it. Sooner or later Naomi would go on break or leave for the day and she'd get her chance then. At the worst, she'd have to pay for a sandwich during her break.

She was in luck today. After Kaitlin finished picking up trash and threw the bag into the dumpster out back, Naomi headed into the little office to do paperwork, leaving Kaitlin at the register.

All she needed was thirty seconds in the kitchen to snitch a slice of American cheese and a piece of bread. She didn't take time to put any mayo or anything else on it. She just rolled it into a tight cylinder and stuffed half of it into her mouth, chewing and swallowing it as fast as she could and then stuffing the other half in. Some things were tracked more closely than others, but a piece of cheese and a slice of bread wouldn't be missed.

Now she was thirsty, and she paid for an energy drink out of her own money. She drank up to four of these a day, making them one of her biggest monthly expenses, even with her employee discount. She was allowed to drink them during her shifts as long as she didn't keep them right behind the counter.

It could be stressful sometimes. You had to pay attention and watch the cars at the pumps, because if someone drove off, it would come out of your salary. It happened occasionally, but not at night, because at night people had to pre-pay. That took a load off her mind.

But bantering with the regulars was sort of fun. She didn't mind that part at all. A couple of times she'd recognized an old customer from the strip club, but she didn't think any of them had ever recognized her without her club makeup on.

At the end of her shift, she did her grocery shopping, taking no more than she could easily carry. A canister of sour cream and onion potato chips. A frozen enchilada dinner. An individually wrapped piece of string cheese. A cheap can of spaghetti, just like Mom used to make. Three energy drinks. Sure, things were more expensive here than at the grocery store, but with the employee discount, it all evened out, and without a car, this was just easier.

She watched for her chance, and at the last minute, she added two stale strawberry Danishes and three dried up hotdogs that were supposed to be thrown away, hastily wrapping everything up in waxed paper and adding it to her bag but with the frozen enchilada dinner on top.

Outside, she sat on the curb, lit a cigarette and texted her friend Tommy, asking him for a ride home. She just didn't feel like walking, but if Tommy didn't text back by the time she was done smoking, she would.

But he did. He only lived five minutes away, just outside town in an old farmhouse that had been his grandma's. He was always ready to do her a favor. She let him do just enough favors but not too many.

"Hey, thanks," she said, when he pulled up. "I had a long, hard day." Anything over four hours was a long day to Kaitlin.

"No problem," he said. "What's in the bag?"

"Groceries," she said. "I'm starving. She pulled out one of the Danishes and began eating. "Want one? I have two."

"No thanks. But I could go for a burger. You

want one?"

"Sure," she said, re-wrapping the rest of the stale Danish for later. Tommy drove through and she got a cheeseburger, fries and a chocolate shake. Now she could save the hotdogs for tomorrow. She'd have to invite Tommy in, but after half an hour, she'd tell him she was tired. He was nice. He'd take that hint.

"It was so nice of you to drive me home and give me dinner," she said. "You want to come in for a while?"

He did, of course. Tommy was always so hopeful. He used to work with her at the convenience store but had a better job now, working an early shift at a hospital laundry. That was convenient, because it meant he was never going to try to drop in on her in the morning, and he never wanted to stay too late, either.

He followed her into the trailer and she put away her groceries while finishing off the last of the shake. When he was gone, she might have one of the hotdogs, maybe.

Tommy was turning on her TV, flipping through channels with the remote. "You want to watch a movie?" he asked.

It was too early to pretend she was too tired. "Sure," she said, feigning enthusiasm. He was sitting on the sofa, and she took a chair. A quick look of disappointment flashed over his face and she knew he'd been hoping she would sit next to him on the sofa. He'd chosen an action movie. It was one she'd seen before but she didn't care. She shifted herself into a comfy position, tucking her feet up under her, and let out a yawn.

"You tired?" he asked.

"It was kind of a tough day. You know what a bitch Naomi is. She put me on parking lot duty. It was gross. Somebody had thrown out a dirty diaper and I had to pick that up."

"I don't know why you stay there. You could get a better job."

She had never told him about her DUI. She much preferred people to assume she was still saving up for a car.

"It's a convenient location. I just get tired of Naomi always pushing all the dirty work onto me."

"I could rub your shoulders," he offered. Kaitlin knew this was a ploy but she didn't care. It would be an unsuccessful one.

Without a word, she sat on the floor in front of him. Her hair was already up in a clip and out of his way. He rubbed her shoulders for quite a while before he began the inevitable testing of her limits, reaching forward and over her shoulders toward the swell of her breasts and then wandering into side-boob territory.

He probably had a hard-on, but she pretended not to notice anything. If he got too obvious, she'd have to notice it. But it actually felt really good to have someone lavishing attention on her, even though she knew exactly why he was doing it.

"That's so nice," she said, offering a little encouragement. He kept rubbing and stroking, getting close to the line but not quite crossing it.

Maybe Nathan would be in the mood to have her on top in the morning. It had been a while since she'd had an orgasm. Or maybe, the crazy thought came to her, she should just pull Tommy into the bedroom.

But then he'd be around all the time, and she'd lose control over him. Sooner or later, he'd realize her arrangement with Nathan, and things would get ugly. Better to keep things as they were. Besides, she realized that he had leaned over a little and was actually smelling her hair. He was getting a little too excited back there.

"I'm so tired, Tommy," she said. "I think I should just go to bed early."

He quickly agreed. He really was a nice guy. She gave him a long, tight hug to thank him. Yep, he was excited.

"Thanks for everything," she said. And then she washed off her makeup, brushed her teeth and restored the throw pillows to their proper place. She wiped off the kitchen counters where there was a small puddle of melted shake and threw away the fast-food trash.

Then she crawled over the sex part of the mattress and got comfy on the sleeping half. She set the alarm on her phone and was almost immediately asleep.

CHAPTER 3

Nancy

The problem with managing a mobile home park, Nancy thought, was the people.

She did not include herself in this assessment. She only lived here because the mobile home came free with the job. Besides, her mobile home was a double-wide. It was just as nice as any house. Nicer, in many cases.

She had good taste and had decorated it perfectly, mostly with furniture bought on time from the rental place. They had some really good stuff. She had paid off most of it, other than her new kitchen table and chairs, which would be paid off shortly.

She loved coming home to her mobile home. It was nicer than any other place she'd ever lived, and with her free rent, she planned to start tucking some money away just as soon as she'd made the final furniture payment.

She'd scored the job several years ago after completing her two-year associate's degree in business from the local community college. Not every place was as nice as this one.

Loire Mobile Estates was a mobile home park. It was not a trailer park, and she corrected people whenever they used the other term. It had mostly nicer mobile homes and a convenient little laundry room. The streets were in decent shape. The landscaping around the rental office was really pretty, too.

In theory, the homes were mobile, but once a mobile home found its way here, it was unlikely to ever be moved anywhere else. It was just too expensive. By the time you unhooked all the electrical, water and sewer and paid to have the home hauled elsewhere and hooked everything up again, the cost could easily run $10,000.

In some parks, people would own their own mobile homes and just pay for utilities and lot rent. They could move their mobile homes to another location if they really wanted to. But with very few exceptions, the company owned the homes in this park and rented them out. It was easier. Some of the mobile homes, like the one Nancy lived in, were in close to perfect condition. Others, not so much.

The little one at the end of her street had been empty for a while. A sewage backup had destroyed the flooring and she'd had to make sure everything got cleaned up and fixed up. She arranged new carpeting for the whole thing except the bathroom and kitchen, which each got new vinyl. They had a contract with a flooring place and generally used the same flooring for every job. It was cheaper that way, and they always had extra matching flooring for repairs. They tended to need a lot of repairs.

There was a single mom and daughter moving into the place today. The mother had filled out the application and had proven she had enough money coming in to cover expenses. It came from welfare, of course. She had a housing voucher.

But who else was going to live there? Unlike her own double-wide, or most of the others that had at least a little tip-out to make some extra room for the sofa, this mobile home was cramped, even for a mobile home. OK, let's be real, she thought. That one is nothing but a trailer. And new flooring aside, it was rough.

The cheap old fake-wood paneling was scratched up and the built-in bookcase that served as a divider between the living room and kitchen was missing some shelves. The kid would be sleeping in a room so small it would barely fit a twin bed. The dressers and closets in both bedrooms were built in, which was good, because it would be hard to find a dresser small enough to fit. The mother's room was a little bigger, but still would only fit a double bed. People today thought they needed queens or kings but they didn't. A double bed was plenty.

She'd shown Angel the place a week ago, and

Angel had picked it apart.

"This window is cracked," Angel had complained, looking at the window in the second bedroom. "Is that going to be fixed before I move in?"

It was never going to be fixed, Nancy knew. That window had been broken through two tenants that she knew of, and probably more before Nancy had started managing the park. It was a shitty little trailer that rented for almost nothing. What did Angel expect?

"I can put some clear tape over it for now," she had told her. "If you just leave it alone, it'll be fine." If the kid messed with it and broke it, she'd ding them on the security deposit.

Angel had let it drop but complained that one of the cabinets was missing a handle.

"I'll see if I can get the handyman in there to work on that," Nancy had said. She didn't make any promises she knew very well she wasn't going to keep. The park's handyman had other things to do than worry about a missing handle in this rathole. You could still open the cabinet door just as easy. If Angel didn't like it, she was welcome to try to find another place that would take her voucher.

In the end, Nancy knew, Angel was not a woman with a lot of choices. If she were, she wouldn't be here. And Nancy was right. Angel had stopped bitching and had made the appointment to sign the lease and move in today.

Without a doubt, she was going to show up with a friend's pickup truck. Probably it would belong to some man she was sleeping with. She'd have two beds, a cheap-ass second-hand table and chairs and a sofa from the charity store and not much else. Not much else would fit in there anyway.

Still, it was good to get the trailer earning rent again. She got bonuses in months when she had a 100 percent occupancy rate. She almost never did, because this was often out of her control. It's not like she could have rented the place out when there was raw sewage on the floor, after all. But there were no exceptions to the rule.

If she managed 100 percent occupancy for a few more months, she'd pay off the kitchen set and still have enough for a down payment on a new car in no time. It was embarrassing, driving a ten-year-old car. She managed this place and should have the nicest car.

There were several people on other streets in the park who drove new vehicles. And then there was Shirley, driving around in her boat of a Lincoln. It was old but immaculate, and it pissed Nancy off every time she saw Shirley haul her old Kirby out there to vacuum it. It was a once-a-week ritual, which was overdoing things a bit. Shirley used to live in a big house and thought she was better than everyone else.

She wasn't, though. Her mobile home, which she owned outright, was one of the better ones in the park, but it wasn't better than Nancy's. And if Nancy wanted to, she could buy better outdoor furniture than Shirley's.

Shirley was not the only person who could have a fancy little table and chairs. Nancy just might get her own set from the rental store, but not until she'd paid for her kitchen set. That was her top priority. She was never anything but nice to Shirley's face, though. Single ladies needed to stick together.

One of the things she thought would be a plus when she'd taken this job was the respect she'd gain. She was still in her thirties and managed the whole park. Who arranged for new carpeting or to fix the plumbing? She did. Who was personally emailed by Mr. Darby, the owner of the park, fairly often? That would be her. Who was responsible for getting background checks, verifying incomes, collecting rent? Her again. Who made sure people moving out whose mobile homes passed inspections got their deposits returned?

Well, in truth that didn't happen very often. But when it did, she handled it. It wasn't an easy job. You had to be a very responsible person.

And yet, did anybody here really respect her? Hardly, but there were exceptions. It was clear that the pretty young girl with the older boyfriend, Kaitlin Torsney, respected her. She always enjoyed talking to Kaitlin. That was a girl who understood who her betters were. Nancy didn't always like pretty girls. In her experience, many of them were bitches.

But Kaitlin, pretty as she was, always showed the proper respect. How did Kaitlin get her hair to hold that wave? Nancy had tried everything to get her coarse black hair to look like that. Curling irons, hot rollers, and at last a disastrous perm that had turned her hair into a frizzy mess.

She'd been trying to grow it out like Kaitlin's, but had to cut it into a pixie to get rid of the worst damage. So she was flattered when Kaitlin had complimented her and told her it looked cute. She liked that girl. And she had the sense to date an older, obviously more established man with an expensive car instead of wasting her time with young boys.

"You ought to enroll in community college. You could major in business, like me. It's not that expensive and you could get a better job than just working in a convenience store. You'd earn enough money to get a car," she'd told her.

Maybe Kaitlin would take her advice. If she did, Nancy would put in a good word for her with Mr. Darby. Maybe he would realize there was enough work at the mobile home park for two people. Or maybe there was some kind of promotion Nancy could get and then Kaitlin could manage this place. Wouldn't that piss off Shirley, if Kaitlin ended up in a better mobile home than Shirley's? She smiled.

She loved her job. When the new tenant had

come in to apply, Nancy hadn't liked the look of her. She was one of those women who had let themselves go after having a kid. No wonder she was single. The woman's name was Angel. Stupid name. Who would name a kid Angel? And then she'd gone and named her kid Maya. Another stupid name.

But Angel had been lucky. She had the voucher in hand right when the ugliest and cheapest unit in the park was open. It was just about the only mobile home in the park her voucher would have covered. If Nancy dated the paperwork that very day, she'd have 100 percent occupancy that month, which meant a $100 bonus. So that was that, and Nancy hoped for the best from Angel. She'd be keeping an eye on her for sure.

She was allowed to close the office from noon to one o'clock each weekday for lunch, but she usually didn't. There was a small kitchenette with a microwave in the office, and she often brought in leftovers to eat at her desk. That was how dedicated she was. She had mentioned it several times to Mr. Darby. Just casually. Just letting him know how seriously she took her job and how hard she worked. She didn't even take lunch! Who else could say that?

Today she had a tuna noodle casserole. It wasn't that hard to make. You boiled some macaroni and added a can of tuna and a can of cream of mushroom soup. Then you stirred in some milk and some shredded cheese and baked it. You could add some crushed crackers or bread crumbs to the top if you wanted, but you didn't need to. A little shredded cheese on top was just as good, and faster. She was a damned good cook, and casseroles were her specialty.

Tonight, she was going to try a new recipe she'd seen online. You took a can of ham and beans and put it in a casserole dish and cut up several hot dogs. Then you took a cornbread muffin mix and mixed it up, but instead of putting it in cupcake tins, you spread it over the beans and hotdogs. Then you baked it. Corn Dog Casserole, it was called. She'd have it for supper tonight and lunch tomorrow. She was thrifty that way.

She knew a lot of people would go out for lunch, but she didn't want to waste her money that way. Not if she was going to save up for a new car.

The door jangled and she set her tuna casserole aside. It was Angel and Maya. They weren't supposed to come until one. It would have served them right if they'd come to find a locked office and a sign telling her to come back later. Well, Nancy thought, she'd definitely work that into the conversation.

"Hello! Good to see you!" she said. "I see you've got Maya with you. Hi, Maya!"

Maya was a scrawny, socially awkward 13-year-old who looked even younger. She still had the body of a child. She didn't say anything, just half-smiled and hung back.

"You're in luck. I'm almost done with my lunch and I can get you all taken care of in a few," she said, taking another bite of tuna noodle and chewing it slowly. She was damned if she was going to let her food get cold when it was still only twelve-thirty. Technically, she could make Angel wait until one o'clock if she wanted to. If she weren't so nice and so dedicated.

Angel walked over to the cork bulletin board and was reading the copy of the rules Nancy had posted there.

"Those are the rules," Nancy said. "There's a copy in your packet I'm going to give you, too."

"The trailer park rules?" Angel asked.

"Mobile home park rules," she corrected automatically. "Oh, yes indeed. We are very strict here, for the good of everybody. We provide a clean, quiet, pleasant place to live. As long as you follow the rules, you'll be very happy here. In fact, I live at the end of the cul de sac where your place is, so we'll be neighbors. Where was it you said you lived before?"

She couldn't be expected to remember the details of every single person who filled out the paperwork, after all.

"We've been living with my mom," Angel said.

"Right. Well, you're lucky to have gotten in. We usually like people with recent landlord references. But as long as you follow the rules, you'll be just fine." She finished up her last bite of tuna noodle and pushed the plastic container it had been in aside to make room for a packet of materials. “OK. I’ll take all your paperwork. You have the voucher for your rent. Very good. Your garbage, water and sewer are included in your rent. It’s a fantastic deal. If you want cable, that’s separate. Your rent deposit is separate, too. You have that?”

Angel reached into her jeans and pulled out a ragged roll of money, mostly one-dollar bills. “I have it.”

“Right. You’ll get this back when you move out, if you leave everything in the same good condition it was in when you moved in.” She reached for the money and began counting it. The bills were warm from Angel’s body and she found she didn’t want to touch them.

If the woman hadn’t been so unattractive, she might wonder if she’d earned all those single bills stripping. Most people had a check or money order or carried in a stack of twenties. But the whole $400 was there. She wrote out a receipt and gave it to Angel, and then she came up with an excuse to wash her hands.

“Excuse me, I’m just going to take my dishes to the sink,” she said, picking up the container that had held her tuna casserole and carrying it to the kitchenette. She placed it in the sink and made a show of rinsing it well, and then she lathered up her hands. Relief. Angel’s warm money had made her feel contaminated.

Back at her desk, she produced four keys. "You get two house keys and two mailbox keys. Don't lose them. We charge $10 for lost keys. And you can't copy them. If you have some good reason why you need another one, it's $10 to get a copy. Will you be mowing yourself, or do you want to pay the landscape fee?"

"I didn't know that cost money," Angel said. "I don't have a mower."

"Well, you can't just let your grass grow all summer. It has to be mowed. You can do it yourself or you can pay the park. We have a crew. Or, of course, you can pay someone else to mow it. It's up to you. We charge $30. But if you are going to mow it yourself and you don't keep it up, we'll do it and then there's another $50 surcharge. So keep it mowed."

"I don't know," Angel said. "I can see if somebody I know might be able to do it."

"You can get back to me on that," Nancy said. "It's just been mowed, so you have about a week to figure it out. Don't forget."

"I won't," Angel said.

Nancy was eager to get to the package of cookies she had hidden in her desk drawer for dessert. "Well, that does it. Welcome to Loire Mobile Home Park, Ms. Webb."

"Thanks," Angel said. "Come on, Maya." The two left, and Nancy looked out the window. Sure enough, there was a guy with an old pickup truck full of crappy furniture out there waiting for them.

She withdrew two cookies from her desk drawer, ate them quickly, and then placed two more on her lap, where they were easy to get to but not visible to anyone who might unexpectedly walk in. Nancy didn't like to be seen eating cookies.

It was time for one of the best parts of her day: Reading the complaint emails. There was at least one nearly every day, often several. People liked to rat each other out, and then Nancy would feel a little sense of justice as she dealt with each transgression.

One lady was complaining that the people living at No. 3 Nightingale had a poodle. "I've seen it sitting in the window," the woman said. Pets were not allowed, and that included even temporary pet-sitting. She'd check it out. If they had a dog there, they'd have to let it out eventually. They probably thought they could get away with it, but they couldn't, and there was a $50 fine for that.

Another person was reporting that their neighbor had let their flower bed go to weeds. She would check out that now, in the daylight. She could give them a warning or she could fine them, and it just depended on their attitude. If it turned out they were really sick or had a new baby or something, she could be magnanimous and declare she'd decided to let them off with a warning. But if they gave her any shit, she'd drop the hammer on them. That was a $50 fine, too.

Rules were meant to be followed.

After the irritating interlude with the new tenant, Nancy decided to reward herself with a little spying. She closed up the office and took a circuitous walk toward the mobile home of the people who were supposed to be harboring a dog. Their place was on the other side of the park, and Nancy soon wished she'd brought a can of soda with her. It was hot and still, and she felt the sweat blossoming from her armpits and crotch.

But by taking the long way around, she was able to approach the mobile home from behind. It might be a while before she could catch them. How often did a dog need to pee? Nancy had no idea. She'd never owned a dog or cat. They were nasty, hairy, stinky things. Imagine having a cat pee and poop in a plastic box right in your house! Disgusting. If you had a dog, you had to keep taking them outside and your whole yard would be full of their crap in no time. So gross.

Someone might notice if she just stood around in the tiny yard, so she searched for a place to conceal herself. There weren't many good hiding places in these small lots, but the people in No. 4 next door had left a large plastic wading pool leaning up against the back of their mobile home.

Nancy looked around, and seeing nobody, she crept behind the plastic shell of the pool. It wasn't an ideal spot; if anybody looked from either side, she'd be visible.

However, it looked like the only possibility, so she sat with her back against the skirting of the mobile home and drew her knees up to her chest and wrapped her arms around her legs.

The inside of the pool was slimy with algae; they had probably left the pool sitting out with water in it for days on end. That was against the rules, too.

She very carefully drew her phone out of her pocket to check the time; she'd only left the office ten minutes ago. It sure didn't take long to get hot and sweaty in this weather, especially behind the plastic shell of the pool. An occasional weak breeze teased her, but it wasn't enough to cool her. Sweat trickled down her forehead. The gel she used to maintain her new pixie haircut seemed to be mixing with her sweat, forming a soft layer of goo on her scalp. As it melted down her forehead, she tried to wipe the sticky mixture away from her face with her shirttail. It was impossible, though. Her shirt was damp with sweat and her hair was now matted flat against her head.

She should have waited for night, when she could simply have stood behind a tree. But they might just be dog-sitting, and if she waited too long, there was always the chance the dog would be gone by then.

Her legs and stomach felt uncomfortable, constricted in her tight, sweaty jeans. The waistband cut painfully into her stomach, giving her heartburn. She unbuttoned the jeans and eased the zipper down a little bit, making room for her tuna noodle casserole. That was better. It was somewhat easier to breathe, too.

But her legs were still cramped. If she could just ever so carefully scoot the pool out a little, she would have a touch more leg room. She carefully pushed the bottom edge forward about an inch, but that wasn't enough to improve her cramped position. She tried to shift it just a little more, but she went too far. The pool would have landed upside down and flat on the grass except her head was holding up one end.

But that gave her an idea. If the pool were flat on the grass, she might have room to lie on her stomach and stretch her legs out. It might be better. Anybody walking by would think the pool had simply fallen from against the mobile home.

The pool's size didn't allow her to stretch her legs straight out, but by spreading her legs and then pulling her knees up a little bit like a frog getting ready to jump, she had more room. The dry, crunchy, half-dead grass was rough against her chin and forearms and with the pool sealing off even the small breezes, it was unbearably hot.

Plus, she realized, she couldn't see a thing. She very, very slowly lifted the edge of the pool, just enough to peer out from under it. But she didn't have a good view because there was a large flower pot in the way.

The thing to do would be to very slowly and carefully crawl a little closer to No. 3. If she did it slowly enough, nobody would notice. She army-crawled a few feet in that direction and used her right fist to prop up the edge of the pool. It was hot as blazes under there and the neighborhood was silent except for the thrum of several window air conditioners.

The swampy smell of stagnant water and algae was stronger now that the pool was trapping all the air around her. But it would all be worth it if she managed to cite the residents of No. 3 for the illicit poodle. She couldn't help but smile. They'd certainly underestimated her determination.

As she'd crawled, the rough, crunchy grass had dragged across her sweaty lower belly where she'd opened her pants and now that skin was irritated as hell. Her right fist was still propping up the edge of the pool so she could keep watch, but she carefully navigated her body so that her left hand could reach her lower belly, now covered with rising welts. She'd never get her jeans fastened in this position, but she tried to rearrange her shirt to protect her from the way the dead grass was poking her.

Her shirt wasn't long enough, so she slipped her hand between the grass and her belly. It was terribly uncomfortable and her skin was slick with sweat, but at least the grass was no longer abrading everything between her belly button and the elastic of her underwear. But she wasn't going to let this minor discomfort keep her from nailing the residents of No. 3.

She thought she could hear the door of No. 4 open, but she couldn't risk rearranging her body to take a look. Her view was on No. 3. It sounded like a kid and a mom had walked out.

"Look, Mommy!" Nancy heard a young girl say.

"Your pool tried to blow away," a woman's voice said. Nancy prayed they'd immediately get into their car and drive away. As soon as they did, she was going to get out of here and try again tonight.

"Can we ask Dylan to come over?" the little girl asked.

Oh dear God. Nancy held perfectly still.

"Go ask his mom," came the woman's voice. Nancy watched as a little girl ran to No. 3 and knocked on the door. She could only see the girl's bare feet. Please don't let her be wearing a swimsuit. Please don't let the mother be planning to let them swim.

"Can Dylan come swim?" the little girl asked.

Nancy couldn't catch everything that was said, but the little girl came running back to No. 4. "His mom said yes!"

With no further warning, the mother flipped over the pool and screamed.

Nancy suddenly realized she was lying there on her stomach with her hand thrust into her undone jeans. Quickly, she rolled over, fastened her pants, and stood up. As she got to her feet, she thought she might faint, but she didn't.

Instead, she brushed her wet hair off her forehead. "I've had some disturbing reports of things going on here," she said. "I had to check it out." She began walking away, but then she turned back.

"Those pools are to be emptied immediately after each use. This one has algae in it. I won't cite you this time, but I'll be watching."

As she finished walking across the grass, Dylan came running out in his little swim trunks, a rather realistic-looking stuffed poodle under his arm.

CHAPTER 4

Jimmy

"Take it easy."

That was what his wife, Janiece, said so often that he'd internalized it and now thought it to himself constantly. Just because he had plenty to be angry about didn't mean it was a good idea to let that anger out.

He was repeating it to himself again now. He'd been planning to take off next week, and he and Janiece were going to drive down to visit her brother and sister-in-law. But even though his boss had verbally OK'd the time off weeks ago, it turned out he was also supposed to have filled out an online form, and Jimmy hadn't done that, because that was news to Jimmy. So they'd have to postpone their trip.

He and Janiece wanted to let their girls spend some time playing with and getting to know their cousins. He and Janiece had both grown up with bunches of cousins, and their two girls were growing up without that. But Jimmy and his wife wanted to give their daughters that experience as much as they could.

The job at Loire Custom Metal had looked good at first. It started out at $13.50 per hour, which had sounded like a lot at the time. LCM manufactured industrial machinery parts and was exactly the kind of place he hoped to work for as a mechanical engineer once he graduated. It could be useful to see the industry from the blue-collar side, he'd felt. He'd have more insight. He also hoped such experience might offer him the inside track with the company.

But that was a pipe dream. There was a clear delineation between the guys on the factory floor and the suits in engineering. They weren't even in the same building. It was probably safe to say that not one suit knew one factory floor guy. He may as well have gotten a job in fast food as far as making professional connections went.

He had no idea of how professional networking happened. How could he? That's not the kind of family he'd grown up in.

It was a common story. They were both the first ones in their family to get to go to college. He was working on an engineering degree and Janiece was planning to become a teacher. They were going to be the ones to break out of the pattern that had caught their families.

Then she got pregnant. Well, they decided, they'd press on. He'd finish up and get a good job as fast as he could, and she'd take a year or two off before returning to school. It would be a tough couple of years, but then they'd be solidly middle class. It would all work out. They got married right away.

"I want to do this right," Jimmy told her.

A number of things went wrong. The first problem they ran into was learning that Jimmy couldn't get any more financial aid.

This was because he had started out majoring in education, but switched to engineering at the end of his sophomore year. Partly, this was at the urging of his advisor.

"You're a smart man, Jimmy. You'll never make any money teaching. You've got the grades and test scores for engineering, and you'll make a lot more money that way."

He'd walked out of that meeting with his head in the clouds, feeling gratified that somebody thought his goals, already so much higher than the ones he'd grown up with, should be higher yet. He didn't have to think it over. He changed his major right away. It would take him an extra year to finish, but he didn't mind that.

However, when he applied for his financial aid for what was to have been his fifth and final year of college, he learned that his time was up. He was deemed not to have made sufficient progress toward his degree. He'd had four years. He wasn't eligible for anything for the fifth year.

"OK, Plan B," Janiece had said. "I can get loans to finish my teaching degree. I can do that while

I'm pregnant, and when I've got my teaching job, we can afford for you to finish your degree. It's not how I wanted motherhood to happen, but it'll work out."

It might have worked, except for one thing. Well, two.

They weren't having one baby. They were having twins. Janiece pressed on, but halfway through the semester, her blood pressure ballooning, she was forced to go on bed rest. That meant dropping out of school.

At first, Jimmy was satisfied with a full-time job managing a restaurant, attractive to him because it actually offered health insurance. But the coverage was so poor and the birth so expensive that he realized too late that they'd have been better off going on welfare and letting public aid cover it.

By the time Jordynn and Jazzmyn were born by emergency cesarean almost a month early, their parents were broker than broke. The babies spent three weeks in the hospital. The restaurant closed down a month later. Six months after they dropped out of college, their student loan payments started, but they had no way to pay them so they applied for forbearance.

But that just meant they didn't have to make payments. It did not mean the interest stopped. Each month, their balance grew and grew. The amount they owed on student loans and hospital bills was now more than what they'd hoped to spend on their first house.

Jimmy was bitter. They'd actually have been better off if they hadn't gone to college at all. If they hadn't gotten married. If he hadn't looked for a job with insurance. If they'd just let public aid take care of the medical bills.

After the restaurant, he landed at LCM. So there he was, working in a factory, just like his dad, but with enormous debt. The hospital had ultimately written off a percentage of their bill, but they still owed thousands.

The girls were toddlers now, and he knew how badly Janiece wanted to return to school. Their plan could still work, she always told him. She could still finish her degree, and they could get back on track. The big obstacles now were daycare and transportation.

Daycare for two toddlers would cost more than their rent, utilities and car payment put together. And speaking of car payments, they'd have to buy a second vehicle. Right now, they were able to make do with just one car.

He'd been so proud of himself. A lot of his friends hadn't gone to college at all. Some had gone into the trades. Some had gotten jobs in retail.

Not him. He was going to graduate from college. He and his wife would be professionals. He could still remember what it felt like to be so proud of himself, and whenever he remembered that now, it just made him feel small and ashamed.

If he hadn't changed his major, things would have been so different. He could have been teaching right now, making decent money with solid health care. Things might have been tight, sure, but he'd be making full payments on his student loans. Janiece's would still be a problem, but at least they'd be making progress on his.

Pride goeth before a fall. That was what his Pops had said to him. It pissed him off. On some level, his dad seemed actually to find Jimmy's failures satisfying.

"Did you think it was going to be that easy, Jimmy? You weren't the first one to think you could get ahead. Now you see how the world really is."

That was what he'd said when Jimmy had poured out his angst. Pops never managed to get anywhere in life, so maybe he resented the way his proud son thought it was going to be so easy. Well, now he knew better. Janiece still thought they were going to be able to pull it off once the girls were in school. He only pretended to think so. It didn't matter how hard they tried. Pops had been right. There would always be something that was going to reach out and trip them up.

That's what made him so bitter. The world had convinced him that there were rules, and if you followed them, things would work out. He had believed this. Study hard. Stay out of trouble. Go to college. Set high goals. Color within the lines.

All right, so he'd gotten his girlfriend pregnant, but they'd gotten married right away and they'd both worked hard to make things right. But they were stuck.

He no longer believed that following the rules was going to get him anywhere, and he had started thinking about what rules might be worth breaking.

CHAPTER 5

Shirley

It had been a shock to learn she was poor.

She'd been upper middle class her whole life, until she wasn't. Right out of high school, she'd married John Collins. She hadn't ever lived on her own. That wasn't what you did back then, if you were from a certain kind of family. You lived at home, and then you got married. She had done exactly what was expected of her; she'd married well and had been a good wife.

John was a few years older than she was, but that was fine. Their parents knew each other from the country club and were thrilled at the match. Their dads played golf together and their mothers played tennis together. John's family owned a pharmacy, so he'd become a pharmacist.

The money was good, and then the money was really good. They joined the same country club as their parents.

They moved from their nice house to their really nice house and raised two sons there.

Shirley had loved that house so much. It had four bedrooms and three full bathrooms, plus a powder room just inside the entryway for guests. It had both an eat-in kitchen and a dining room. It had a casual family room and a formal living room.

It's like it had two of everything; one for using and one for showing. What could be more elegant?

In later years, they'd actually added a second kitchen and yet another bathroom and bedroom to the basement. She nagged John into having the basement remodeled. He hadn't wanted to do it, but she thought it would be nice for when the boys had families and came to visit. She'd had a ball designing and decorating it. Besides the additional kitchen, bathroom and bedroom, they had put in a little entertainment area with a pool table.

"You'll see. It will be wonderful for the holidays when the boys come home with their wives and children," she'd said.

Only they never did. Neither of her sons had married. Both had moved to California. Her oldest, Brant, did something technical and non-glamourous with the movie business. Something with computers and special effects.

Then her younger son, Chad, had followed him out there. He wanted to be an actor, but he'd only had a few non-speaking roles. Sometimes he did commercials. She had seen several of them.

Mostly, he waited tables. Well, he could be doing that in Loire. You could wait tables anywhere.

They didn't even come home for Christmas last year. That broke her heart, but then again, what was she going to do? Were the boys going to share the twin bed in her guest room?

When John passed away, she had had a terrible shock. Shouldn't a pharmacist have left her enough money to live well? There had always seemed to be plenty of money through the years. She began to wonder if that was part of his hesitation when she'd wanted to turn the basement into a showplace. She had thought he was just being cheap.

Why hadn't he told her they didn't have that much money anymore? If she'd only known, she'd have taken an interest in their finances. She had gone her whole life without ever balancing a checkbook. He always did it. By the time she had to learn how to handle money, checkbooks weren't even a thing anymore.

"But where did all the money go?" she'd asked their accountant, tears running down her face, a week after the funeral. "Wasn't it your job to take care of things?"

The accountant had cleared his throat. She could see he really felt bad for her, and she realized later that was probably the only reason he'd taken her abuse.

"I'm sorry this is such a shock to you, Mrs. Collins. There are two problems. One of them is that John liked to follow his hunches with the stock market. And he was a pharmacist, not a stockbroker. He liked to think he could beat the market. Many of his stock picks did not do well at all. You know, there's a reason people hire stockbrokers. But even so, the pharmacy business isn't what it used to be. Little independent places like yours have been closing everywhere. The big chains have squeezed out most of the little guys. The pharmacy had been losing money for years. I advised him to take an offer he'd gotten years ago, but he was sure he could turn things around eventually. So that accounts for the debt."

"But what am I to do?"

She hadn't liked his answer. Her only real asset was her house, and it had a second mortgage on it. Just paying off that, the property taxes and normal upkeep was going to finish her off in a few years. But if she were to sell it, she might get enough to purchase a small house. Or maybe she could rent. But if she wanted money to live on, her best bet was to sell the house as soon as she could.

The real estate lady hadn't been nice at all. She said some of the improvements that Shirley was so proud of didn't really add to the house's value. "I wouldn't have put money into the basement project," she said, and Shirley wanted to stab her.

In the end, the price she got was much lower than she'd thought it would be, and the prices of the houses she was looking at were higher than she thought they would be. So she thought about renting, but the accountant had some harsh advice for her. He made her look at a spreadsheet on his laptop, and pointed out how much money she would be able to spend every month if she did one thing or another.

"Why, that's scarcely enough to live in a trailer!" she'd exclaimed.

Never in her life did she think that was exactly what she'd end up doing, but in the end, she got a lot more bang for her buck in a trailer than she would have any other way. She was able to buy outright a surprisingly nice like-new trailer already situated in the trailer park for $35,500. Her monthly lot rent was $300, and that included her water and garbage.

She couldn't have reasonably lived on just her widow's Social Security and investment proceeds otherwise. The proceeds from the sale of her house — invested into a fund the accountant recommended — would give her a semi-OK amount of spending money that should last the rest of her life.

It was ironic, she realized, that if she'd been in charge of their finances, she'd be living in a nice condo in Florida right now. She'd assumed John knew what he was doing and it hadn't ever occurred to her to ask him how things were going. Every year he lived, their debt deepened. If he'd lived much longer, she saw now, even living in a trailer would have been a stretch: She might have ended up in public housing. Once she realized that, she saw things a little differently.

It was surprising what you could get used to. She had always assumed trailer parks were full of druggies and prostitutes, or welfare mothers with half a dozen children by a dozen men, but everyone on her street worked, with the exception of the black lady with twin babies, and that man two doors down. But he had a bad back, supposedly, and was on disability. He was her worst neighbor.

He had told her he used to play guitar, and he had bumper stickers for bands she'd never heard of all over his beater car. He played his music too loud and had some very disreputable-looking female company. Luckily, Kaitlin's trailer blocked Shirley's view of most of his shenanigans.

She was lucky to be located between Kaitlin and Nancy. Both were nice, and all three of the ladies got along quite well together. It was nice to live near other friendly single ladies.

The only other woman in the park was the black lady, and she seemed friendly enough, but she was married with small children, so of course she had a different kind of life. It had nothing to do with her being black that Shirley didn't socialize with her. She had never been prejudiced at all. Some people her age were, but she wasn't. It was absolutely OK with her to live across the street from a black family. She never gave it a thought.

The thing about that black family, though, was that they all had weird names. The lady had dropped off Christmas cards to all the neighbors, which was nice, but how were you supposed to pronounce her name? It was spelled J-A-N-I-E-C-E. Was it pronounced just like "Janice"? If so, why was it not spelled that way? Why did black people always have to spell things weird?

Nobody ever had to wonder how to spell or pronounce her name, Shirley. That was a nice, normal name. But Janiece had given both her girls names as odd as their own.

That was going to hurt them. Everybody would know they were black just by their names. Try getting a job with that kind of name. Probably the main reason the husband had a decent factory job was that his name was completely normal. No hiring manager would have looked at his name and known he was black. And that mattered, because you couldn't just assume everyone was as accepting of others as she was.

She was curious about who was going to move into the new trailer. All Nancy had told her was that she'd rented it out to a single mother. Kaitlin had shown no curiosity at all, but Shirley couldn't wait. She sat out front having a cigarette and a cup of coffee and reading a magazine. With any luck, it would be another nice lady she could have coffee with.

CHAPTER 6

Darren

He was surrounded by bitches, and it was just going to get worse, he saw.

The kitchen table was littered with empty take-out containers and two overflowing ashtrays. He put his cigarette out in a pool of sweet and sour sauce. Tomorrow was garbage pick-up day, and he would need to be sure to get his trash out.

He'd forgotten last week, which was the only reason he hadn't cleared the table. His kitchen trash can was full, and so was his outdoor can. When they picked up the trash tomorrow, he could empty his kitchen and bathroom trash cans, and then he could clear his table and counters, and that would give him room to wash his dishes.

He ate a lot of take-out and frozen foods because he'd never learned to cook. He had assumed he'd eventually get married and his wife would do it. But when he was younger and playing every weekend in a band, it made no sense to settle down.

He closed his eyes and remembered those glory days. It had been one hot girl after another. He worked on a road crew and made damned good money during the week, and on the weekends his band, Government Cheese, played in local bars and hoped to make the big time.

They hadn't, of course. They mostly played covers because that was what the bars wanted. Bar managers had no interest in paying someone to play songs their customers had never heard before; they wanted familiar tunes that their drunk customers would sing along with and maybe even dance to, so that's what Government Cheese delivered. It was great fun and girls always loved a guy with a guitar.

He was the only guy in the band who made good money at his day job, so he tended to throw in more money for the stuff you always needed to play gigs. New amps, cables, better speakers. He still had two guitars and a bunch of equipment but he didn't play anymore. The band broke up years ago, and anyway, he didn't want to lose his disability by playing for money. You had to be careful.

It had never occurred to him he wouldn't always be able to make all the money and lay all the hot girls he wanted. But once his back got all fucked up, things changed.

Disability paid shockingly little. And once he

was basically sitting on his ass all day, he started putting on weight, which just made his back hurt more. It turns out that being old, fat and broke made it a lot harder to get laid than when he'd been young, in good shape, in a band and with a little money to spend.

He still went out sometimes to hear some live music and check out the ladies and sometimes bring one home. He'd gone through a long dry spell while he got used to the idea that the girls he used to pick up with ease were no longer within his grasp.

He finally realized he was going to have to drop his standards or get used to being celibate. Once he stopped going after the hot young girls, his luck improved. And honestly, if he was drunk and the lights were low, what difference did it make, really?

Some of them he liked enough to keep around for a while. That was kind of nice. They'd clean his place, cook his food and give him a little bit of what he needed. But he'd never wanted any of them around enough to marry them. He liked variety. He'd never been able to stick to one woman for long.

Even with a bad back and not much money, you could still enjoy your life. If you turned up your music and had a few beers, that was almost as good as partying. You just had to watch out for Nancy, a frigid bitch who couldn't stand it if anybody else was having a good time. He'd made the mistake of thinking she might be interested in a little male attention one time.

"Why don't you come on over?" he'd suggested. "I've got a twelve-pack. We can listen to my old band recordings if you want."

Maybe he'd been a little drunk when he made that suggestion, but still. It was a perfectly nice offer, and he'd have given her a good time. She didn't have to be so rude about it. She could have just said no instead of telling him she wouldn't go out with him if he were the last man on earth.

But there was an upside to having flirted with Nancy. He discovered, quite by accident, how easily he could fluster her. All he had to do was flirt a little.

"Damn, Nancy," he'd say, looking her up and down slowly. "You're looking good today, girl. You about ready to come over and listen to some music with me?" He did that every single time she tried to cite him for loud music, and now she never bothered him about it.

Although, if Nancy had ever responded to his flirting, he would have taken whatever he could get. It didn't matter that she wasn't much to look at. You couldn't be picky when you got to his age, and it would have been convenient to have a woman right on his street.

Now Darren watched as across the street the new woman sat on her porch. That's all she'd done all day so far. She'd moved in just a few days ago, and she had a pile of cardboard boxes out by her trash can. That had given him an idea — he'd wait until it was dark and get rid of a little bit of his trash by mixing it in with hers. She'd never notice it. Except she was fucking always on her porch.

At first, he assumed she was sitting outside to smoke. Things sure had changed over the last thirty or forty years. Used to be, people just smoked in the house. Even non-smokers didn't care if you smoked in their house, usually. They'd go get an ashtray they kept for company and you could light right up, even in their living rooms.

Then it suddenly became rude to smoke in other people's houses. You'd have to go outside to do it. That made sense, he guessed. If you didn't smoke yourself, maybe you didn't want it in your house.

But now, smokers who lived alone would go outside to smoke! That was just crazy. You'd see Kaitlin and Shirley out there smoking away in their tiny front yards, even in the winter. Both those women lived alone, and both of them smoked, so what was the sense in going outside? He himself enjoyed his heat in winter and his air conditioning in summer and comfortably smoked his cigarettes indoors. As far as he could tell, there was no downside. It smelled just fine in his trailer, other than the garbage, which he would definitely take out tonight.

Kaitlin and Shirley were both bitches, but in different ways. Kaitlin was a hot little number he wouldn't kick out of bed, but she thought she was too good to give him the time of day. Shirley was just as stuck up, but she was too old for him, so he'd never hit on her. It would be like doing it with somebody's grandma. He reconsidered. Shirley was probably more like his mom's age. But either way, no fucking way.

How those two ended up so friendly was beyond him. Maybe Kaitlin, too, thought of Shirley as a grandma figure.

The new woman across the street, though. She just might be a possibility. She was fat but he'd had fatter. She was no knock-out, but he was used to that. He watched her, assessing his chances. On the downside, she had a kid. He was guessing her daughter might be ten or so, but he hadn't been around kids enough to know.

Anyway, the woman just sat there for hours on end. Sometimes she was looking at her phone or reading a magazine, but sometimes she was just staring off. As far as he could tell, she didn't even smoke.

He'd make an introduction later. He should shower first. And maybe clean things up in here a bit, just in case she wanted to come over. A lot of women would try to hide things from their kid, and if that was how it was, she'd probably come over here.

He looked around at the empty pizza boxes and take-out containers and the two bags of trash he had sitting on his kitchen floor. He had been a little hung over on trash day last week, so he'd missed it. He hadn't done the dishes because he had the two trash bags inconveniently sitting right in front of the sink.

This was Nancy's fault. He'd drag the damned trash can to the street right now if he could, and he'd pile all the full garbage bags around it. Then he'd have a fresh start and could do his dishes and wipe down all the surfaces that currently held dishes and food containers.

However, Nancy pitched a fit if anybody carried their trash out to the street sooner than the night before trash day. Maybe he'd be able to get away with it by flirting but maybe not. He hadn't tried pushing that particular boundary. The woman across the street would find out how strict Nancy was soon enough, or maybe Nancy let people break that rule if they were still in the move-in process and had extra junk.

Now that he was thinking of getting to know the new woman, he felt eager to get his place cleaned out. He wasn't naturally this messy. It was just the bad back and Nancy's stupid trash rules that had gotten him here.

He could change his sheets and do his laundry in the meantime. But first, he'd take a shower and shave, in case she saw him out running around looking rough. He wanted to make a good first impression. He'd put on a decent shirt, even.

Looking at himself in the mirror, he did not feel displeased. With his hair combed and his good shirt on, he looked pretty damned nice, and not all that many years older than her. Besides, she was fat and not very good looking. How picky could she be?

He loaded up the trunk of his car with all his laundry, waving to the woman as he stood in his front yard. Then he made the one-minute drive to the trailer park's laundry facilities. There were three washing machines and three dryers, and they were all free at the moment, so he dumped all his sheets and towels into one and all the rest of his clothes in the other.

Various wanna-be wives had taken him to task repeatedly for not separating out his clothes, but he had never seen that it made a damned bit of difference. This was how he'd done it all his life and it was fine.

He could have walked back home while the laundry washed, but he didn't bother. There was a little picnic table sitting outside where you could smoke. They didn't allow it in the laundry building. There were snack and soda machines and he had a pocket full of quarters, so he treated himself to a root beer and a bag of chips. He scrolled through his favorite porn site while he waited.

Of all the advances in technology Darren had seen in his lifetime, perhaps the most underappreciated was the ability to privately view porn for free anytime, anywhere. The first time he'd seen what a naked woman looked like had been at his friend T.J.'s house.

T.J.'s dad had a stack of dirty magazines hidden in his garage workshop, and on any given non-school day, as soon as T.J.'s parents went to work, the boys would let themselves into the detached garage and very carefully get the magazines out and look at them together. They were very solemn and quiet at first, like acolytes being given their first look at a secret, sacred text.

But as time went by, they started bragging about what they'd do to this girl or that one, and arguing which ones were prettier or had the best tits. And then one day, T.J. had pulled his thing out. Darren had been hard too, of course, but he had tried to hide it. T.J. was done hiding it; he pulled it out and did what Darren had only done in the bathroom or his own bedroom.

"What's the matter? Don't you like girls?" T.J. had taunted him.

"Sure I do."

"Then what's the problem?" He was yanking away and Darren tried not to look.

"I mean, it's private." But his hand crept toward his fly. It was no longer up to him.

"It feels better when you can see the picture. Try it."

Darren hadn't wanted to do it in front of T.J., but he did wonder what it would feel like to do it while looking at the pictures. He'd been going home, closing his eyes and doing his best to remember, but now he took his favorite magazine and turned right to the blonde with enormous hooters. She was the one he liked to think about.

He was already very hard, and it didn't take him very long, even with T.J. watching, because T.J. had been right. It was much more exciting to do it while looking at the magazine.

"See, I told you," T.J. said. And after that, they masturbated to the magazines together every chance they had. It stopped being embarrassing soon enough. They competed to see who could finish faster or shoot it farther.

But one day, while they were distracted by what they were doing, one of the neighbors walked right into the garage. Their hard-ons had disappeared instantly and they'd rushed to fasten their pants and turn over the magazines.

"What are you boys up to in here?" Mr. Abbott had asked, although there was zero chance he didn't know exactly what they were up to.

"Nothing," T.J. said.

"Didn't look like nothing," the man said. "I see you two boys make a beeline for the garage every day. I had a feeling you were up to no good." Mr. Abbott picked up a magazine. "You boys have dirty minds. I wonder what your parents would think."

"Please don't tell my dad," T.J. had begged. Darren still remembered the deep shame and hopelessness he'd felt. Mr. Abbott was going to tell their parents and they were going to be disowned. Their parents would probably kick them out.

But then came the reprieve. "I tell you what. I've been planning to enlarge my garden. It's going to take a lot of digging. You boys tell your parents you're going to help me with some yard work tomorrow after lunch. I'll even pay you both for it. You do that for me and I won't tell."

Relieved, the boys immediately agreed. The next day, they hadn't been digging five minutes before Mr. Abbott said it was time for a lemonade break and had invited them into the air conditioning to cool off.

"I know you boys like dirty magazines. You ever see a dirty movie?"

It was shockingly easy for him to use their shame, terror and sexual curiosity to make them do what he wanted them to do. At first he said he only wanted to see how they did it for themselves. But as soon as they'd compromised themselves that far, he had the power to make them do things to him, and to let him do things to them.

It only ended when T.J. started crying. And not just play tears, but real, full-out girly sobbing. Mr. Abbott suddenly seemed concerned about how it was going to look if he sent home a crying kid.

"That's enough of that. Get your asses outside and get that garden done. Here's your money," he'd said, handing them each a five-dollar bill. And they'd taken their money, and then they'd sweated their asses off digging through the grass, turning it over and breaking up the clumps. They knew he was watching them from the window. Neither of them said a single word to each other.

Two hours later, when they were burned and broken, he'd told them it was enough. "You're done here. You tell a soul and I'll find out and I'll tell your parents and everyone else everything you did."

Darren had sworn a solemn oath to himself to never, ever look at porn ever again. He and T.J. stopped hanging out.

But he was to break his oath to himself over and over, especially once he was old enough to buy magazines. He'd buy them, use them, throw them out and swear never to buy another. Then the internet came along and that was all she wrote. And now that he had the internet on his phone? He abandoned himself to it. Resistance was futile. If he had five minutes to kill, that was what he did.

Right now, people could drive by and they'd just assume he was reading the news. As long as he arranged his legs to hide his erection, he appeared perfectly respectful. Just a man smoking a cigarette and reading about the situation in the Middle East or how the stock market was doing as he waited for his laundry to finish up.

When he got home, he knew just what he was

going to do. First, he'd pop a pain pill. Doing the laundry had shifted something in his back.

But as soon as the pill kicked in, he was going to sit at his kitchen table, bring up some noisy porn on his phone and watch the new woman sitting on her porch as he jacked off. Suddenly, he didn't mind at all that that's all she ever did.

CHAPTER 7

Janiece

The break she'd been counting on for weeks wasn't going to happen.

She and Jimmy should have been visiting her brother right now. She had been counting on it. Their daughters were 3 now, and they would have had so much fun playing with their cousins. She had been yearning to see her family and get a break from everything. Jimmy's boss was such an asshole to rescind the vacation he'd approved. Now she didn't know when they'd be able to go.

Twins sounded like fun, but they were twice the work. They had finally weaned and were potty trained and sleeping through the night, but these were recent developments, and she still felt like she was catching up on years of lost sleep.

Two active little girls could destroy a trailer in no time. They were so full of energy. She tried to worry less about keeping the trailer in order and prioritized things like reading to them and making sure they learned how to count and recognize their colors. Her children would always have to work harder than anybody else. It was a double whammy, being black and female. Nobody had to tell Janiece that.

But it would get better. It was just a waiting game now. They'd be eligible for free preschool next year, and then she could at last return to school. She'd made sure to keep her student loan situation in order. Yes, the amount was growing alarmingly, and it was going to get worse before it got better, but it *would* get better. Once she had her teaching degree, it would be so much better. It would. It had to.

People said teachers didn't make much money but their salaries looked good to Janiece. And as soon as she got a teaching job, her plan was to try to support the household on that salary so Jimmy could get back into school.

She dreamed of what they could do with an engineer's salary plus a teacher's salary. She had it all planned out. They'd stay in the trailer park for at least a year, so they could pay their loans down as quickly as possible. They were used to living on not much money, so the trick would be to stay here for a year or maybe two after they had moved on with their lives, and use all that money Jimmy would make to drop their loan balances like a rock.

She had a whole spiral notebook full of her figures. If they lived here for one year. If they lived here for two years. If her first year of teaching paid $40,000. If his first year of being an engineer paid $80,000. It might pay more.

They could, conceivably, be in decent shape in four years. One more year before the girls were in school. One more year to finish her degree. One year of teaching while Jimmy finished his degree. And after that, they'd be home free. Writing out possible budgets soothed her and made her feel like she had a handle on things.

In the meantime, they lived as cheaply as they could. They kept just one car, and they wouldn't get a second one until they absolutely had to. It might be possible for her to get a ride to campus, or it might be possible to take the bus. There were all kinds of ways it might pan out. She had imagined all of them.

She cooked everything from scratch and could feed them all for less than $350 per month, and that included Jimmy's lunches. Her mother and grandmother were both excellent cooks who had taught her how to cut up a whole chicken and turn it into dinner for a week. Traditional foods like collard greens were cheap. She'd cook them with just the littlest bit of ham.

She took nutrition seriously. They loved sweet potatoes and ham and chicken, yes, but she made sure they got plenty of fresh vegetables and fruits. Her kids would not grow up eating boxed macaroni or chicken nuggets or junk. They were poor and they were black, and they had enough to overcome. She would give them every advantage it was in her power to give them.

She did a little homeschooling session every morning after breakfast. Both girls knew all their colors and could sing the ABCs with her. She was working on teaching them how to write letters and numbers now. And she read to them all the time.

Kids books were mostly cheap and she bought lots of them, but they also went to the library and checked things out. The girls loved the library. It was a far cry from the plain old buildings full of books she remembered; now there were activities and storytellers and even toys you could check out for free. Janiece took advantage of everything they offered. Her kids were going to know everything the rich white kids knew. She would teach them herself if she had to.

Her kids would probably scarcely remember being poor and living in a trailer. By the time they were making memories, they'd have a proper house.

In the meantime, she had turned the trailer into a little preschool. She had cut letters and numbers out of construction paper and posted them on the hallway walls at kid height. Their artwork was hanging everywhere. She kept the TV off when the girls were up, other than some children's programming on public TV.

She needed one more semester of classes and a semester of student teaching. She'd talked to her academic advisor, Martha Givens, and had her plans all laid out and ready to go. All she needed was to wait until her babies were old enough for free preschool.

Her advisor had been surprised she was planning to wait.

"Why wait? The sooner you get done, the sooner you can start your career," Ms. Givens had said. "They'll be fine in daycare."

Janiece had asked if there was any free daycare available through the school.

"No, you'll just have to bite the bullet and pay for it. I know it might mean giving up on some extras, but it's very worth your while."

Janiece had cocked her head and regarded Ms. Givens, who had been her advisor since she had first enrolled. She was a nice enough woman, but it appeared she'd never hit any roadblocks in life. She was married to a math professor and Janiece knew they lived in one of the big old houses in the historic district and had no children.

"The cheapest full-time daycare I can find costs $800 a month, and I have twins. So that's $1,600 per month," she said.

"Yes, high-quality care is expensive, but you wouldn't want to put their children just anywhere."

"Oh, that's not the high-quality place. That's the cheapest place. The nice places cost a lot more. But since we're already living on less than $2,000 a month, I think it might be kind of hard to pay $1,600 of it just for daycare."

Ms. Givens stood up, signaling the meeting was over. "If you really want to succeed, you'll find a way. I believe a positive attitude makes all the difference. If you're determined to look at it from a negative point of view, you're only going to see the negatives. I myself have always made it a point to look for the positives, and I believe it's paid off for me. I wish you luck, Ms. Jackson."

The hell of it was, Janiece did think of herself as a positive person. At every roadblock, Jimmy would react with anger, and Janiece would always be the one to offer a more positive perspective. "Take it easy," she'd say. "We'll get through this."

Part of her had wanted to force Ms. Givens to listen. She'd wanted to list what they paid for rent and utilities, for the car payment and insurance and gas and for food, and to ask Ms. Givens just what items she thought her family could do without so they could pay $1,600 every month for daycare.

She was very proud of how thrifty she was. It wasn't easy to live on Jimmy's salary but they managed, because she did things like make big pots of red beans and rice and buy most of their clothes at the thrift store.

She hung the wet laundry on the bathtub shower rod instead of paying to use the dryers. That saved about two dollars for every load, and that added up fast when you had twin girls and a husband whose clothes got factory-filthy. Hanging everything up to dry saved about $10 per week, which was $520 every year! Gosh, that would be enough to cover several days of daycare for one of the girls.

Sometimes the futility of her situation did get her down. She was doing her very best, but it seemed like other people had so much easier lives. Others thought nothing of feeding quarters to the dryers until their clothes were dry.

Looking around their street, most of her neighbors smoked. How anybody could afford that habit was beyond her. It cost a fortune. But then again, she and Jimmy were the only ones with children, unless the new lady at the end of the lane had some. She hadn't seen any yet.

She didn't have a warm relationship with anybody in the park. She'd tried. Last Christmas, she had dropped off a beautiful Christmas card at every trailer door, hoping to get to know a few of her neighbors. It would be nice to have friends. But nobody had reciprocated.

She resisted thinking it was because they were the only black family in the park. Maybe they were all stand-offish in general. But you could see Kaitlin and Shirley gossiping and smoking like mad nearly every day. You rarely saw Darren or Nancy.

Jonesy was the friendliest one. They exchanged greetings now and then, but he worked as much as Jimmy did. You'd see Jonesy coming and going at all hours, always dragging a big camera and a notebook. He was a reporter. She'd thought reporters made more money, but apparently not Jonesy. He seemed to do little more than work and sleep.

They'd had a conversation about it once, early on. Janiece had strung a clothesline from the corner of the trailer to a small tree, and was hanging up a load of Jimmy's work pants to dry in the sun, when Jonesy had emerged from his trailer for a read and a smoke.

"I hate to tell you this, but Nancy isn't going to stand for that." She read the title of the paperback he held: *Deadeye Dick*. She'd heard of Vonnegut but had never heard of that book. "It's against the trailer park rules." He rolled his eyes. "Apparently this place is too high class for clotheslines."

"Are you kidding me?" She kept hanging up the pants anyway.

"I wish I were. I hung one up when I first moved in and she made me take it down. I thought I was going to be able to save a few bucks a week, but she threw a fit. Kills me to throw away a handful of quarters every week when the sun is free."

"I always thought reporters did OK," she ventured, hoping he didn't take offense. His response was to laugh.

"No. Almost all of us would make more

waiting tables. You'd be surprised. Even the local TV anchors are making nothing. They look good on camera, but they're poor. Sometimes the station works out a promotional deal with clothing stores so the anchors can have the right look." He pointed at his own clothing. "They don't bother with newspaper reporters. It's OK for us to look like slobs."

Jonesy had been right. Nancy had marched right over that night and threatened to fine Janiece if she didn't take the line down. You'd have thought Janiece had put a rusty clunker up on blocks on the front lawn of a mansion the way Nancy carried on.

Not allowing poor people living in a trailer park to save money with a clothesline was immoral, in Janiece's view. Probably, the owners made bank on the mildewy little laundry room. Janiece couldn't avoid washing her clothes there, but she'd be damned if she was going to pay for their dryers, so she stuck to hanging everything up in the bathroom. It wasn't convenient but it worked.

And in the end, everything is temporary.

Being on bedrest had been boring but it had not lasted forever. Visiting the babies at the NICU all day and pumping her milk around the clock and learning how to care for fragile babies and never getting enough sleep, all while recovering from surgery and preeclampsia had been an exhausting, painful blur, but it had not lasted forever.

Caring for two tiny babies mostly by herself, never getting more than three hours of sleep at a stretch for months on end, changing as many as twenty-five diapers a day, perfecting the art of getting two babies correctly latched on at the same time and being so tired she often forgot to shower had been the hardest thing she had ever done, but it had not lasted forever.

Two rambunctious toddlers climbing everything in the trailer with absolutely no regard for their personal safety, causing her to feel terrified one of them was going to fall off the kitchen table and break her arm or worse so that she couldn't take the risk of even peeing by herself and would make them come into the bathroom with her if Jimmy wasn't home ... that was pretty hard but it had not lasted forever.

Now the girls were easier to care for. They could talk a little now and that made a big difference. They'd settle down and listen to her read them stories. They were better sleepers. Very soon, they'd be in all-day preschool, and she'd be back in college. It was all going to work out.

This would not last forever.

CHAPTER 8

Angel

It was such a relief not to have to live with her mom anymore.

She was 35 years old and had lived with her mom off and on her whole life, mostly on. And she hated it — she ought to be married and living with a husband. She was a traditional girl with traditional values but she'd had bad luck with men.

Maya's dad, for example. She had really thought he was going to marry her. He'd even given her an engagement ring, at one point, but then they'd had another one of their terrible fights and she'd flung it back at him. She hadn't meant it. She was just being dramatic. But afterward, he refused to give it back, so that breakup was for real.

Before Maya, she'd gotten pregnant two other times, and those babies were in Heaven. She was 17 the first time she got pregnant. It was Robby, the son of her minister. She had gone to that church her whole life. Her mom liked that they only allowed the King James Bible rather than the liberal versions of the Word so many lesser churches had settled for.

Angel had only let Robby put the tip in. She knew it was wrong, but he had been so persuasive. And she didn't think you could get pregnant just from the tip.

But then she missed her period and started feeling sick every morning and knew what had happened. She dreaded the looks of judgment everyone at school and church was going to direct to her once they knew she and Robby had broken the rules and done it. Although they'd barely even done it.

"We have to get rid of it," Robby had said, crying. "Think about it. If we have a baby, my dad will lose his job! No church is going to keep a minister with a bastard grandchild. And everybody is going to say you're a whore."

"We could get married," Angel had said.

"Angel. They can count. They are still going to know what we did. There's a place about an hour from here. I can take the money out of my savings account. Nobody will ever have to know."

She knew it was wrong, but then again, Robby was right when he said it was also wrong that his dad would lose his job and they'd all be shunned. God would forgive them, he said, and they could get married and have a baby later.

It might even be the same baby — couldn't it

be true that the baby would return to Heaven and come back in a couple of years when they were ready? That was the argument that finally swayed her. They weren't really going to kill the baby. They were just going to sort of put it on layaway and have it later.

Robby broke up with her the next day, though. He said he couldn't look at her without feeling guilty and he said he could never marry a girl who would kill her own baby. So she guessed that baby wasn't just on layaway after all. That baby was actually dead.

Angel had pretended to be having terrible menstrual cramps and didn't leave bed for almost a week. Her mom had no reason not to believe her, because she sure was bleeding enough.

Angel had looked at each sanitary napkin carefully, searching for any little baby parts there might be. There were a lot of clots, and she carefully probed each one with her finger. Just in case. She saved all the pads from that time and later, when she was home alone, dug a deep hole in the backyard and buried them all, wrapped carefully in a pretty pillowcase. Then she transplanted some marigolds there and said a prayer.

The second time she got pregnant, she was 21 and was dating another nice boy. They worked at the same grocery store and went to the same church. It was a different church than the one

Robby's dad preached at; Angel never went back there after the break-up.

Bill had a gorgeous singing voice and she half fell in love with him just watching and listening to him perform in the church choir. This time she knew very well she was sinning, but she was in what she later thought of as her bad girl phase.

Unfortunately, Bill liked to drink, and he occasionally hit her, so she wasn't quite sure whether she should marry him or not. While she was making up her mind, she had a miscarriage, probably because God knew she didn't deserve a baby.

She tried very hard not to feel relieved when it happened. She planted some more marigolds in her mom's yard.

After that, she felt fatalistic about it. Contraception being a sin, it was in God's hands. So the third time she got pregnant, while dating a guy named Jeff she'd gone to high school with, she didn't tell anyone. She would wait and see what God had in mind for her. When she was four months pregnant, Jeff noticed her larger breasts and her baby bump, and she pretended she hadn't known.

He was maybe not totally thrilled, but not totally upset, either, and he gave her the ring, which she wore for a whole month before throwing it back at him.

By this time, she was nearly six months pregnant and it looked like God intended this one to be born. So she told her mother everything. Her mother screamed and cried and threatened to throw her out on the street and then, a few hours later, said they'd go out shopping for a crib the next day.

Besides the grocery store, Angel had worked at a video rental store, a pizza place and at the front desk of a motel. But once she had Maya, she never worked again.

"Maya needs a full-time mama," she insisted when her mother prodded her to look for a job. "Jeff should be paying more child support."

Jeff worked the same kind of dead-end jobs she had worked and paid very little in child support. He lived with his mother, who doted on Maya and wanted to see her grandchild every week, but Angel often found excuses to prevent this. Nobody could watch Maya as well as she could. If Jeff and his mother wanted to see Maya, he would have to cough up child support. Often, his mother paid it for him, and then Maya would go spend the weekend at her other grandma's house.

Living with her mom, and getting sporadic child support and some welfare, Angel didn't need to work. She was too tired, she said. Raising a child by herself was a lot of work, and she mostly preferred to watch TV all day. Once Maya was in school, Angel's mother got all bossy about money.

"Maya's not a baby. It's time you went back to

work," her mother said. "They're hiring at the grocery store. You could walk there from here until you saved up for a car."

"I don't want Maya to be raised by a working mother," Angel said. "A mother's place is in the home."

"I'm your mother, and *I* work, in case you haven't noticed. Somebody has to pay the bills around here. I'm getting tired of being the only one who does."

She even shamed Angel for her weight, and eventually, Angel could no longer tolerate such abuse.

"If you ever want to meet a nice man to be Maya's stepdad, you might want to lay off the potato chips and chocolate ice cream, is all I'm saying." That was no way to talk to your daughter. Angel just wanted a little peace but there was none to be had at her mother's house anymore, and there was no husband on the horizon. So she had looked into housing vouchers.

"No, her dad hardly ever pays child support," she'd explained to her caseworker. "And my mom is a very negative person. I don't think it's good for Maya." But she was surprised by how expensive rent was. She'd had in mind a cute little two-bedroom house with a nice yard, but as it turned out, she could qualify only for a trailer.

Jeff had come through, though, borrowing his uncle's truck and helping her move their stuff.

He'd even hinted he might come around a little more now that she had her own place. She hadn't said yes and she hadn't said no. You never knew when you were going to need a favor.

For now, her favorite thing was just sitting peacefully on the little porch in front of her trailer. It wasn't very big, but it had an awning, and Jeff had been nice enough to bring her two of his mom's old lawn chairs and a little plastic table. She could sit out there all day if she wanted to, and nobody bothered her. Maya preferred to stay inside and watch TV, and that was fine with Angel.

She had peace and quiet at last.

CHAPTER 9

Nathan

Having it all was not enough for Nathan.

He had made good money as a mechanical engineer, and he started making even more once he moved into managing a team of mechanical engineers. Having plenty of money meant he was able to procure everything that made him happy.

He had a classically beautiful wife with Nordic cheekbones and a platinum bob. He had a brand-new Lexus and a big boat. He had just built a new house, which his elegant wife, Amanda, had very tastefully and expensively decorated with the help of an interior designer. They went out to eat most evenings, and he cultivated a taste for good scotch and cigars.

So he already had far more than most men had, but it wouldn't be enough if he didn't also have Kaitlin to visit every morning. She was his wonderful dirty little secret he had all to himself. The reason he'd gotten away with keeping her all this time was simple: He had never told a soul. Even his best friend had no idea that Nathan had a sugar baby. Bragging was what got you into trouble.

Kaitlin was ideal because she didn't insist on the full sugar baby experience. She did not hanker after fine jewelry or her own car. She didn't even insist on a fancy apartment. She knew better than to even ask for him to take her on trips. She asked no questions. She made no demands.

Once in a while she'd request a little extra money, but she always had a decent reason, and she always made it worth his while.

If she tried, she could have scored all the extras. She had the face, body and bedroom skills to demand real spoiling. She could be getting a luxury condo, a car and all the rest. But she didn't seem to realize that. She was satisfied with getting enough money to pay for the rent and utilities on a trailer.

Since his promotion, he could easily have upgraded her living situation, but he had never told her about his improved position. She thought she was getting as much as he could afford, and he would let her keep thinking that.

It was better that she lived in a crappy trailer park. If she'd been in a nice condo, there would always be the chance somebody might see him coming or going from her place every day. But a trailer park? None of his friends or colleagues was ever going to see him there. It was practically on the way between his house and his office. Detouring to her trailer took about two extra minutes of driving, and he almost never stayed more than half an hour, including the quickie shower he always took before he left.

Kaitlin seemed to assume he needed her because his wife didn't take care of him in bed. He encouraged her in this belief, but nothing could have been further from the truth. Amanda was just as hot as Kaitlin, and maybe even more beautiful, in a more upper-class sort of way. And their sex life was great. He made love to his wife most nights during the week and usually even more on the weekends, when he didn't see Kaitlin.

But he always made sure Amanda enjoyed herself in bed. He frankly didn't care if Kaitlin enjoyed their sex or not.

He wasn't really paying for the sex. He was paying for Kaitlin to be available exactly when he wanted her and he was paying to be able to leave when he was done and not have to speak to her until he was ready to have sex with her again.

Getting sex was easy. Having it ready every morning when he wanted it? Not having to deal with the woman the rest of the day?

That was worth paying for. Her number was in his phone under the name Ken Stonecipher, an engineer he used to work with who had moved out of state years ago and to whom he had no reason to ever speak again.

Kaitlin was under strict orders never to call him and to text him only in a life-or-death situation, and then only to text something innocuous so he'd know to call her as soon as he had privacy. She'd never once broken that rule, because she understood very well that if she did, that would be the end of their arrangement.

For now, she was perfect. He was sure his performance at work was better because he showed up every morning in a positive state of mind, feeling entirely satisfied with his life. Some of his colleagues talked about how a morning run really paid off for them.

But in his opinion, a morning fuck beat a morning run all to hell. And the knowledge that he was secretly screwing two different women almost every weekday? He was sure if he ever had his testosterone checked, it would be off the charts.

He'd always had a crazy-high sex drive. If he thought he could get away with it, he'd have another sugar baby for nooners and yet another for after work, but he knew that was just asking to get caught.

But if he'd been alive hundreds of years ago? He'd have been one of those guys with a harem, absolutely. Or maybe he should have been a Mormon back when they were officially in favor of polygamy. Two women were barely enough to meet his needs. He often jacked off to his favorite fantasy, which was having a large apartment complex full of hot women who all paid their rent with sex.

He looked at those poor fools in the trailer park and wondered how they could endure such a life of privation, but then he looked at the engineers he managed in much the same way. Did these people not have an appetite for all that the world offered? It was so, so easy to take what you wanted. Why didn't everyone do it? What made a person content with such a limited life?

That would never be him. He saw no reason he shouldn't keep striving for more. The C-suite beckoned. And once he had that, he'd be able to help himself to just about anything he wanted. Maybe one of those smart little college student sugar babies. It would be worth coughing up the big bucks to enjoy that kind of pussy.

At some point, he would trade up. But for now, Little Miss Kaitlin was absolutely perfect for his needs.

CHAPTER 10

Shirley

Another Loire landmark had bitten the dust. This hardly seemed the same town she had grown up in anymore.

Shirley subscribed to the local paper and generally read it every morning with her first cigarette and cup of coffee of the day — when it was actually delivered. A lot of times, it wasn't anymore.

Apparently, the bowling alley had burned down, but this was the first she'd heard of it. The story must have run on one of the days she hadn't gotten the paper. But here was a big feature story by the reporter fellow who lived across from her, talking all about it. He'd interviewed the owner, Charles Darby.

Shirley used to bowl and play bridge with Linda Darby back in the day. Charles and Linda owned one of the oldest strip malls in Loire, the bowling alley and some small apartment buildings — when Shirley sold her big house and thought about moving, she immediately rejected the idea of living in one of the Darby apartments, only to land in his trailer park. If she'd known Darby owned the place, she'd never have signed a lease.

No matter how nice Linda was, her husband was the sort who gave landlords a bad name. No wonder Linda had eventually left him.

The strip mall wasn't what it used to be. Half of it was vacant and the other half had gone from tenants like jewelers and baby boutiques to things like vape joints and payday loan places. One of the apartment buildings showed up a lot in the police news. If you read the addresses of people arrested for shoplifting and domestic battery and that sort of thing, an awful lot of them seemed to have Charles Darby as a landlord.

But anyway, Jonesy had interviewed all kinds of people she knew.

In its heyday, the bowling alley served as a civic meeting place. Churches and local businesses often formed leagues. Loire Custom Metal sponsored three of them.

"I bowled here every Tuesday night for 20 years," said Carol Findley, who bowled as a member of the Methodist Ladies Aid Society team.

"I only missed one time, when I went into labor on a Tuesday morning. I gave birth to a 10-pound baby that night and I was back the very next week with my baby. I bowled a 120 that night. My doctor

scolded me for it," she said with a chuckle.

"He said, 'I thought I told you not to pick up anything heavier than your baby for a month.' I told him, 'If I can push out a 10-pound baby, I guess I can throw a 10-pound bowling ball.'"

Shirley remembered Carol. They'd never been on the same team, but they'd been in the same league.

Owner Charles Darby declined to be interviewed.

That was a first. But maybe he was too embarrassed that all his businesses had gone to pot to want to talk to a reporter.

It was Sunday morning and Jonesy was home. She knew because his car was parked in front of his trailer. So she marched right over to his trailer, coffee in one hand, cigarette in the other and paper tucked under her arm.

He answered right away.

"I read your story," she said.

"Which one?"

"The bowling alley story," she said. "In today's paper. Why didn't Charles Darby want to talk?"

"You'll have to ask him."

"You should have interviewed me. I bowled there for years, and Linda Darby and I were pretty good friends back then. I could have told you a lot more."

She should call Linda. She'd drifted away from all her bowling and bridge friends, but it seemed like Linda might have come down in the world far enough that they might have some things in common again.

"Let me grab my cigarettes and I'll come over," he said.

"How do you take your coffee?" she asked him once they were seated at her little patio table.

"Black is fine," he said as he lit a cigarette. She had a fresh pot ready and she fetched him a cup.

"Carol Findley didn't bowl a 120 a week after having a baby. She did show up, but she mostly just sat there showing off her baby."

"It made for a good story."

"Yes, but I was there and she's lying. Who cares, right? But Charles Darby turned down a chance to talk to a reporter? I never knew that man to miss a chance to get his picture in the paper. Are you sure he didn't burn that place to the ground himself?"

"What makes you think he did?" He took a sip of his coffee but he looked interested, she thought.

"Look at all his properties. They all look terrible. Run down. Bad tenants or no tenants at all. He can't be making much money at any of them, and when he and his wife were together, they were always running and doing. He always liked to throw his money around. One of his apartment buildings burned to the ground about ten years ago. Maybe it was more like twenty. I don't remember. I do remember they said it was lucky nobody was living there because they were getting ready to do a big remodel. They were going to re-do all the wiring and the plumbing. They said it was the old wiring that caught on fire, but I always wondered about that and I wasn't the only one."

"If they knew the wiring was bad enough they cleared everyone out so they could fix it, that kind of proves the point that the wiring was bad, right?"

Shirley made a little scoffing noise. "He didn't rebuild it, though. He just pocketed the insurance money. Empty lot there to this day. I bet you anything he doesn't rebuild the bowling alley, either. He'll just keep the money."

"Do you have any evidence to back it up?"

"Well, that's your job, isn't it? You're the reporter."

CHAPTER 11

Kaitlin

She had the trifecta: an IOU, an IUD and a DUI.

Back when she first got the sugar baby gig with Nathan, Kaitlin recalled, Sapphire felt she was owed for acting as her advisor.

"I told you, girl. You and me are gonna celebrate. You owe me, and I'm collecting on the IOU. Let's go to the Loire club and party our asses off tomorrow night."

Kaitlin had counted the money Nathan gave her when he guessed her name. It was almost a grand, and she figured she did owe Sapphire a favor. Besides, she thought, it would be fun to go to a different strip club as a customer.

She picked up Sapphire in the car she'd bought herself three months after she started dancing. She'd paid cash for it; she paid cash for almost everything.

"Nice car," Sapphire said. "Now when are you going to get a better place to live?"

"I like my trailer, actually. It was the only place

that would rent to me when I was 18 and wanted to get away from my creepy stepdad."

"We all got a creepy stepdad or uncle somewhere in our past," Sapphire said.

Kaitlin changed the subject. "This will be my first time in a strip club with my clothes on."

"If you get drunk enough, you'll probably feel like taking them off. But I never take my clothes off for free."

Kaitlin laughed. "Not even to shower?"

Sapphire laughed. "I got to have a horny little man in my bathroom with money in his hand or else I just get ripe."

The two women were in a party mood and did everything in reverse. Kaitlin bought Sapphire a lap dance and laughed hysterically all the way through it.

Next, they went up to the stage and clenched dollar bills between their teeth and tilted their faces toward the dancers on stage so they would give them "the boob treatment," taking the money by pressing their breasts together. It was a move Kaitlin and Sapphire knew well. They tucked money into the dancers' bikinis.

"It's more fun this way!" Kaitlin said. "I get it now!"

The drinks cost a mint but Kaitlin didn't mind. It was all free money as far as she was concerned. And the funny thing was, the patrons paid no attention to them at all except when they were interacting with the dancers. Otherwise? The men paid little more attention to Kaitlin and Sapphire than they did to the doorman.

"What's your real name, Sapphire?" Kaitlin asked. She'd already told Sapphire to call her Kaitlin, not Karma.

"It's Ruth! Don't ever tell anyone, OK? I think there's a law that you can't be a dancer if your real name is Ruth."

She didn't look a damned thing like a Ruth. She looked more like a Sapphire for sure, even dressed in fairly normal street clothes.

"You'll always be Sapphire to me," Kaitlin had said. She was pretty drunk at that point. Then Sapphire ordered a bottle of Dom Perignon.

"Are you insane?" she hissed. "Two hundred bucks for a bottle of wine?"

"Live a little, honey! You're a sugar baby now! You can afford it. Besides, this isn't the most expensive Dom. I've had the top stuff before. This ain't it." She pulled the money out of Kaitlin's purse and handed it to the bartender, and then handed him another twenty of Kaitlin's money as a tip, and the bartender filled two flutes.

Kaitlin didn't think it tasted any different than any other sparkly wine, but she drank up. All those little bubbles making a show before disappearing made her think of all her money doing the same; she wanted to capture at least some of them.

"You never told me how much he's paying you. Two thousand? Three?"

"Noooo," Kaitlin said, suddenly quiet.

"Four thousand? Is it more than four thousand bucks a month?"

"It's eight hundred," she whispered. "Is that bad?"

Sapphire suddenly looked almost sober. "Jesus Christ, that's bad. You're giving it up for less than a grand? How often is he visiting you?"

"Every morning before work. But he's only there for half an hour."

"You're fucking him 20 times a month, for $800, so that's ... that's less than $50 a throw. There's crack whores getting more than that for a half-and-half. I thought I told you not to take his first offer."

"I know! But what if he picked somebody else?"

"The very least you shoulda got was two grand. How are you going to pay your bills on that? I thought you said he wanted you to stop dancing?"

"I was going to get maybe a part-time job at a store. He said it would be better if I did something like that so nobody knows my private business."

Sapphire snorted. "He's just cheap. Did he agree to pay for any extras?"

"He paid for me to get an IUD and to get all checked out so he wouldn't have to wear a condom."

"Oh, big spender. Well, at least charge him more for the blowjobs. You didn't talk about blowjobs, right?"

"No."

"Well, they're not included. If he wants one, he has to pay extra. He knows damned well he's cheaping out. He'll pay up. If you need extra money, get it that way. And next time you pick out a guy, get a better deal. If you wanted to just give it away, you'd have picked a guy your own age."

The night wasn't fun anymore. Sapphire had pulled some money out of her own purse and handed it to Kaitlin. "I'm sorry, honey. I thought you had it to blow tonight. But you need it more than I do."

Kaitlin miserably forced down the champagne. Her stomach felt bloated and she didn't want to drink anything else, but it was too expensive to waste. Suddenly, it just felt like she was at work. Why had she even come here? She could be making a fortune here tonight, not spending one.

She tipped up her glass and drank it as if it were medicine, and then filled up and did it again. Sapphire finished off the last of the bottle.

"I guess I'm ready to go home," Kaitlin said, and Sapphire quickly agreed.

She couldn't remember where her car was parked until she hit the panic button and heard the alarm go off. "This way," she told Sapphire, who cracked up.

"That's one way to find your car."

They got in and Kaitlin very slowly drove across the parking lot.

"Be really careful," Sapphire said.

"I know it." It was all going fine until she saw the flashing lights come up behind her.

"I wasn't even speeding!" she told the officer, and she was almost sure that was true.

"License and registration."

Her fingers dove through the sea of loose money in her purse and finally dredged up her license. Then she reached past Sapphire and rummaged through the glove box for her registration.

"Have you been drinking, ma'am?"

"I had a couple of drinks of champagne," she said. That was true. It was also true that she'd had a bunch of other drinks before that, but he hadn't asked how much, now had he? Sapphire sat there absolutely silent.

The cop went back to his car and just sat there with his stupid lights flashing everywhere for a long time.

"I'll be all sobered up by the time he finally comes back," she told Sapphire.

"Don't say nothing to him. Not one word."

He finally came back. "Step out of the car, please."

He said he wanted to put her through some field sobriety tests. She didn't know why he was bothering. Even if she passed them, he'd make her breathe into a tube and she knew she wasn't going to pass.

Still, when he asked her to stand on one foot, she gave it a go and thought she did pretty well, probably because she was no stranger to being drunk while balancing in heels a lot higher than what she was wearing tonight.

He asked her to walk a straight line, and she pretended she was on the catwalk at work. She held up her head, smiled big, put her hands on her hips and did it with attitude, singing her favorite song to dance to at work and keeping her eyes on an imaginary stripper pole just ahead. Maybe he'd think she was too hot to arrest. You never knew. She was willing to try anything to avoid the breathalyzer.

But in the end, he held it up to her face and told her to blow into it.

"Don't do it," Sapphire said. "They can't make you do it."

"If you don't do it, you'll lose your license," the cop told her. She later realized he had been full of crap. She was going to lose her license whether she did it or not. But as with a broke girl in the VIP room, blowing was inevitable.

Soon thereafter, she sold her car and applied for a job at the only business within walking distance of her trailer. That car wasn't doing her any good just sitting there undriven. Sugar baby in the morning, convenience store cashier in the afternoon. That was her life now.

But actually, Nathan had been right. Nobody

questioned how she paid her rent, because they knew she had a job at a convenience store. Nobody questioned why she didn't have a car, because she worked at a convenience store. They just assumed she couldn't afford to own a car.

It was all very convenient.

CHAPTER 12

Nancy

The first thing she did when she got into the office every day was check her email for anything from Mr. Darby. You never knew. He might be impressed by all her extra efforts and give her a raise eventually. Just because it hadn't happened yet didn't mean it wouldn't happen eventually.

Today she did have an email from him, and she opened it first.

"Oh shit." It wasn't good news. He was selling the park to some big company. He said he had been assured by the new people that no changes were planned, that it had been a pleasure working with her, that he wished her all the very best and that someone from Sterling Communities would be in touch.

Nancy reached into her desk and pulled out the package of sugar cookies she kept there, eating two as she scrolled through her email looking for something from the new company.

Sure enough, there was another email, similar

in tone to the other, welcoming her to the Sterling Communities family. As she read it, she reached for another cookie.

Maybe this wouldn't be bad. They were a huge company that owned not just mobile home parks but also some condos and apartment buildings. That could mean more money, and potentially a raise. She brightened. It was unbelievable how little she was paid.

Of course, her free double-wide was a good part of her compensation, but even so, once she paid the premium on her health insurance, she had very little money to live on. That's why she was so thrifty with her lunches. Still, she was almost done paying for her furniture, so she got by. This could be a good thing if it meant a raise.

The new company had instructed her to make copies of an attached tenant letter and distribute one to everyone in the park. She printed it out and began making copies so she could place one in every mailbox. She was a conscientious employee, and soon enough they'd see that.

Mr. Darby was an old creep. But there might be somebody single at Sterling Communities. You never did know.

CHAPTER 13

Jonesy

Jonesy had dedicated a lot of time to learning to write well, but he recognized he'd probably have more money if he'd instead learned to paint houses or groom pets.

He had taken a few business classes in J-school because he'd wanted to be a business reporter, but all he'd ever managed to get were jobs as a general assignment reporter. The specialized gigs at newspapers were few and far between now. Other than at a few top papers, there were no longer any such animals as arts reporters, medical reporters, business reporters or anything else. There were only reporters, and they had to know how to do it all.

He'd covered city hall shenanigans, murder investigations, inquests, elections, the local schools, the local farming economy, feature stories of all kinds and whatever else his editor dreamed up. The closest thing he'd gotten to the business beat lately was the grand opening of a boutique that had just opened in Loire's sad little downtown square. He'd written up a short story and shot some pictures and videos there that morning.

He filled out his hours as if he worked eight to five each day, with an hour off for lunch. The night the bowling alley burned down, he'd worked from eight a.m. one day to three-thirty a.m. the next day. But his time card claimed he'd worked the same eight-to-noon, one-to-five as every other day. All those pictures he'd shot in the middle of the night had obviously been taken when he was off the clock, but such things were never questioned.

Early on, he'd occasionally put down hours for breaking news that had popped out of nowhere. If he'd been roused from his bed late at night to cover a fire or a murder, surely that warranted a couple of hours of overtime, right?

Wrong. Dani had jumped his editor's ass, who had in turn reluctantly told Jonesy to keep his hours at forty. Jonesy had angrily called Dani to demand an explanation, but she wouldn't budge.

"Managing your time is a basic skill we expect of all our employees," she'd said. "It's really very simple, Gilbert."

Even his mother didn't call him anything but Jonesy anymore, but he gritted his teeth and said nothing.

"This is the newspaper business. You know there are going to be times when things come up.

It's the nature of the beast. So set aside some time every week for the unexpected. And one more angry outburst like this from you and you'll be written up. Chain of command, Gilbert. You answer to Carl. Talk to him. He gets it. He holds himself to the same forty hours we all do."

Carl, the paper's editor, worked at least sixty hours most weeks and Jonesy was sure Dani knew that. He hung up on her and went back to lying on his timesheet every week.

He was just finishing up the boutique video when Carl yelled at him.

"Hey, Jonesy. You know anything about Charles Darby?"

He looked up. "I know he sucks."

"How so?"

"I've been living in his trailer park for a while now."

"Oh, it might be a conflict of interest for you to check into this, but I don't know who else would."

"Check into what?"

"It looks like the little fish has sold his trailer park to a big fish called Sterling Communities. They sent us a press release."

Jonesy walked over to Carl's desk and started reading over his shoulder. Carl hated that, but Jonesy didn't care.

Darby had owned the local trailer park for a couple of decades. New company was vast, and owned properties across the Midwest and into the South. There was a quote from the CEO of Sterling Communities that said he looked forward to bringing Loire Mobile Home Park into the Sterling family. No big changes planned. Seamless transition. Blah, blah, blah.

"Forward me the email and I'll look into it."

"Nah," Carl said. "We'll just run a brief on the biz page. You get that video up and then let's get you out of here. How many hours do you have left for this week?"

"Keeping it at eight every day," Jonesy said. "Just like always."

CHAPTER 14

Nancy

Nancy loved the sense of justice and power she felt when she evicted a bad apple. Or anyone, really.

It didn't happen all that often. People had to pay a deposit, first month's rent and last month's rent before they moved in, so people mostly tried hard to keep up. When people did do a scoot in the middle of the night, it was typically because they were a month behind and realized eviction was the next step.

The company usually was still ahead of the game, though, because they still had the deposit, and they'd go after the rest of the money whenever possible.

It was a different story for those few people who owned their own mobile homes but rented the lot. Twice now, Nancy had dropped the hammer on people who fell behind on their lot rent.

The Fergusons were an older couple who had

moved their own mobile home here about a million years ago. They'd paid their lot rent right on time every month until the husband died.

The widow, Catherine, kept trying to make late and partial payments but company policy didn't allow that. You had to pay the full amount. Besides, it was only $300 a month.

"I'm having trouble without Roy's Social Security," Catherine had told Nancy. "I didn't realize his checks were going to stop when he died. You understand. You must have a mother."

"I do have a mother. She pays her rent every month," Nancy said. Her mom lived in subsidized senior housing and only had to pay on a sliding scale, but that was beside the point. She paid it, and that was what mattered.

It was too bad, but you couldn't just let people not pay their rent, and eventually, Mr. Darby directed Nancy to evict Mrs. Ferguson. There was a company lawyer who handled the legal part of it, and Catherine had brought the letter into the office, crying.

"How can this be?" Catherine had asked her. "I own the trailer. We paid it off years ago."

"Yes, but you didn't buy the land. The company owns the land, and you haven't been paying your rent so now the company is seizing your mobile home. It's all very legal."

"I know I'm three months behind, but that's less than a thousand dollars. The trailer is worth much more than that, and it's my home. I don't have anywhere else to go!"

Nancy thought the old woman might start yelling, but instead, she just looked broken. It was true that it was too bad she lost her home, but she should have paid her lot rent.

In the end, Catherine ended up living in the same senior housing complex Nancy's mother did, and there was a decent chance she had to pay more than $300 every month. Nancy had seen her there once, but she pretended she didn't recognize her.

Anyway, Catherine Ferguson should have understood it wasn't really Nancy's fault. She didn't make the rules.

CHAPTER 15

Shirley

Shirley picked up her mail and noted a mint green sheet of paper tucked in amongst her cable bill and a sheaf of junk mail. All notices from the trailer park were printed on that distinctive green, so she sat on her little outdoor table and lit a cigarette before settling in to read it.

New owners. Apparently Darby had sold out, probably because he needed the money. Who cared? She would have to call her bank and arrange a change before her next lot rent was due.

Instead of transferring her payment to one company, she'd send it to another. There were directions on what to do if you paid by check or money order. Cash would no longer be accepted.

Shirley didn't give a crap. She had never written a check in her life. She'd skipped all that and gone straight to online banking. Her accountant had shown her how to do everything the modern way.

She tucked the note in her purse and looked through the rest of her mail before chucking it all in the trash, including her cable bill. That was paid automatically every month by direct deposit, so she never had to worry about it.

Shirley had met the new woman, Angel, finally. She could not say she was a fan.

Angel had no idea how to hold up her end of a conversation. Shirley had walked over there, friendly as could be, and had introduced herself. During the painfully short conversation, Shirley had learned only three things about Angel: She was a single mother, her child's father seldom paid child support, and she was a Christian who did not agree with any of the local churches, which were all far too liberal. Everything Angel had to say touched on one of those topics.

"Are you a church-going woman?" Angel had asked her.

Shirley had been, years ago. She'd stopped going after John died and she'd moved; it seemed more like a social club with people she no longer had anything in common with. But she thought it was a rude question and she wasn't sure how to answer.

"Once in a while," she'd said, and then she tried to change the subject. "How old is your daughter?"

It was as if Angel hadn't even heard her. "I'd go to church every Sunday if there was one around here that actually followed Jesus Christ.

But they're all fakes."

The daughter, Maya, had not been part of the conversation at all. The child sat inside, absorbed in the TV, while Angel explained that she had had to get Maya out of her mother's house because her mother was a very negative person.

Angel didn't ask Shirley anything about her life, so she was not able to tell her much about the big house she used to have, or about the pharmacy she and her husband had owned, or her two boys who lived in Los Angeles. Angel had zero interest in any of those things, so after a few attempts at conversation, Shirley gave up. She stayed long enough to be polite and then lied.

"It was good to meet you, Angel. I hope you enjoy living here." And then she marched right back to her own trailer.

The truth was, it was excruciating trying to talk to Angel, and she did not give a shit whether she enjoyed living here. Kaitlin would chatter pleasantly all day long about anything and everything, and she was always up for a story from Shirley's past, when her life had been the way it was supposed to be.

CHAPTER 16

Angel

There were three men living on her street, Angel had immediately determined. One was black, and he was married anyway. Another was single but worked in the lamestream media, so he was just as out of the question as a black man. But there was a single white man right across the street from her, and he was surprisingly nice.

His name was Darren. She had had him all wrong at first, because he listened to trashy music and drank beer. However, he'd been on the drunk side when he'd come over to meet her, and she could immediately see he wasn't one of the mean drunks. He was a happy drunk.

He'd carried over a little cooler full of beer and while she didn't ordinarily agree with drinking, he was in a good mood so she'd taken one, just to be polite, and then a couple more.

Darren had a lot of funny stories about when he was in a band, and he told them non-stop. She didn't even need to talk, which was fine with her.

She didn't even really need to listen; he just liked to talk. He'd smoked and he'd talked and she had drunk a few beers and he had drunk the rest of them, and it was the first company she'd had since moving out, other than Shirley, who had marched over just to tell Angel all about the big fancy house she used to have.

Well, she didn't have it now, did she? So why should Angel care?

She could tell Darren was interested in her. He probably just needed a good woman to turn him around, and maybe she'd be the one to manage it. A lot of men drank too much until they had a good woman to steer them into behaving. Not only that, but he'd solved one of her big problems by offering to mow her yard for her.

There was every reason to think he might be willing to drive her to the store occasionally. She did not have a car and she hadn't thought through the logistics of grocery shopping by bus. She and Maya had gone just one time, and it had taken forever.

By the time they got home, the ice cream was soft and their arms ached. Besides, she had confidence that given enough time, she could bring Darren to God. That was reason enough to give the man a chance. Getting her lawn mowed and rides to the grocery store were not the important things here, but saving this man was.

"Don't you ever miss home cooking?" she asked him.

"I miss a lot of things when I don't have a good woman around," he said.

She knew what he meant but pretended she didn't. "Well, if you give me a ride to the grocery store every week, I could fix you some good food."

"Do you know how to make spaghetti? I've got the stuff for spaghetti right now." It was one of the few things he knew how to cook for himself, but he hadn't gotten around to making it.

"I can do that." Spaghetti was easy. You boiled the pasta and browned the hamburger and added a jar of spaghetti sauce.

Her mom had made her do some of the cooking, so she did know how, even though she normally didn't bother for herself or Maya.

"Let me just go check in on Maya." She went inside and asked Maya if she wanted to help her make spaghetti at Darren's place. Maya said she wanted to eat a can of soup instead, so Angel cooked at Darren's house and ate supper with him there.

His trailer was a lot nicer than hers, and it was clean. She'd been surprised by that. He'd talked a mile a minute while she cooked. It was like playing house. The spaghetti came out fine. They both had a good appetite and finished it off fast.

She thought for sure he would try to kiss her before she left but he hadn't, which threw off her plans. She'd wanted to refuse him so he'd know what kind of woman she was. But how could she let him know she was old fashioned if he didn't even try anything?

Finally, she decided he must be just as old fashioned as she was. And if that was the case, he might just need a little encouragement. He was probably too shy or too afraid of being rejected.

So she gave him a quick kiss after she finished doing the dishes. He'd looked surprised, but then he'd given her a longer kiss, and she'd let him. Old-fashioned men weren't easy to find nowadays, and she was lucky to have met one. Then she went back home before he could get too encouraged.

"Maya, did you eat some soup?"

The girl, still sitting on the sofa watching her shows, nodded. An empty can of cream of chicken with a spoon in it sat on the coffee table. Angel often ate it cold right out of the can, and Maya had learned to like it that way, too. It was thick and extra salty.

Angel returned to the porch to sit and think for a while before bed. Across the way, she could see Darren through his kitchen window. He was watching her intently, something she'd noticed him doing a lot lately. The man was clearly smitten.

CHAPTER 17

Maya

Living in the trailer was better than living with Grandma because now they had the deluxe cable package and she could watch uninterrupted all day long.

Grandma had only basic cable. She said it was a waste of money. And she was always trying to get Maya to go outside and play. Or read a book. Or do something besides her favorite thing, which was watching TV.

She missed Grandma's cooking, but she didn't miss being nagged. Mom had never been very interested in cooking before, but now she went over to the neighbor's house almost every night and cooked there, leaving Maya to eat cold soup. She always said Maya could come over if she wanted, but Maya had no interest in getting to know Darren, and she liked having the whole place to herself and being able to watch TV endlessly.

She hadn't seen her dad or either grandma

since they'd moved, although she knew her dad knew exactly where they lived, because he'd helped them move. She was sure they'd come get her at some point, and her other grandma would probably buy her some new clothes and give her cookies. That was cool, although she barely got to watch any TV when she was there.

When she got home after a visit with her dad and other grandma, her mother would always ask her a million questions. Did they take you out to eat? Did her dad have any other woman around? Did he ask about Angel? Did they give you a check? Let's see that outfit they bought you. Just one pair of jeans? Did you forget to tell them you need new shoes?

Mom said she'd go to the same school here that she had gone to when they'd lived with Grandma. She wasn't sure if that was a good or bad thing. She wouldn't have to start over at a new school, but she didn't have any friends at her old school. It might have been possible to make some friends at a new school. Or maybe not.

Her mom had talked about possibly homeschooling her, though, and she was all for it. There was no way her mom was really going to do that. She'd be able to watch TV all day long.

One of the very few new things Mom had bought before they moved was this TV, and Maya loved it. It overpowered the little living room, but she liked it that way. She'd settle in under a blanket, remote in hand, and binge on all the shows she wanted.

A lot of shows had twenty-two episodes, and if they were the half-hour ones, she could watch an entire season in one day as long as Mom stayed out of her way. Sometimes it wasn't possible; sometimes Mom wanted to watch something else or made her clean her tiny room or go take a shower. But if she got up and started watching right away, and ate her meals on the sofa, she could fit them all in.

She had a little notebook she used to keep track of everything she wanted to watch, how many episodes it had and how many seasons it had. She marked each episode off as she watched it, which brought order to her days. On days when she was able to finish an entire season in one day, she slept well.

What she didn't like was having a handful of episodes left over at the end of the day. That meant she'd have to finish them in the morning, and then her whole day would be thrown off because it would be all the harder to complete any other season. Sometimes, she'd instead fill up the rest of the day with something entirely different, like movies. There was nothing worse than finishing up one show at noon and knowing any new show you started would have to be abandoned halfway through. Mom would pitch a fit if she tried to stay up late to finish the season she was on.

It had been easier lately, though. Mom was

always across the street, almost every night, and that made it possible to almost always fit in a whole season.

Her notebook was filling up. She liked writing down all the names of the shows in her very best handwriting, using extra curlicues and making it fancy. She dotted every "i" with a heart and drew little flowers off to the side. The front of it was decorated with hearts and flowers and said "Maya's TV Shows" on it in her very fanciest handwriting. She liked flipping through it and seeing all the shows she'd already finished.

It gave her a feeling of accomplishment.

CHAPTER 18

Jonesy

Only in modern-day America, Jonesy thought, could a broke guy in a trailer be accused of being a greedy media insider.

He'd met the new renter that afternoon. He'd been smoking and reading on his front step when he saw her, and had walked over to introduce himself.

"Hi, I'm Jonesy." He'd extended his hand for a handshake but the new woman had rejected it.

"I hear you're a reporter."

"I work for the *Loire Daily Register,* yes."

"You're all a bunch of communists who will write anything to sell papers."

Jonesy laughed, which seemed to surprise her. "I'm a communist out to sell papers? That's a new one."

"Laugh all you want. I know the truth. Stay away from me and my daughter."

Great. A right-wing nutjob in the neighborhood. He turned around and walked back to his own trailer, feeling her eyes on him the whole time.

If he were just out to sell newspapers, he thought, he probably would have more than seven bucks in his wallet. But sure, he was part of a secret international media cabal out to run the world.

The truth was, Jonesy had become a journalist because he wanted a job that let him read and write all day. He had always been a hardcore reader.

Growing up, he'd devoured science fiction, especially Isaac Asimov and Ursula Le Guin. Then he discovered Kurt Vonnegut and plowed through everything he wrote, and after that he'd expanded into the classics. He was probably the only kid in his high school who loved to read Russian novels. *War and Peace. The Brothers Karamazov. Anna Karenina. Crime and Punishment.* The longer the book the better. He hated it when good books ended.

Now he read non-fiction just as voraciously. History. Biographies. Economics. Philosophy. His trailer was full of cheap bookcases stuffed with second-hand books. He remembered his teachers urging their students to read more.

"Knowledge is power," claimed his history teacher, Mr. Perry. "The more you read, the further you'll go in life." Jonesy had somehow believed that.

Most of his friends were as well-read as he

was, and none of them had ever made much money. In fact, he'd go so far as to say there was an inverse relationship between being well-read and being wealthy.

He'd very often noticed, when going into people's homes for interviews, that wealthy businessmen tended to have few to no books. If they did, they were more often the think-positive sorts of business self-help books that whipped people up into a frothy zeal.

He'd read many such books, and they were all shit. Most of them would start a chapter with an obviously made-up little anecdote about a man who wasn't meeting his business goals, but then he absorbed one of the vague principals promoted by the book and put it into practice, and suddenly his success increased by a zillion percent, thus proving the importance of the vague principal.

He'd given real thought to attempting to write a series of such books. It would be easy, he thought, to interview a few self-important businessmen and spin a yarn about how they'd become successful through positivity, vision and hard work, blah blah blah. He'd wanted to be a business reporter, after all.

But while he found economics fascinating, he found most business books worthless. What he had found, in a lifetime of reading and writing about such things, was that success in business could very often be predicted by three major things: family money, luck and connections. He had never interviewed a single businessman who had credited his success to that, however. Not one. It was always vision and hard work that got the credit.

He'd seen some genuine exceptions, usually women or immigrants. In those cases, sometimes it was a matter of intelligence, vision and hard work, but these things were almost always accompanied by a degree of luck.

These views were not popular and he knew it, so he kept them out of his reporting and gave his editor and the public what they expected. But it didn't escape him that he himself was a very good example of how knowledge was not necessarily power. He was intelligent, educated, well-read and hard-working, yet here he was, sweating the rent increase on a trailer.

All those times he'd applied for jobs in communications, he'd done his very best to impersonate the business people he'd interviewed. If the ad said they were looking for someone with a passion for insurance, that's what he'd try to channel. He would craft an ideal cover letter and resume.

The few times he actually got an interview, he would get his hair barbered and spend more on a new suit than he could afford. Still, they could always see through him. They somehow recognized that he wasn't what they wanted. He didn't know why.

He felt like he could answer an ad that said something like, "Seeking a middle-aged, broke, balding man who smokes too much, reads constantly and lives in a trailer" and they would respond with something like, "Sorry, but we are going with another candidate who is a better fit."

At this point, he knew he was never going to get a high-paying job. His chances of winning the lottery were just as good, and he had never even bought a ticket. He would keep working fifty or sixty hours a week at a newspaper and claiming he worked forty, and when he eventually got laid off, he would get a job tending bar, and he would do that until he was too old to stand on his feet all night, and then he'd do it a little bit longer, and then he'd probably just kill himself, because he'd checked what his Social Security was going to be, and it was a joke.

He had about $60,000 in his 401(k), and he wasn't sure why he'd even bothered. He had stopped putting any money into it about four years ago, when his health insurance premium jumped and he had to find some way to make his weekly check cover his basic expenses. Only one of the newspapers he'd worked for had ever offered a match, anyway.

He hadn't had a raise in a decade and didn't expect to ever get another one, so he would never be able to save anything more for retirement. A paltry $60,000 wasn't enough to make a difference in his old age. He probably should just withdraw it all, pay the penalty, and take a fantastic trip around the world.

Until a few years ago, he'd believed doing good work would eventually get him noticed by a bigger paper, but now even the bigger papers weren't safe havens. He'd been humiliated when Carl asked him to take over the obit desk once a week.

"I'm busy with that opioid story we talked about. The county's OD rate spiked after the hospital closed its chronic pain clinic. You want me to put that aside and do obits tonight?"

"Yep. I do. If you don't, there's nobody else to do it tonight. I did it last night while you were at the school board meeting, so don't think you're too good to do the obit page. Everybody's got to pitch in. And don't forget you owe me tweets today, too. Dani will have my ass if we don't keep up with that."

He'd confessed his humiliation to his friend Dave, whom he'd known since their days at the college paper. Dave had always been more successful than Jonesy. But Dave had no sympathy for him.

"You think you've got it bad? My editor has me putting together the Sunday society page now. Who gives a fuck about weddings and engagements? And anniversaries? But we charge big bucks to run that shit, so we all have to do it."

If even Dave was dealing with engagement announcements now, Jonesy knew, just getting hired at a bigger paper was no protection anymore. Things would suck wherever he went.

He had one dream left, and that was his sci-fi novel he was writing. He didn't often have the juice after writing about other things — the school district's finances, a local nursing home being fined following a resident's choking death, one of the grocery stores having a grand re-opening after its remodel were among this week's disposable compositions — but on days when he did have juice, he'd write as if someone were holding a gun to his head.

He understood that the chances of this novel making him any money were slim, but writing the book fed his last dream.

He only needed one dream to keep him alive.

CHAPTER 19

Darren

This was the sweetest setup Darren had had since his guitar god days.

Angel came over every night and made his dinner, had sex with him, and then went home. He had barely met her daughter, which was fine with him. He had no interest in daddy duty.

Angel was not much of a talker, and that was ideal, too. She sometimes veered off into religious mumbo-jumbo, but she never tried to drag him to church. None of the churches in their area fit her requirements, thankfully. He catered to her by expressing agreement with everything she said about religion. It was all the same to him.

"You notice these school shootings are always in public schools. When we took prayer out of the schools, that's when it started. You never hear about shootings in Christian schools. But instead of just putting God back in schools, they want to take our guns away."

"You've got a point," he said. He had no idea whether she did or not. He was supremely uninterested in God and guns. Neither had a thing to do with him.

"If Maya's dad paid child support like he should, I'd be able to put her in a good Christian school. I didn't understand how important it was to choose a Godly man then. I know better now."

He didn't know what to say about that, but he did know how to put a cap on the God talk.

"Come here, woman," he said, and pulled her shirt up. She never said no. Ever. It was the best way to change the subject. Were all religious nuts this compliant in bed? If he'd known this perk, he would've joined a church years ago.

So she wasn't much to look at. Well, you couldn't have everything, could you? But he didn't see anybody else jumping to provide food and sex and then going straight home.

It was even better than the deal Kaitlin was providing the rich guy. Darren was certain that man was a sugar daddy. No regular boyfriend showed up early on weekday mornings and stayed for just half an hour. But God only knew how much that man was paying for his pussy, whereas Darren not only didn't pay a dime, but got dinner out of the deal.

He mowed Angel's little yard about once a week when he mowed his own, which took him maybe five extra minutes. The lots here were tiny. He gave her a ride to the grocery store when he went, which was ideal because she was cooking for him most nights anyway.

Listening to a little bit of God talk was a very small price to pay.

When Darren met a woman, he liked to imagine what she was like in bed. He'd see a woman in the store and would think, "I bet that one won't do shit" or "I bet she's dirty as fuck."

He hadn't had high hopes for Angel, but he'd been wrong. The woman would do anything. Absolutely anything. There was nothing he had suggested so far that she hadn't gone right along with. A couple of times he'd pressed his luck and had thought, "This will be the thing that pisses her off. I've gone too far this time."

But Angel hadn't missed a beat. She seemed to have no limits at all. Anal? Sure. Letting him finish all over her face while calling her a dirty slut? Not a problem. Ripping off her clothes and pretending to force her? That was OK as long as he agreed to replace the torn clothes. She'd showed up for the next visit with a spare outfit tucked into a plastic grocery bag and said he could do what he wanted.

And holy shit, she wasn't kidding. Darren watched fake-rape porn often. It was his favorite. But he'd never dared ask a woman to let him do it.

"If you want me to stop, just say the word 'spaghetti' and I swear I'll stop right away," he said.

She had whimpered and cried and begged him not to force her. She had told him he was too big and it was hurting her. She had held her legs tightly together and fought him off so that he had to really work to get it in there.

But what she didn't do was say the magic word, "spaghetti." Darren was obsessed with their new game, and he'd bought her a number of outfits so he could rip them off her. It was the biggest thrill he'd ever had, and he couldn't get enough.

She never came over until it was time to cook supper. She still sat on her front porch doing nothing all day, and he'd sit in his kitchen and bring up some noisy gang-bang porn to listen to as he looked at her and jacked off, thinking of how good it was going to be to take her hard that night. It had been at least a decade since he'd had such a sexual appetite.

No other woman had ever satisfied him like Angel could, and he dropped all his other kinks to concentrate on this one.

The important elements were to rip off her clothes, to force her legs apart, to hear her beg him to stop and to pound into her as hard as he could until he finished. The rest of the scenario could be different every night, but he needed those specific things, and Angel was fine with providing them.

Afterward, she acted as if nothing unusual had happened at all. In fact, there had been times she'd lain there afterward in her torn clothes, catching her breath, and had started talking about why going to a liberal church was worse than going to no church at all.

He told her he agreed with her 100 percent, and she smiled.

CHAPTER 20

Nancy

It was the worst day of her life.

It had been a few weeks since Sterling had bought the park, and she'd been very careful to show the new people how responsible she was, hoping some kind of raise or promotion might be forthcoming.

Instead, here she was sitting with Sarah the Sterling HR bitch, who was explaining that they had their own management team that would be taking over. Nancy had just booted up her computer when Sarah had walked in. The woman hadn't even made an appointment or tried to break it to her nicely. She just walked in, introduced herself and announced that they had decided to lay her off.

"I have this paperwork for you," Sarah said, handing her a thick packet. "You'll need this information if you intend to apply for unemployment."

"What about my house?" Nancy had asked.

"We won't have on-site management moving forward. As a courtesy, we're extending your occupancy until the end of the year, so you have plenty of time to make other arrangements if you choose to do that. However, if you choose to stay, we're happy to have you as a tenant. You'll pay $500 lot rent plus $750 for your mobile home."

"That's over a thousand bucks!"

"Well, you're currently living in the largest home in the park," Sarah had said. "As you know, there are a number of less expensive housing options in the park, and under the circumstances, we'd be willing to waive the transfer fee."

Nancy had found a cardboard box and she'd filled it with her personal items, such as the box of cookies in her desk, the ham and potato casserole from the refrigerator and a decorative candle that she had never lit because it was against the rules.

"This is my own executive desk set. I bought it with my own money when I got the job, and I'm not leaving it here," she said. It had an imitation leather desk pad with matching business card holder, pen cup and in-box and out-box trays. Her set had really classed up the otherwise rather utilitarian-looking office, and there was no way she was letting Sarah have it.

"If nobody is here at the office, who will run things?"

"We're contracting with a local property management company," she said. "All tenants will receive an informational packet later today."

Nancy looked around the office one more time, searching for any little thing she might have forgotten.

"I have another appointment," Sarah had said. "Are we ready to wrap this up?"

"Just about," Nancy had said. "I want to remove my personal pictures from the computer." Her screensaver was a repeating collage of her junior college graduation pictures. She took her time going into the hard drive and deleting them one by one.

While she was doing that, Sarah's phone buzzed and she walked across the room to take the call, explaining that she was still at the Loire property but expected to be done soon. She pronounced "Loire" the snobby way out-of-towners did, so Nancy reset the computer password from the one she'd been assigned to "SarahIs#1Bitch" and then she shut it down.

"I have some personal items in the restroom," she called out.

She picked up her big purse and went to the little restroom, where she had a box of tampons under the sink she wasn't about to leave for someone else. Also under the sink was a small coffee can she emptied every day to catch the slow drip from the plumbing leak. She'd reported it but had never gotten authorization to hire a plumber. That had been months ago, and there was no doubt it had been forgotten.

Instead of emptying it, she filled it to the brim and carefully replaced it under the sink. Now, every new drip would spill over the edge and eventually rot out the vanity and she couldn't be blamed.

It served them right.

CHAPTER 21

Janiece

Janiece was always thinking.

Jimmy was paid twice a month, and on paydays Janiece would pay whatever bills were due and check the balances on all their accounts. It was frightening to see how fast their student loan balances grew, but she focused on thinking about how fast that number would go down once she and Jimmy were both working at the jobs they were meant for.

She hadn't been surprised to learn the new trailer park owners were jacking up their rent by $300 per month after the first of the year. That was going to hurt. It might be worth looking for a little apartment instead. They'd chosen this place because it was cheap. If it wasn't going to be cheap, what was the point of staying here?

Because Jimmy wasn't eligible for further student loans, they'd focused on figuring out how she could finish as fast as she could. But after her fruitless visit with Ms. Givens, she wondered if they had it backwards.

Would it, in fact, be possible for Jimmy to finish first? His salary potential would be twice what hers would be. The problem was, he needed that fifth year of school, and had been deemed not to have made satisfactory academic progress. Could they appeal? Could he enroll for the fall semester? And if he could, what would they live on? Could he work full-time while attending? Could she find something with a schedule that would allow Jimmy to watch the girls while she worked? Or maybe he could attend part-time?

"I think we should try again," she told Jimmy that night as she finished making dinner. "I know it would be a lot for you to work and go to school at the same time, but it would just be for a year. Really, just for nine months. Or I could waitress at night while you watch the girls. They're getting easier. No more diapers now. They can feed themselves. I think maybe we could swing it. What do you think?"

"I've thought about it," he said, glancing into the living room. It was in complete disarray, with the sofa cushions arranged to make a fort around the coffee table. The girls were yelling and crawling in and out of their fort, entertaining themselves. "We probably never should have gotten our own place. If we had kept living with one of our parents, even if we kicked in a few bucks every month, we could have swung it. I was just too proud."

"It wasn't just you. I was too proud, too. But one really hard year might make all the difference for us later. We should look into what we might be able to do. Maybe you should go talk to your advisor. We aren't the only people out there who have had to figure out how to finish school while raising kids."

She set bowls of ham and beans on the table for Jimmy and herself and fixed two little plastic bowls for the girls. The cast iron skillet she'd baked the cornbread in was too hot to put on the table. The girls were sure to touch it no matter what she said, so she transferred individual servings of cornbread onto plates and called in the girls, who ignored her.

"I'll email him about an appointment. It won't hurt to ask." He went into the living room. "Girls! Your mom called you in for dinner. Come on and eat now." He scooped up Jordynn and deposited the giggling child into her seat and went back for Jazzmynn, who was hiding under the coffee table. He lifted it away and she shrieked in surprise before he picked her up and popped her into her chair.

They were happy kids, because they didn't yet know the nature of the world. Everything they could possibly want at this stage of life was right here in their trailer.

He dreaded the day when they'd figure out what a struggle life really was.

CHAPTER 22

Jonesy

Jonesy looked forward to winter, when he would sleep soundly again.

All summer, he melted into his damp sheets. He used to have a small window unit he ran just in his bedroom, but it had conked out about mid-July, and he had not replaced it, first because he was considering whether he really wanted to spend a couple hundred bucks on a new air conditioner, and then, once he'd gotten news of his rent increasing, he had decided he'd likely just move.

The trailer was supposed to have central air, but it didn't, just as the refrigerator didn't have a working ice maker. He'd reported both shortcomings to Nancy, but nothing was ever done.

He couldn't prove it, but he suspected she played favorites and had deliberately not gotten around to fixing his issues. He knew for a fact that Kaitlin had successfully lobbied to get new carpeting and paint. That was unheard of in this park except when a tenant moved out and left behind a mess.

He had stripped his bed to nothing but a bottom sheet and a pillow, and he had placed a fan in the window to bring in a little cool air at night. He couldn't wait for more comfortable temperatures to arrive. There was nothing like burrowing under a warm blanket and thinking his thoughts while cold air freshened the room. Everything seemed worse in hot weather, when he couldn't sleep worth a damn. But when it cooled off, life wouldn't seem so bad, and he'd work on his book more.

Sweater weather was better than sweating weather for his creativity. He'd written a good deal of his book sitting cozily in bed, laptop on his lap. Where else should a laptop go? Certainly not on a desk. He didn't own one.

His book had to do with memories, and what it might be like if you could revisit them more fully. He knew he wasn't the first person to come up with the idea, but that didn't stop him from using it as a premise.

In his book, scientists had designed a way to fully immerse you into a memory. It involved a microscopic implant that was placed specifically into the portion of your brain where that memory was stored. You were inserted into a sort of MRI machine and asked to concentrate on the memory you wanted optimized. That part of your brain would light up, and they'd very carefully introduce the implant.

One of the main characters of his book wanted to optimize his memory of a trip he had taken to Paris. It cost more to optimize the memory than it had taken to pay for the trip in the first place, and he had to borrow the money.

But at first, it was worth it. He enjoyed lying in bed, closing his eyes and being back in Paris.

He had chosen the most stereotypical part of the trip. He could experience sitting down at a sidewalk cafe and ordering a croissant and a cappuccino. He could feel the flaky bits of the croissant breaking away as he brought his teeth together. He could taste the milky foam and the strong espresso of the cappuccino. He could feel the cobblestones under his feet and could see the Eiffel Tower in the distance.

He could people-watch all the Parisians walking by and it was, in every sense, just like being there again, except that he retained a faint consciousness that he was not truly there, but was reliving it.

If there were a fire or something, he could snap himself back into reality at will. Otherwise, it really felt like he was there.

The problem was, the man had gone through a breakup and a job loss soon after this, and instead of fixing his life, he preferred to lie in bed.

"I'm going to Paris," he'd say. He wouldn't look for a job, wash his sheets, or, eventually, eat anything. He could escape every unpleasantness by "going to Paris." Jonesy wasn't sure what was going to happen eventually, but there was a good chance he'd decide the character was going to starve to death. He saw it as a metaphor for a culture that refused to face reality as the world went to hell.

Jonesy enjoyed exploring the idea that people would prefer to live in the past rather than try to work on the future. You just needed one really perfect memory and enough money to optimize it. He imagined people planning what they wanted to experience and spending all their money to take a fantastic trip so they'd always have it to return to.

The name of the book was *The Happy Place.* An ex-girlfriend of his years ago had seen a therapist who had instructed her to "go to your happy place" when she was stressed.

He found it amusing, but typical of the culture, that a therapist would advise people to ignore reality by going to their happy place instead of trying to fix their current problems.

CHAPTER 23

Angel

Of course, you had to make allowances for men. They were what they were.

You couldn't judge them. There was a reason God wanted men in charge of things. They were stronger and they had needs that women didn't. It was a woman's place to take care of those needs, and in return, you could count on a good man to take care of you.

Even though he had a bad back, she was confident that if she needed saving, Darren could do it. He was a big guy.

It wasn't that Angel was afraid of living alone. The trailer park was a pretty quiet place, all in all. And if it came down to it, she had her dad's old gun, which she and Maya kept right behind the large-screen TV, right on top of her King James Bible. The Second Amendment gave her the right to keep a gun, and the Bible taught her that if you took care of your man, he would take care of you. So she was doubly protected.

Darren hadn't asked her to marry him yet, but

he would. He couldn't keep his hands off her. She'd expected a man his age to have certain limitations in the bedroom, but he didn't. He had to have her every night.

Some nights, they hurried through their meal to get to the bedroom stuff faster. Lately, he didn't even wait to get into his bedroom. He was grabbing her breasts even during supper.

Last night, he'd jumped her as she walked through the living room, and had roughly undressed her and taken her right on the middle of his living room floor. She'd been so surprised that she'd let out a little surprised yell for real, and that had seemed to really get him going.

Each night, she talked a little bit more about her beliefs, and he hadn't disagreed with any of them. Strictly speaking, having sex before marriage was a sin, but she was well aware she was already damaged goods, so it didn't matter. Once she had let one man touch her, what would the point be in pretending to be pure? If she were a virgin, that would be different, but she wasn't.

She had two babies in Heaven and a living child, all by different men. She knew what that made her, and even though God had forgiven her, it didn't change what she was. It would all be better once they were married.

She hoped he'd ask her pretty soon, before her pregnancy started showing. Of course, her weight helped her hide it. She had plenty of time, and could wait until Darren asked her to marry him before she revealed it. Also, in January her rent was going to jump.

She had called her caseworker, but she didn't yet know if she'd be able to get more money on her housing voucher. If she could move in with Darren before her rent went up, that would be just fine. She'd bring her big TV and Maya would have a bigger bedroom here. It might be possible to put Darren's current TV into the bedroom that Maya and the baby would share.

In the meantime, she decided to stop paying the cable bill, because it was hard to come up with the whole amount, and pretty soon they could just watch Darren's anyway.

They'd have to be quieter when they played their games if Maya lived here, which was probably going to disappoint him. He really liked her to yell. But it might also be possible to allow Maya to spend more weekends at her dad's house. That would give Darren an opportunity to do it the way he wanted without worrying about Maya hearing them.

It would all work out, she was sure. Anyway, it was in God's hands.

CHAPTER 24

Kaitlin

It looked like there might be a lot more blowjobs in her future.

Her rent was going to go up the first of the year. She had mentioned it to Nathan but he had been noncommittal, and Kaitlin was worried and waiting for the right moment to talk to him about it. She'd never asked for him to increase the monthly amount and wasn't sure if he'd be willing to increase her monthly allowance or if he'd want her to earn the extra on her knees.

Of course, she could try to work a few more hours at the convenience store, but Sapphire had been right when she said Nathan was just cheaping out. This was her chance to get him to pay what he should have been paying her all along.

Tommy assumed she paid for her trailer out of her convenience store earnings and she didn't tell him any different.

"Talk to Naomi," he urged her as they halfheartedly watched a movie one night after he gave her a ride home. She'd sat next to him on the sofa instead of the chair for a change. It was like throwing a dog a bone. "She'll give you more hours, I bet."

"I might," she hedged. "We'll see." She stretched and repositioned herself, ending up just almost but not quite touching Tommy. That perked him up a little.

"Or get another job that pays better. I don't know if I could get you on at the hospital laundry, but maybe. It pays a lot more than the convenience store does."

"I can't work anywhere else but the convenience store," she said. "Remember? The hospital is too far to walk. I've gotta work close to my place. Anyway, I kind of like living here. I know it's just a trailer, but it's actually just right for one person."

"I grew up in a trailer," he said. "It wasn't as nice as this one, though. It was a piece of junk."

"I didn't know that. Was it here?"

He helped himself to another piece of the pizza he'd ordered. "No. It was at my house where I live now. When my grandparents were alive, my mom had a trailer on my grandma's lot. You can do that out in the country. You just have to have a way to hook it up to a septic tank and a water line. My mom moved out of the trailer years ago and I had it junked after I inherited Grandma's house. You could even move this trailer out to my place if you wanted to. Free lot rent." He looked at her like a puppy dog.

"I don't own the trailer. I just rent it. Otherwise, I would."

"Well, anyway, if you want me to, I might be able to help you get a job at the laundry. You could ride to work with me every day."

That would mean working full time in a hot, steamy laundry, washing gross hospital sheets, and it would mean giving up the easy money from Nathan.

"I'll have to think about it." She picked up another piece of pizza. It had been nice of Tommy to order it. He would never take the leftovers home with him, and that would mean she could have a piece of leftover pizza for breakfast as soon as Nathan left. That was something to look forward to.

She never ate anything or had a cigarette until he left. She didn't want garlic or cigarette breath. Nathan didn't like it that she smoked. If he made it a condition of paying her, she'd quit, but he hadn't.

She wasn't sure how likely he was to agree to pay her more. Yes, he was cheaping out, but maybe he couldn't get away with paying her more. It could be that he was afraid his wife would notice the missing money.

She'd found his wife on social media, and had learned her name was Amanda, and was surprised to see how good she looked. Stuck up, but good. It had inspired her not to get too lax with her grooming.

She'd just assumed he had a frumpy wife, but he didn't. In fact, his wife was hot enough to be a dancer or a sugar baby if she wanted. Most likely, the woman was frigid. She looked like the type who might dole out monthly sex. Kaitlin never, in even the smallest way, made any reference to Nathan's wife, and she certainly never told Nathan she'd looked up his wife on the internet. She knew instinctively that that was exactly the sort of thing that would make Nathan drop her.

She glanced at Tommy. His eyes were glued to the movie and he was eating yet another piece of pizza. She hoped he was getting full; she had been counting on pizza for breakfast.

"Can I have a tiny little backrub?" she asked, and watched his eyes light up. He put down his pizza. Good. He couldn't eat pizza and rub her shoulders at the same time. She stretched out, placing a throw pillow on his lap and laying her head down. He'd no doubt been expecting her to just sit in front of him. The suggestiveness of the position was not lost on her, but she pretended otherwise.

"Oh, that's perfect. You give the best back rubs," she said, as his hands kneaded her back and shoulders. He really did give wonderful back rubs and was probably good in bed. Sooner or later, she just might find out, but not now. For now, this was enough.

He was probably hard, but she couldn't tell through this thick pillow. It was so relaxing that as he continued stroking and rubbing her back, she closed her eyes and actually fell asleep briefly.

"Tommy, you're too good to be true." She closed her eyes again, then she opened them wide. If they both were to fall asleep, it could be disastrous. What if they fell asleep and Tommy was still here when Nathan arrived? She was always afraid of that, which was the biggest reason she never let anyone spend the night. Even the few guys that she had sex with had to go home afterward.

She sat up. "That was great. My back feels so much better now. But I need to go to sleep."

Tommy didn't argue, just reached out and crammed the rest of the piece of pizza he'd been eating into his mouth and stretched.

"All right. Don't forget, think about the laundry job." He gathered up his phone and keys and let himself out.

"I will, Tommy. Good night."

There was still a piece left for breakfast. Perfect.

CHAPTER 25

Jimmy

There are days in your life when everything changes.

Like the day they found out Janiece was pregnant, or the day she had to drop out of college. Like the day his student loans for his last year of college were denied.

Today, things were going to change again, and none of it would have happened if Janiece had not specifically suggested he call his advisor when she had. He had splurged on a bouquet of grocery store flowers for her, and when he walked into the kitchen where she was peeling potatoes, he thrust the flowers at her, grinning like an idiot.

"What's going on?" She looked surprised and no wonder. As far as he could remember, he'd never bought her flowers before. He didn't come home smiling very often, either.

He'd practiced how he was going to tell her, but all that went out the door and he blurted out his news.

"I got an engineering internship that'll cover a semester of tuition!"

"What?"

"LCM has an engineering internship. They offer it to two senior mechanical engineering students every semester, and this year one of the guys they offered it to just now had to drop out for some reason. If I'd met with my advisor a week earlier or later it wouldn't have happened. But my advisor talked to the company guy and we all had a conversation and got it all worked out."

The smile hadn't left his face all day. He hadn't been this happy since … well, he hadn't even been this happy when the girls were born, because they were so little and it was so scary.

"Jimmy, for real?" She clutched the flowers in front of her, using both hands, looking as uncertain as a teenage bride.

"For real. And just about the best part is, it comes with a fucking stipend!" He was shouting at this point. "They will pay me more than I'm making now!"

Jordynn came running in from the living room, excited to join in whatever was making Jimmy so happy. "Daddy!" He picked her up and hugged her. Jazzmyn was right behind her, and Jimmy held them both in his arms and swung them around, both girls giggling and happy and then struggling to get back down.

"This is real? This is really real?" Janiece still looked like she was afraid he was going to tell her it was all a joke.

He lowered the girls to the floor, and seemed not to even notice them trying to climb his legs as he spoke slowly and seriously to his wife.

"This is really real. You always tell me to take it easy, and everything is going to work out in the end, and I never believed it. But you were right."

Finally, Janiece smiled. "Oh man, there will be no living with Ms. Givens now. She's going to say it's all because of your positive attitude." She carried the flowers into the next room and started searching for something to put them in. They didn't have a vase, but she found an oversized plastic cup with a faded convenience store logo on it to use.

Jimmy laughed. "I didn't get it because of a positive attitude. I got it because this is one of their recruitment tools. It's a corporate-academic partnership thing they do. They get some influence with the college curriculum and they get a line on promising engineers. Most of the guys who go through this program end up working for them after graduation."

"How much is the stipend?"

"It works out to not much more than I'm making, but it's a little more. I'll have classes in the morning three days a week and the rest of the time I'll be working in the engineering department. The hard part will be the second semester, because we'll have to figure out how to pay for that. But we'll manage somehow. It's just one semester."

Janiece dropped her face into her hands and her whole body shook. "I'm just overwhelmed."

"So that's the main thing, but there's another."

Janiece looked at him. "Don't tell me there's a catch."

"Not a catch, but something I'm a little bit worried about. They sent me up to meet the engineering department and you are not going to believe this. The guy in charge is the same guy we see across the street every morning. I'd bet money he's that girl's sugar daddy."

"Oh shit." Janiece glanced at the girls, who had drifted off to play, and was relieved that they hadn't heard. "Did he recognize you?"

"Nope. Not in the slightest. Obviously, I didn't say anything."

"What were you going to say? 'Oh, hi! I think you're boinking my neighbor?' "

"He probably thinks one black dude looks the same as another. And that's fine with me. Far as I'm concerned, it's better if he never knows what I know."

CHAPTER 26

Shirley

Shirley dreaded the end of summer.

She hated winter, which was why she'd always assumed she'd spend her retirement years in Florida, in a nice beach condo. She smoked less in cold weather because she disliked standing outside, but she also didn't want the smell in her trailer.

When she was young, it was common and perfectly acceptable to smoke. At some point it had become a lower-class habit, but she'd never been able to shake it. And here in the trailer park, it was no social liability. It was almost the other way around. Most poor people smoked, she'd noticed.

At first, she thought that was odd. Smoking had become a very expensive habit. However, if you were broke, what else was there? These people couldn't travel or go out for nice dinners or afford a thousand other of life's ordinary pleasures, but they could afford a pack of smokes.

Looked at that way, cigarettes were a cheap luxury. It was that or sex, and she didn't see herself having any more sex. She'd never had sex with anybody but her husband. She didn't mind it while she'd had it, but she didn't miss it now it was gone, either. Certainly she didn't intend to start something with some new man at her age. Maybe if she'd been younger when John passed away, but not now. She liked living alone, as long as she had somebody to talk to now and then.

Shirley herself didn't plan to move, even though she was quite pissed about the increase in her lot rent. She might have made a different decision than to move here if she'd known they were going to jack it up so high. She was one of the few in the park who owned her trailer outright, and theoretically she could just pick up and move, but it was an expensive proposition to move a trailer, and anyway, she'd have to pay lot rent wherever she went.

The new owners had required everybody to make their decision by midnight Friday. It seemed hasty to her, but she'd returned the form and committed to renewing her lease for another year.

At least she could absorb the cost. Her expenses were few. She had lots of nice things from years past. She barely ever bought a new piece of clothing, because her wardrobe was full of classic pieces that had been very expensive when she'd bought them years ago.

She still had all her fine jewelry — John had been very good about buying her nice things for her birthday every year. Her trailer was full of her good Ethan Allen furniture. She still had her Lincoln. It was old but as classic and stylish as Shirley herself, and she hoped both of them would keep going for a long time. She would keep it for as long as she was able to drive.

All in all, though things in her life could have gone better, they also could have gone worse. Probably her main regret, besides not having paid attention to her finances before she was widowed, was her lack of grandchildren. She had assumed she'd have some by now, but apparently that was never going to happen. It would be one thing if only one of her boys had remained single and childless, but both of them? That was really unfair.

She talked to her boys once a week. Brant was doing fine. She didn't really understand exactly what he did, but she knew it had to do with computerized special effects. When you watched a movie, there would be all kinds of credits for people doing jobs that nobody outside Hollywood knew a thing about. One of the companies you might see listed on the screen was the place where her oldest son worked.

It was just like working in any other office, the way he explained it. He made what sounded like a lot of money, but was merely a solid middle-class living in Los Angeles because things were so expensive there.

But Chad. What was Chad thinking? He was 52. If you had not made it as an actor by 52, it was time to face reality. Who ever heard of waiting tables at 52? She still hoped he'd give it up and come home, though what he might do in Loire, she couldn't say.

Her boys had grown up with all the advantages, and yet Chad was living the sort of life you might expect one of the kids from the trailer park to be living. It made no sense. They'd grown up in a very nice neighborhood with excellent schools, and Shirley had been a room mother every single year, something she was very proud of. Hadn't it been her duty?

So many mothers had started working outside the home and couldn't do it, but she could, because John made a good living in those years. You could make a lot of money owning a pharmacy then. Not now, she finally understood, after her accountant had pointed it out. But when the boys were growing up, you could.

Both her boys had gotten college degrees that John and Shirley had paid for entirely. They didn't have all this debt from student loans she'd read about.

It was sort of interesting, the two halves of her life. She'd been well off and now she was poor. Yet, when it came right down to it, her life hadn't changed so very much. If John had lived a few years longer and lost a little more of their money, it would have been a different story, but as it was, she had a comfortable, attractive place to live in a safe, quiet neighborhood and didn't have to try to work. She'd narrowly escaped having to get a job as a grocery store cashier or something like that.

She had nearly said as much to Kaitlin that morning before realizing how rude it would have been to have suggested that being a grocery store cashier would have been horrible. The girl worked at a convenience store. Close enough. So she'd changed the subject to the leases.

"I went ahead and committed to another year," Shirley had told her. "I assume you did, too? I've heard a lot of people ended up signing the new leases just because tonight's deadline came too fast to make any new arrangements."

Kaitlin had suddenly looked frightened. "Tonight? I thought it was next week."

"No, it's tonight. Midnight tonight."

"I gotta go," Kaitlin had said. "I thought I had another week."

She jumped up and ran back to her own trailer, abandoning her freshly lighted cigarette.

CHAPTER 27

Nathan

He had known it would end someday. But he thought the end was several years away.

Kaitlin had told him a couple of weeks ago her rent was going up, but she'd said it wasn't going to happen until the first of the year, so he hadn't worried about it. He hadn't made any promises, but he fully intended to go ahead and increase her allowance by whatever she needed to pay her rent. He had always been surprised at how quickly she'd agreed to his opening bid of $800 per month. He just didn't want to agree right away and make it look too easy.

"OK. Well, let me look into things," he'd said, and then he'd opened his pants and sat down on the sofa.

But now, here he was at work when his phone pulsed in his pocket. He pulled it out and looked at it: He had a text from Ken Stonecipher.

"The hell I do," he murmured to himself.

He opened the text and read it:

"I know I'm not supposed to text you but those new owner BASTARDS say I have to commit to staying or moving by midnight tonight!! I thought I had longer. Sorry!! I need to know if you think you can get the extra $200? Because I need to know ASAP!!"

He quickly tapped out a reply:

"I will stop by at 5:20. Be there."

CHAPTER 28

Darren

Darren could go months without needing to take more than an occasional ibuprofen, and then he could spend a week doped up in bed.

This was one of those times. He got up only to go to the bathroom or to eat enough crackers so he could pop a pain pill without tearing up his guts. If he took the pills on an empty stomach, he threw up, every time. He often wondered if his propensity to puke was what saved him from becoming addicted to opioids. He took them only when the pain was otherwise unbearable.

His back was so messed up right now that he couldn't even manage to fake-rape Angel. She still came over every night to cook supper, though, and right now, that was almost as good.

"What do you want to eat tonight?" she asked, and he said he wanted a sandwich and french fries. Those were things he could easily eat while lying in bed.

"There isn't any bread, though," Angel said.

"Or any frozen french fries. We need to go to the store."

"You go ahead and take the car. I'll give you the money." There was no way he was going to haul his ass to the store right now.

She stood in the door of the bedroom, looking down at him. "I don't have a license."

"I don't give a shit. Just take it. They aren't going to catch you on a five-minute drive." After a while, the discomfort was almost as bad as the pain. Every single part of his body was urging him to find a comfortable new position, except his back, which would scream if he tried to flip onto his side.

"I don't know how to drive." She didn't seem embarrassed. It was as if she were acknowledging she didn't know how to fly a plane.

"Ah fuck." Well, there certainly had been times in the past when his back had flared up and he hadn't had a woman around. This wouldn't be the first time he had had to suck it up and do something.

"When my back gets better, I'm going to teach you how to drive." He slowly and painfully rose from the bed. "I'll drive, but I'm not getting out of the car. You'll have to do the shopping and carry everything."

Once he was standing, he took one more pain pill. He was never going to be able to get in and out of the car otherwise.

CHAPTER 29

Shirley

One of the best parts of Shirley's week was having her hair done.

She went every Friday afternoon to have it washed and set, and trimmed or permed as necessary. She had gone to the same stylist, Diane, for years. Diane kept Shirley's hair silvery bright with a rinse formulated to keep gray hair from yellowing. Almost all Diane's clients were older ladies, as was Diane herself.

Girls today talked about pampering and self care, but they didn't usually get their hair done once a week and they should. It was relaxing and Diane was a hoot. Shirley had given up a lot in recent years, but she'd never give up her weekly hair salon appointment.

Diane never seemed to tire of Shirley's stories. On some level, Shirley understood that Diane had a professional obligation to listen and might actually be less than thrilled to hear Shirley gab. But she didn't care. It was just so nice to talk to somebody who had known her in her good years.

She told Diane she was thinking about getting some new houseplants. "But did I ever tell you about the time I bought the paperwhites?"

She waited a beat for Diane to reply that she hadn't. She probably had, but no matter.

"It was winter, and I wanted a taste of spring in the house. I hate winter, you know." Diane nodded, indicating she did know that. Shirley mentioned it every winter.

"Well. I bought some paperwhites and eventually they bloomed and were just beautiful. But at the same time, I kept smelling cat urine, and we didn't have a cat. I made John take out the garbage. Well, that wasn't it. I got down and sniffed all the carpeting but couldn't smell anything. Brant came down and saw me standing by the shoe closet, sniffing all the sneakers. He was like, 'Um, Mom?' And I said, 'This whole house smells like cat pee and I'm just trying to figure out where it's coming from!' So anyway, after sniffing this and that all day, I finally realized it was those darned flowers. I haven't bought a paperwhite since. They used to smell so nice, too. The ones you buy now just reek. It's too bad. They're pretty."

"Huh." Diane was clipping the hair at the very nape of Shirley's neck.

"I'm thinking maybe of some African violets. I used to have those. I don't know whatever happened to them. I probably killed them.

They're pretty, though, and they don't have any smell at all. Flowers in the house are kind of a mood-booster in winter, I think. I always assumed at this point I'd be in Florida with a flower garden all year long."

"That sounds nice. I'm just going to put you under the dryer now, OK?"

After her appointment, Shirley stopped by a florist and purchased two African violets, one in a round pot and one in a square pot. She placed them carefully on the floor mat on the passenger side. Then she drove home, even more slowly than before.

The last thing she wanted was to get the inside of her immaculate Lincoln dirty.

CHAPTER 30

Jonesy

His rare day off had gone splendidly, once he got past an excruciating morning conversation with Nancy.

He had learned to avoid unnecessary interactions with Nancy because she liked to gossip about how poorly everyone in the trailer park handled their money and their lives. Darren blew his disability checks on booze. That black family wouldn't be so poor if the mother would get off her lazy ass and get a job. Kaitlin had ignored her advice to get an associate's degree and that's why she was still working at a convenience store. Shirley must be spending a mint to keep that big boat of hers in gas. She should trade it in for something smaller.

Nancy offered no criticism of how Jonesy spent his money, but he was willing to bet that when she gossiped with other people, she didn't leave him out of it. He idly wondered if she criticized him for wasting money on cigarettes or for not being smart enough to get a better job. Probably both.

Jonesy had watched one day as one of the rental furniture places delivered a kitchen table and chairs to Nancy's place. He was aware of what a bad deal those places were; he'd written about them before. Like pawn shops and title loan joints, they preyed on the poor, ignorant and desperate. Yet Nancy believed herself to be a paragon of budgeting. Well, we all have logs in our eyes, right?

He'd gotten up early for a walk around the neighborhood, and there was Nancy, striding down the sidewalk to her car, and looking right at him as he approached his sidewalk. There was no good way to avoid her.

"Good morning, Nancy." He offered only a second's eye contact and maintained his stride, hoping that the polite greeting would also function as a goodbye, but Nancy stopped moving, and he felt the pull of etiquette force him to a stop.

"How are you, Jonesy?" She'd persisted in calling him Gilbert for quite a while.

"I'm good. Just felt like taking a short walk before settling down to work." Maybe she'd take the hint that he didn't have time for a long conversation.

"I meant to get up early today, too. I have so much work to do. Sometimes I come in early to catch up. There's really too much work in the office for just one person."

"I think it's like that everywhere," he said. He had seen her car come and go enough to understand she worked a very standard forty-hour week, but he bit back an urge to launch into a rant about how much harder he worked.

It is a truth universally acknowledged, he thought to himself, that everyone was hopelessly overworked. Everyone's workplace was barely holding on, surviving only due to the immense sacrifices of the person telling the story.

"How many people work in your office?" she asked. He could see where she was coming from a mile away — she was going to speculate that any workplace with multiple people must indulge its employees in endless hours of leisure.

"About half as many as we had five years ago, but the workload has doubled."

"I don't know if I mentioned it before, but I have an associate's degree in business. I know a lot about workplace efficiency. Did you know most people are only productive for about three hours a day? They could probably cut your staff again and nobody would even notice."

Jonesy bit back another urge to spill his guts. "I'll probably find out soon. We're about due for another round of layoffs." He formed his lips into an approximation of a smile and walked down his sidewalk. He had his front door open and was close to freedom when she spoke again.

"You should come over and see my new furniture sometime!"

She had suggested this several times. Jonesy was never quite sure if she meant it as a friendly overture or if she was trying to flirt. Either way, he wasn't interested, but he knew better than to say no. Better to make vague positive noises.

"I'll have to do that one of these days." And then he escaped. Having a cigarette was part of his pre-writing ritual, but didn't want to go back outside and take the risk of meeting Nancy or anybody else, so he set up the fan in his bedroom window to blow the smoke out. It was a move he'd first picked up as a teenager, sneaking smokes in his bedroom.

If you sat a box fan on the sill, right up against the screen, and you carefully held your cigarette right in front of it and exhaled every breath right toward the middle of the fan, all the smoke went straight out and you did not stink up the room.

He felt like a kid sneaking around, but he did it, and as usual, the smoke got him into the right mental state to write.

One cigarette unlocked the mental juice to crank out several chapters of *The Happy Place*, and he thought they were some of the best writing he'd done yet.

In his story, the optimized memory technique had at first been performed only for those who were willing and able to shell out big bucks, but then everyone realized there were many other possibilities for the technology.

For one thing, some overweight people signed up for the procedure to serve as the ultimate diet. You gathered a spread of all your favorite foods, stuffed yourself with every delicacy imaginable, and then had that memory optimized. Forever after, you ingested only a prescribed liquid diet, returning to the memory of your ultimate indulgence as you drank it.

It didn't take long for the government to realize the procedure's usefulness in quelling dissent and keeping the population docile. If troublemakers or the very poor had suitable happy memories, they'd optimize them. But if they didn't, there was a Disney contract.

Problem people were given a deluxe three-hour trip to Disneyland, and then their memory of that was optimized. It was presented as a humanitarian solution, but in reality, it was just an updated version of bread and circuses.

Even better, government researchers perfected a bigger breakthrough that would allow them to implant happy memories without the bother and expense of helping people experience anything happy. They were able to chemically "copy" another person's memory and implant it into anyone's brain. The idea was to provide happy virtual memories to keep people with perfectly shitty lives content.

You'd be able to choose. Did you want a trip to Disneyland or Vegas? Did you want a false memory of that moment when you ascended Mt. Everest or won an Olympic gold medal? Divorced people could ignore the reality of their broken marriage and relive their weddings and honeymoons or enjoy an implanted version of someone else's romance that felt like their own.

However, people who indulged themselves in too-frequent visits to their happy place tended to accomplish nothing else from then on.

Why should you subject yourself to boring hard work in order to get a feeling of accomplishment, when you could easily re-live your glory days or even experience someone else's? People who had scarcely gone jogging before signed up for an implanted memory of winning marathons.

He hoped the story was managing to get across his point about the folly of chasing pleasure instead of satisfaction. That was something he saw wherever he went, and it was no less true of the wealthy and powerful than it was of the poor and powerless. The same people who shake their heads at the stupidity of poor people wasting a hundred bucks on a pair of sneakers usually see nothing odd about spending the same amount on a pair of work shoes.

But now that he had spent several hours satisfying his desire to create good work, it was time for him to pursue one of his favorite pleasures. He browsed his bookcases, located an old paperback copy of *Breakfast of Champions* and perched himself on his front steps to smoke and read.

Writers had always understood how fucked up the world was.

CHAPTER 31

Nathan

Nathan pulled up in front of Kaitlin's trailer and counted the money he'd just withdrawn. She might get nasty, but if she did, bringing out this wad of money would likely calm her down.

He intended to give her the equivalent of four months' allowance as a goodbye gift in any case.

He knocked on the door this time. It was part of their routine for him to walk right in for their morning visit, but this was not part of their routine.

In fact, he had never before visited her at any time but early morning. There was seldom anyone around when he visited her in the morning, but there were some people hanging around outside now, which made him uncomfortable. A middle-aged guy down the street was sitting outside smoking and reading a book. Nathan knocked and hoped Kaitlin would answer quickly.

She did. She looked different than usual,

because she was fully dressed. Her hair and makeup were as well done as always, but she was wearing jeans and an ordinary shirt. It was the first time he'd seen her in regular clothes.

When he'd met her, she'd been stripping, and when he visited her for sex, she generally wore a robe or some kind of little silky thing that she took off immediately. So that's what she looks like when she's not stripping or getting ready to screw, he thought. It was a good look for her, and he wondered if she'd allow one last goodbye session. But his wife would be texting him if he ran too late. Best not to risk it.

He said nothing until he was seated on her sofa, and then he cleared his throat. "I was perfectly clear when we first met about my need for discretion."

"I know, but —"

"Texting was for emergencies only, and you were to say nothing that could conceivably cause a problem for me if anybody were to see my phone screen. I believe I suggested something like a simple 'call me,' which would let me know I needed to contact you as soon as I reasonably could."

Kaitlin stood in front of him and bit her lips. It was in a worried way, not a sexy way. She stood there, not sitting down, as if she thought he was about to open his pants.

"Look, I can't have this. I'm sorry, but moving forward, this just isn't going to work out."

Tears began spilling out of her eyes. "I can find another way to get the extra money!"

It was good that she was crying, not screaming. Sadness was a better response than anger.

"It's not the money. It's the text. You knew better than to send that text." He stood up. "I've really enjoyed this, but we both knew it was not going to last forever." He pulled the money out of his pocket and placed it on her coffee table.

"This covers the next four months, plus a little more. That should be plenty of time for you to figure out your next step. I wish you the best."

She didn't look hot when she was crying, and he could not wait to escape. Without another word, he removed his copy of the trailer key from his pocket and placed it on top of the money, and then, to his intense relief, he got away.

CHAPTER 32

Darren

He could not imagine enduring pain more excruciating than what he felt right now.

It was a good thing the grocery store was only a few minutes from his place. Just the tiny movements of driving hurt like a bitch. The pain clinic where he got his pills had recently closed and he was going to have to find a new doctor who would take his Medicaid, because he couldn't endure much more of this.

Angel had told Maya they were going to the store, and she reported that Maya had requested fish sticks and some more soup. Angel had food stamps, but they didn't cover much, and he'd been paying for some of her groceries. He didn't mind. Even as low as his disability payments were, he was still in better financial shape than Angel was.

He was relieved when he reached the store. Angel went inside to shop and he tried to get comfortable, but there was no position that didn't hurt. It didn't feel like the last pill had even kicked in, but his stomach was jumping around and he felt miserable.

He hoped he wouldn't have to open the car door and vomit onto the parking lot, but he unfastened his seat belt just in case. Even that small movement was torture. You never knew how much you used your back muscles for the simplest things, like reaching around to fasten or unfasten your seatbelt.

When his back was doing OK, he took ordinary movements completely for granted. Now? Every successful change in position was a hard-fought victory.

Jesus, what was taking that woman so long? She knew he was in agony. Or she should. He concentrated on fighting down a wave of nausea, braced for the pain he knew he'd feel if he had to open the door and lean over to puke.

There she was. She was wheeling a cart up to the car. He hit the button on his keyfob to pop the trunk, and she transferred what had to be a thousand little plastic bags into it. They always put about three items in each stupid little sack. He had a million of them under his kitchen sink.

Finally, she left the cart in the adjacent empty parking space and climbed into the front seat.

He was sitting back, his eyes closed, breathing deeply but not too deeply, because even that hurt.

"You OK?" It was as if she didn't understand the concept of pain if she weren't feeling it herself.

"No." But he opened his eyes and concentrated on driving home. He could do nothing automatically. Every movement had to be thought out and done consciously. She chattered on about what she was going to cook and he ignored her. He just wanted to get back into bed. To hell with supper. His stomach wanted no part of food right now.

"You bought more crackers, right?"

"I think so."

Finally they got home and he stopped the car, pressing as slowly as possible on the brake to avoid jarring his back, and popped the trunk so Angel could carry in the groceries.

"Give me a minute here," he muttered, a wave of dizziness mixing with the pain and nausea washing over him. As Angel began carrying the bags from the trunk to his porch, he closed his eyes and took a few deep breaths to steel himself for the pain of getting his body out of the car and back into bed.

Jesus, this was bad.

CHAPTER 33

Shirley

"Well, darn it," Shirley said to herself as she unfastened her seatbelt.

Despite her extreme care in driving home, as she parked in front of her trailer she realized one of her new African violets had rolled over and spilled soil all over the floor mat. It was the one in the round pot.

She leaned sideways, stretched her hands toward the passenger side floorboard and tried to gently scoop the spilled soil back into the pot. With any luck, the flower would be fine. The roots hadn't been exposed for very long. She'd drag her Kirby out here later and make sure she got every last bit of dirt out of her car.

CHAPTER 34

Nathan

Nathan didn't like all these people being around, and the sooner he left this place for good, the better.

The middle-aged guy was still sitting on his front steps, smoking and reading, and both Kaitlin's next door neighbors had returned home in the short time he'd been in her trailer. The old lady's Lincoln was parked right in front of his Lexus, and the fat older guy in the beater Chevy was just sitting in his driver's seat, doing God knows what.

Then his phone buzzed, and he knew before he looked it would be from Amanda. Sure enough. He groaned. Instead of answering it, he'd later tell her hadn't heard it.

He'd just started his car and had been at the point of pulling out when the beater Chevy suddenly lurched forward and hit his Lexus, shaking the hell out of him and causing his car to slam forward into the ancient Lincoln that was parked just ahead of him. He turned off the engine and jumped out of his car to survey the damage. It was minor.

But his immediate concern was how he'd explain his presence in this trailer park if the cops came out. He did not want any documentation that he'd been here to possibly give him away to his wife. It would be better if he could just drive off right now.

Smoker Man, he saw, had rushed over immediately, phone in hand, and looked to be calling 911. Damn it. Now he couldn't just leave.

The fat old guy in the Chevy was moaning and groaning, even though the collision hadn't been that bad. Possibly he'd rammed into him on purpose, hoping for a payout? He had some idea that Kaitlin had said the man was on disability for a bad back, which was likely a scam. While he was thinking this, a fat, disagreeable-looking woman came boiling out of the trailer yelling.

"Darren!" the woman yelled. "Darren!" She seemed to be looking after the man, who in any case didn't look injured.

Nathan turned his attention to Smoker Man, who had opened the door of the old Lincoln and was talking to someone. Nathan peered into the window of the Lincoln.

Oh Jesus. It was an old lady, lying on the front seat with a bloody head, moaning. He hadn't even known she was in the car. Now the police were sure to have questions and he had nothing good to tell them.

And then a black guy came running out of the trailer across the street, straight up to Smoker Man. "What happened? Is Shirley OK?" The old woman was moaning and holding her hand to her bloody forehead.

"Get a towel for her head. I already called 911," Smoker Man said. The black guy ran back to his trailer and Smoker Man addressed Nathan. "Don't just stand there. Go check on Darren!"

Nathan did as he was told. This was a clusterfuck.

The guy in the crappy old Chevrolet didn't have a mark on him but was moaning. His wife or girlfriend or whoever she was stood there crying her eyes out.

But when Nathan asked him what happened, he just grunted that his back hurt. He didn't offer an explanation for why or how he'd hit him. The sirens were approaching and Nathan knew they'd ask him questions. At least Kaitlin had not come out of her trailer. That was a plus.

The black guy had returned with a dish towel. His wife was pretty good-looking for a black woman. She was standing in the open doorway of their trailer, watching, blocking at least two small children who were trying to get past her.

The black guy handed the towel to Smoker Man, who placed it on the old lady's head as he reassured her. "Take it easy, Shirley. You're all right. Head wounds just bleed a lot."

Then Smoker Man turned to the black guy. "I don't think she's hurt as bad as it looks. She was leaning over when the car hit and happened to cut her head on a radio knob or something."

The police arrived first and started providing first aid, and a few minutes later the ambulance was there. Nathan decided to get back into his car. Amanda texted him again, and he again ignored it. He wasn't going to answer until he had a better idea of what to say; anything he texted now could end up constraining his options.

And then the black guy was knocking on his window. He rolled it down.

"I'm Jimmy Jackson. I think I can be of service."

CHAPTER 35

Jimmy

Of course, Nathan Clark had no idea who he was. Jimmy patiently explained that he worked at LCM and had an engineering internship there.

"We met today during orientation."

"Yes, of course," Nathan said, but Jimmy could tell by the look on his face that he had no idea who he was. "Listen, Jimmy, this isn't the best time for me."

"Cops are going to want to talk to you. Why don't you come on into my trailer?"

Nathan just looked confused.

"I'd do it quick, if I were you. Be more convincing that you're mentoring me if you're sitting at my kitchen table in front of a pile of books."

"OK." That was all Nathan said, and Jimmy wondered if the man was stupid or what. Wouldn't be the first stupid boss he'd seen. But after a few seconds, Nathan got out of his car and followed Jimmy into his trailer.

"This is my wife, Janiece," Jimmy said. "Janiece, why don't you take the girls to the other room?" She methodically said it was nice to meet Nathan and led the children away.

Jimmy placed a couple of textbooks on the table. "So we met today at LCM and you took an interest in me and decided to mentor me. Nice of you. Thanks. That's your story, and we're sticking to it. And as far as I know, that is the *only* reason you came to this trailer park today."

"What do you want?" Nathan asked. "Do you want money?"

"I don't want a thing. I have everything a man could want already. But it never does hurt to have a friend, does it?"

CHAPTER 36

Kaitlin

She watched everything very carefully from her bedroom, peering through the blinds. Nathan had to be shitting a brick.

She was relieved to see Shirley looking fine, but they took her off by ambulance anyway. She didn't dare go outside, with Nathan there. He'd be furious, and she didn't want that. It was still possible he'd change his mind, but for now, she'd stay out of his way. Besides, she didn't want to talk to the cops. She was still bitter about her DUI.

It was odd that Nathan had gone into the black couple's trailer. She'd have to find out later what was happening there. And another ambulance had taken Darren to the hospital, too. Jonesy had gone back to his trailer, and now she could see the cops knocking on the black folks' door and going in. They weren't there very long, and then the street was silent again.

She kept watching, and after a while, Nathan

came out and got into his car and drove away without even looking her way.

He'd miss her, though. That frigid bitch he was married to would never be able to make him happy. Nathan would be back. In the meantime, she had counted her money. It was enough that she could use it as a deposit on a real apartment if she wanted. She would have to get online and commit one way or another by midnight.

She hid the money in the back of her closet and fixed her makeup before texting Tommy. He'd cheer her up.

CHAPTER 37

Angel

It was terrible, the way the cops were treating an injured man. The ambulance had taken him to the hospital, but the cops had said he'd get a tox screen there. She'd asked them what that meant, and it meant they'd see if he were under the influence of drugs or alcohol.

Well, of course he was taking his medicine. His back had been hurting him really bad, and that's why he got distracted and forgot to turn off the key. But he had to drive to the store. What choice had they had?

If welfare paid what it should, or if Jeff had lived up to his responsibilities as a father, she'd have a car of her own and she could have driven to the store. But that just wasn't how it was. How could anybody else have done any better in this situation?

She took the fish sticks, soup and other groceries she needed home to her own trailer.

"You want soup or fish sticks, Maya?"

"Fish sticks." She didn't look up.

Angel turned on the oven. "Your grandma will probably come later to give me a ride to the hospital, soon as Darren's ready to come home. I bet they don't keep him overnight."

Maya seemed uninterested. She was watching a new cop series, and, ironically, had paid no attention to the police cars and ambulances that had been right outside her window.

Angel knew this was probably going to delay the wedding proposal. She wasn't showing yet anyway. She hadn't seen the doctor yet to know her due date. The baby's well-being was in God's hands, and even if she did go, the doctor wouldn't have done anything but weigh her and tell her she was eating too much. Waste of money until you were further along.

She'd thought Darren would have proposed by now, but first his back had gone out, and now this little accident had messed up her plans. But he'd be better soon, and she had an idea to ramp things up.

He had mentioned, before his back went out last week, another little fantasy of his. She generally believed in being passive and going along with your man's needs, but it just might be time to move things along. Just a little. Sometimes men needed a little nudge.

"I'm going to go lay myself down while the oven preheats," she told Maya, and went into her bedroom and got into her unmade bed.

She needed a rest; the day's events had been very hard on her. She usually did her best daydreaming on the front porch, but she was worn out and shaken up and wanted to lie still right now. She burrowed under the counterpane, curling her body around the tiny baby bulge only she knew was there.

And then she indulged herself in her favorite routine, imagining what her life was supposed to have been like. She loved to visualize the alternate life she'd just missed out on. By rights, she should be married to Robby and living in a nice house right now, with their baby.

She never imagined the baby grown up; it was always a cute little baby in her fantasies. Her alternate universe was a comforting place to be, and she escaped to it as often as she could.

Robby was the sweetest boy she'd ever kissed. They'd dated a year before they'd done anything bad. But once they started feeling each other under their clothes, all he could talk about was his desire to put the tip into her. He didn't want to actually have sex until they were married, he'd said. He just wanted to get an idea what it was going to be like.

Robby had been such a good kisser. It still hurt to remember how things ended. So when she felt sad, she concentrated on remembering how things had been between them before they'd killed the baby. She only liked to reminisce about the earlier times. When they would get into the backseat of his old car and kiss and kiss and kiss. That had been the best.

If she had had the strength to prevent him from getting into her pants, they'd be married today, and she wouldn't have to do all the sinning she was doing.

But she'd been weak.

"Just the tip," Robby would say. "Please. I won't take your virginity."

It seemed like a reasonable request, so finally she let him. He pulled her panties to the side and rubbed the tip all around. She had an idea he didn't quite know just where the actual opening was. But then, neither did she.

After that, that was all he wanted to do every time they went out. He developed a routine. First, he hooked his thumb around the crotch of her underwear to move it aside. Then he'd slide the tip of his thing around for a while, rubbing himself as he did, and then he'd put just the tip in and keep rubbing himself.

He really enjoyed that part. She'd noticed there was always a heck of a mess in her underwear afterward, but she wasn't sure if that was something from her body or from his. She knew what it was now, of course.

Somehow, their mostly innocent making out had been more exciting than any of the things she'd done with anybody else. She never reminisced about the things she had done with any other boy, but she did like to close her eyes and remember every detail about Robby. Everything that had come afterward had been her fault for breaking God's law. She could reimagine the past, but she couldn't undo it.

She was what she was, now.

CHAPTER 38

Nancy

She was definitely not staying here, but she had no idea where she was going to go.

In order to qualify for a lease on a new apartment, she needed to have a job, and so far she hadn't managed to find one.

The annoying thing was, now she had all this wonderful furniture she'd just finished paying off, but she was going to have to pay to have it moved to her new place. After she moved. After she got a new job.

In spite of her associate's degree in business and her experience running a trailer park, she'd been unable to find another job, which surprised her. She was hard-working and talented and had been to community college, so what exactly did employers want? So far, she'd applied to more than a dozen different jobs, and most of them never even bothered replying to her.

Every day, as she drove by the now-shuttered rental office, she remembered the coffee can under the bathroom vanity and smiled. The bottom of the vanity was probably rotted by now. Good.

Even if she could afford the exorbitant rent the place was going to charge, she no longer wanted to stay here. The other day when she was doing laundry, she'd attempted to commiserate with another tenant who was folding clothes as Nancy was transferring hers into a dryer.

"The new owners are nothing like the old one," Nancy remarked. "They're going to ruin this park."

"The old one sucked just as bad," the woman said.

"Oh, no, the old one was really nice!"

"Maybe you don't remember when you fined me a hundred bucks while my car was broke down in front of my trailer. I was trying to save up to get it fixed. I sure haven't forgot it, though. You had it towed. I had to pay all the money I was saving up for a new alternator to get it out of the impound lot." The woman piled the rest of her laundry, unfolded, into her basket and flounced out.

Nancy was hurt and offended. Was that woman seriously going to blame her just for doing her job?

It felt very unsettled, not to know where she was going to be living in a few months, or how she was going to get the money to pay for it. Or where she was going to move her furniture. At least she'd paid off her kitchen set.

But she was starting to think she wasn't going to be able to get a professional job, and had begun, slowly, to come around to the idea of waiting tables or something like that. It was incredible just how unfair life could be! When she thought of all the times she'd worked through her lunch hour, or stayed late to answer emails, or devoted extra effort to catch people breaking rules, she felt betrayed.

Why had she even bothered to get her associate's degree if she wasn't going to be able to get a professional job? It was just so wrong.

There had been times she'd resented the amount of work they'd piled on her. Now she looked back on those long days as among the happiest she'd ever had. But the joy and satisfaction of coming home every night to a beautiful home full of new furniture had been spoiled, because now she was afraid she wouldn't be able to afford the right kind of apartment to hold it all.

Selling it was unthinkable, but she'd had to start thinking of it, nonetheless. Did Mr. Darby even think about what a bad position he'd put her into?

She doubted it.

CHAPTER 39

Janiece

They settled right into the latest new normal.

Before she and Jimmy got married, it was hard to imagine what it would be like to actually live together, but within two days, it was the new normal. Same with becoming a mother. And with having to put college on hold. It was amazing what you could get used to, and how quickly you could do it.

And now, Jimmy was back in school like nothing had ever happened. He was actually away from home less now than when he'd been working on the factory floor, although he had to find ways to fit studying into his schedule. She was careful to keep the girls occupied when he needed quiet, and redoubled her efforts to get them to sleep at a decent time.

She took pride in her mothering, but she had to admit, getting the kids to sleep was not her strong suit. What she mostly did nowadays was get into their bed — the twins had to share one right now — and read book after book after book.

They fought sleep with every fiber of their being, and if one was still awake, she was likely to wake up the other one. It drove Janiece nuts. She couldn't wait until they had their own rooms, even though it was achingly sweet to see how they snuggled up and (eventually) slept together like two puppies.

She no longer worried about what they'd do when they stopped wanting to sleep cuddled up together. Unless they bought bunk beds, there was no way to fit a second mattress in there, and they were too little to trust either of them in a top bunk. But now that Jimmy had a clear path through to graduation and a good chance of an engineering job at LCM, she knew they could figure something out.

They'd decided they didn't want to pay the jacked-up rent they were going to be charged if they stayed, so she had started checking out little apartments. Getting one with either an extra bedroom or at least enough room for two twin beds would be a priority. The cheaper the better; she had already written in her notebook a whole plan for buying a house, just as soon as she was working and they'd knocked their loans down.

The key would be to make double payments for a year, and she thought they could do that if they pretended they still had less than $2,000 per month to live on. Then they'd have to start setting money aside for a down payment on a house. It would all work out somehow, she was sure.

The one thing she was still worried about was paying for Jimmy's second semester. They still didn't know if he'd be able to get any kind of loan.

"Maybe Mr. Clark will find a way to smooth things out for you," she'd said one night in bed after finally getting both twins to sleep. "You sure smoothed things with him with the cops that night."

"He's just waiting to see if I'm going to ask. I can feel it. He's kept up the 'mentoring' charade just to keep an eye on me."

"Don't ask."

"I know. If I ask, I'm sunk. He's expecting me to ask. And then he's going to consider it a bribe, and then I won't get hired after graduation. I know it just as sure as if he said it. But he might do it if I don't ask."

"Or maybe I should get a waitressing job right away. Start putting money back."

"You're not going to make enough to pay a whole semester's tuition all up front." He spooned up around her, his hand resting lightly on her hip.

"Might." She moved her bottom suggestively and he gave it a playful smack.

"Not after the cost of buying another car."

"You're right." She scooched her butt away from him, just a little. "Damn it. Why does every single damned thing always have to be so hard?"

"I don't know. But I'm going with my gut with this one. I have a feeling he's going to come up with a way to fund next semester because I'm so damned promising, or he's going to figure out something on the side, as long as I don't in any way act like I think I've got it coming."

"He's not visiting Kaitlin anymore, so that probably freed up enough money for him to pay for all your expenses."

"I'm sorry to disappoint you, wifey, but I'm not giving the man no blowjob."

Now Janiece was the one giving the playful smacks. "Oh, and here I thought you were dedicated."

CHAPTER 40

Jonesy

Holding a towel to someone's bloody head is a bonding experience.

Jonesy hadn't written up anything about the crash on his street. Ultimately, it was small potatoes. Shirley was given a couple of stitches and an X-ray and released. Jonesy was the one who drove her back home, since none of her close family was nearby, and he had been there when she was injured.

As for Darren, he was apparently arrested for driving under the influence, but Jonesy didn't follow up. It appeared he'd been on painkillers he took for perfectly legitimate reasons but had driven when he shouldn't have. He was lucky he made it home without killing anyone.

If Shirley hadn't been leaning over to fuss with her plants, it's unlikely there'd have been any injuries at all. Kaitlyn's sugar daddy — well, her reputed sugar daddy — hadn't been hurt at all. He had gone into the Jackson family's trailer, where the police had questioned him briefly, and then he'd left. As far as Jonesy could tell, the man hadn't been back to the trailer park since.

Jonesy had found a small upstairs apartment in a restored Queen Anne that had been subdivided into separate living spaces. He would have his own side entrance for privacy. He wasn't crazy about the thought of climbing up that exterior staircase in winter, but he found the apartment itself charming.

It had polished wood floors, elaborate woodwork and high ceilings. There was no fireplace in his section, he was disappointed to see, but the bathroom was original and gorgeous, all black and white tile and gold fittings. The living room was rather small and oddly shaped, but elegant. The kitchen was even smaller and had been tucked into what he guessed might have been a dressing room at some point. His bedroom, in contrast, was oversized. This was what you got when you adapted part of a house into apartments, he knew.

The owners retained the entire downstairs for themselves, and had turned most of the upstairs into two apartments. He was interested to learn that the woman who lived on the other side was a teacher, though he hadn't seen her yet.

He put down a deposit and looked forward to being warm in winter and cool in summer. As for any potential loss in privacy he might experience as a result of living in the same house as others, he wasn't concerned. Everyone on his street in the trailer park knew entirely too much about each other anyway. This couldn't be much worse.

He planned to splurge on an antique desk or table that he could set up in his bedroom, since it was the largest room by far. That would be where he would finish his novel, which was coming along nicely. It was at about 40,000 words, and he guessed he was about half-way done with the first draft.

He was at the point in the story that a small band of people were trying to spread the word about the dangers of optimized memories. His main character was a man named Killian Pike, who nearly starved to death because he wanted to do nothing but "go to Paris."

But after many, many trips to Paris, Killian Pike had begun to notice something he had missed when he was actually there for real, as well as the first hundred or so times he'd returned in his mind.

It was such a small detail, and it was this: While he took his first bite of croissant, he'd briefly closed his eyes from enjoyment of a perfect and still-warm croissant. When he opened them, the first thing he'd seen was a man standing in an alley and glaring malevolently at a woman who was seated several tables away.

The woman was beautiful and striking in that way only a self-possessed Parisian woman can be. She was just as typically French as his breakfast that day had been, and just as unforgettable. Yet, the man was staring at her not with the pleasure of looking at a beautiful woman, but with what looked like intent to do her harm.

After that, Killian Pike could no longer enjoy his optimized memory. Instead, he became obsessed with learning who the woman was and whether anything had happened to her. He'd gotten his life back together and scraped up enough money to fly back to France, and when he got there, he spent as much time as possible at the same cafe, hoping to see her again.

He never did, but eventually, the owner began chatting with him. He was one of those French men who pretended he didn't speak English, but would immediately switch to very good English as soon as he decided it was in his best interest to do so.

Killian Pike told the French man the entire story, including a precise description of the woman he feared for, a bit embarrassed because when he said it out loud, he realized he sounded completely insane.

But the Frenchman knew exactly who he was talking about.

"That's Aurelie Laurent," he said. "She disappeared three years ago."

"I knew you would tell me something like that," Killian Pike said. Further conversation revealed that she'd disappeared around the time of his visit to France, and he was convinced the man he'd seen staring at her must be guilty of doing her harm.

He was able to provide a very good description of the man, and in fact, just to confirm everything to the police officer, he slipped into his optimized memory once again and came back with an even more precise description.

That was where the story stood so far. Jonesy was trying to decide whether it would be better to have Killian Pike be able to identify the man from a book of police mugshots or whether he should run into the man in person and recognize him.

He couldn't decide, so he put the story aside to think about it for a day. Sometimes, something would bubble up from deep inside his consciousness when he did that, and he usually produced far better writing.

But he felt his book might be going off the rails. Here he was, trying to make some big points about society, and his book was devolving into a murder mystery.

Well, at least he'd managed to keep out the crazy sex subplots. At least, so far. He'd eventually given up on every other book he'd tried to write, because the characters always seemed to be involved in kinky sex. He didn't know why, either.

If ever there were a man who liked his sex vanilla, it would be Jonesy. Yet his abandoned manuscripts were full of prostitution and perversions of every sort.

Jonesy's mother was still alive, and there was no way he was going to publish a book that he'd be ashamed for her to read.

CHAPTER 41

Shirley

Nothing was going right.

Kaitlin said she was going to move away. She hadn't found an apartment yet, but she hadn't renewed her lease. Nancy was also moving. Well, that was expected, of course. No wonder Nancy didn't want to stay, as badly as she'd been treated by the Sterling people. It was unconscionable how they just fired her like that.

Plus, she had gotten a couple of stitches in her forehead. Right after she'd had her hair done, too. She'd looked a mess all week.

Her new African violets were doing fine, though. She placed one on an end table next to her sofa and the other on her kitchen counter.

If she sat in one particular chair in her living room and looked straight ahead, her living room looked very much like the one in her old house. If she didn't look left and see the narrow hallway. If she didn't look right and see the small kitchen. If she didn't glance upward and see how low the ceiling was. But the carpeting she'd chosen to have installed before she moved in was a very good match for what she'd had in her formal living room, and it went well with her nice furniture.

She'd debated, when moving into her trailer, whether to go with her formal living room furniture or her more casual family room furniture. Both were Ethan Allen. She liked their style and had decorated her entire house using Ethan Allen pieces.

Of course she would keep as much of her furniture as possible. That wasn't the question. The question was whether she was going to concentrate more on style or comfort, and she had decided to go with style. After all, she'd had to give up so much. The one thing she would not ever give up was a sense of her own style.

She did not really belong in a trailer park, and if anybody doubted it, her Lincoln Town Car confirmed it, as did her wardrobe full of pieces from places like Talbots and Neiman Marcus, and her collection of fine jewelry.

With Kaitlin and Nancy both leaving, there was no telling who her next door neighbors might be. She hadn't heard what Jonesy's plans were, or the Jackson family, and she didn't give a darn what Darren did, or that awful new woman, Angel.

Jonesy had been quite nice. She'd not really talked to him since the morning she'd told him

Charles Darby had probably burnt down his own bowling alley on purpose, but he'd helped her when she needed it.

She made a mental note to buy him some small gift. Maybe a small plant? No, that was too much like the reason she'd been injured. Maybe just a gift card to a restaurant. He was so thin.

Apparently, Darren had been driving under the influence, which did not surprise her one bit. Couldn't the man lay off the drugs and alcohol at least on the way to the store? She couldn't even sue him, because she knew he didn't have any money.

Kaitlin's friend undoubtedly had more money, but it hadn't been his fault. Darren was the one who pushed the car into her, after all. Anyway, all they'd done at the hospital was check her out and stitch her wound, and she had decent car insurance and Medicare.

It was going to be lonely here, soon, unless somebody good moved into the trailers.

CHAPTER 42

Maya

It had been nice having Mom at home for a change, even though she was in a pretty bad mood.

Mom said Darren was fine and would be home in a few days, but she seemed mad about it. At least she was making dinner every night. Maya had grown tired of cold soup. Fish sticks and frozen pizza were more to her liking.

School had started, which had cut into her TV viewing. Krystal and Emma still bullied her, but they had a new victim now, which was a relief to Maya. There was a new girl named Aaliyah who made a better target because she was black. There weren't that many black kids in the school.

Her mom didn't like black people. She kept complaining about the lazy black people next door. Maya had seen the two little girls playing outside and asked her mom if she thought she might be able to get a babysitting job, but her mom said if she wanted to babysit there were plenty of white kids she could be watching.

But there weren't any white kids. There were only the two little black girls. It would have been nice to have made some money that way. She couldn't think of any other ways to make any. The good thing about babysitting was she could have done it while still seeing her shows.

How hard could it be to take care of children? You just made them sit on the sofa in front of the TV, and if they didn't behave, you smacked their butts. It would have been an easy way to make money.

If she had some money, she could buy herself some new clothes. Her mom hadn't taken her out to buy new clothes before school started. Neither had either grandma. Her jeans from last year still fit around her waist but they were too short, and Krystal made it a point to bring that up every day.

"Nice socks," Krystal kept saying. "You must want everyone to see them." Maya knew better than to tell her mom she needed new jeans.

Her mom believed she was going to marry Darren. If she did, he would be Maya's stepdad, and he might buy her new clothes. But probably not. He did not seem to have a lot of money, either.

Her other grandma would probably buy her new clothes, but she hadn't seen her for a while. Her mom said she'd see her dad and other grandma when the child support was paid up.

Walking down the hallway at school, Maya felt

as if her ankles had flashing neon lights on them, and she scurried from class to class as quickly as she could. Her short jeans were less noticeable when she was sitting down, she thought, so the less she was seen standing or walking, the better.

It was good to have Aaliyah at the school. Maya hoped the other girls would focus so much on the new black girl that they'd forget about her.

When her mom was in a better mood, she intended to ask her if she could have new jeans. She could wear them every single day. Just one pair would be enough.

But first, her mom needed to be in a better mood. When Darren finally got home from the hospital, maybe. Her mom hadn't been visiting him there, probably because she didn't have a car.

CHAPTER 43

Kaitlin

It was time to make a choice. Kaitlin hated making choices.

Tommy said they were hiring at the hospital laundry, and he was almost sure he could get her on if she wanted. He had also suggested she move into his house with him, where he'd lived alone ever since his grandmother died. Kaitlin had only seen the place once. It seemed OK.

But if she moved in with him, sooner or later she would need to start sleeping with him, and that would mean no more arrangements like the one she'd had with Nathan. On the other hand, she liked Tommy a lot more than she'd liked Nathan. Tommy was her own age and he was cute. She'd be getting free rent from the deal, and she could ride with him to and from work, so she wouldn't have to worry about that.

But on the downside, she'd have to work full time. She had never worked full time before. It was just so much easier to have a guy like Nathan pay some of your bills. And while she could probably find somebody who would pay more, these things were unpredictable. It could take time to find a good Nathan. But she would need to give Tommy an answer soon.

Kaitlin understood that when Tommy offered her the chance to live with him for free and get rides to and from work for free, these things weren't really free. He said she could have her own room, but that wouldn't last. Probably she should have sex with him when he came over tonight. Better to know ahead of time what she might be getting into.

Glancing at her phone, she saw she had a couple of hours before Tommy would get off work and come over. Then she opened her bedroom blinds and saw Shirley sitting outside, smoking. She could shoot the shit with Shirley for a while and still have plenty of time to make herself look pretty for Tommy.

"Hey, Shirley," she said, and plopped down on one of the fancy chairs. "Your head is healing right up."

There was still a little pink line on her forehead, but it wasn't all bruised up and swollen like it had been.

"That Darren should by rights pay my hospital bill, but there's no chance of that." She made a little sound of annoyance.

"What happened to him? I haven't seen him around."

"They took him from the hospital to the jail. This wasn't his first go-round with a DUI."

Kaitlin remained silent; she'd always let Shirley think her reason for not having a car was because she couldn't afford one. Instead, she got busy lighting a cigarette and tried to change the subject.

"Angel's back to sitting on the porch all evening."

"I wish you and Nancy were staying, but I hope Angel goes."

"Why don't you go?" Kaitlin asked.

Shirley sighed. "It's expensive to move a trailer, and I'll have to pay the lot rent no matter where I go. I might pay all that money to move my trailer and then the new place might raise the rent, too. So I expect I may as well just stay here."

It was on the tip of her tongue to invite Shirley to move her trailer to the empty trailer pad at Tommy's place, but she decided she should bring it up with him first. Maybe he wouldn't like the idea. Or maybe he would; he'd probably be willing to do just about anything if she suggested it.

And Shirley was always handy to have around. Right now her old-ass Lincoln was at the body shop, but normally by now, she'd have offered Kaitlin a ride to work. Kaitlin didn't need a ride today anyway, though. Naomi hadn't scheduled her for a couple of days for some reason. That was fine. She had plenty of money from Nathan hidden in the back of her closet for now.

"My friend Tommy's coming over in a little while. He might be able to get me on at the hospital laundry. Pay is a lot better there. But it's going to be hot and sweaty."

"Now that sounds like a good move, Kaitlin. That convenience store job isn't ever going to get you anywhere. And have you found a new apartment yet?"

"No, but Tommy has a house. He said I could have my own bedroom. I'm thinking about it."

Shirley stabbed out her cigarette in the little ashtray she carried outside each time she smoked; it never had more than a couple of butts in it at any one time. She was fussy that way.

"I'd be careful having a boy for a roommate. He might not just want a roommate." Shirley gave her a pointed look, and Kaitlin held back a smile. Shirley was awfully innocent for a grown woman.

Shirley and Sapphire were as different as could be, but they were alike, too. They both seemed to think Kaitlin couldn't manage a man without following their rules.

"Tommy's all right. I haven't made up my mind just yet. But I think I'll head home and get a shower before he comes over. You never know. I might even let him kiss me tonight." She winked at Shirley before she turned around and returned to her trailer.

Kaitlin vacuumed and did her dishes, then

cleaned her toilet and shower. Nathan was persnickety, so when he was coming around, she kept everything nice. Without him, she'd let her standards slip. But she wasn't sure how fussy Tommy was. Best to clean things up a little just in case.

Then she got ready. She hadn't been going all out lately, because there was little point in looking pretty when she wasn't getting paid for it, but tonight she wanted to wow Tommy. It wouldn't be smart to make it too obvious.

The best way was to make her hair and makeup look perfect but to wear an ordinary pair of jeans and just a regular shirt. That way he wouldn't think she'd gone to any extra trouble to impress him.

She was all ready long before he came over, and she tried to think about something interesting she could be in the middle of doing when he got there. It's too bad she didn't have a puzzle or some kind of game. Cards. She had a deck of cards. She could be playing solitaire, and then they could play rummy after that.

First she played a game of solitaire, which she lost. Then she laid out another hand, but left it in the middle. When he came over, she'd pretend to be engrossed, and he'd sit there and advise her. She'd noticed before that if anybody played solitaire, everybody around them couldn't help but point out every potential move.

People seemed to enjoy directing others

how to play more than they enjoyed playing themselves.

Sure enough, when he came over, one of the first things he did was point out a move.

"Five of hearts on that six of clubs."

Kaitlyn had just been waiting for him to point out that move, and she pretended she hadn't seen it before he pointed it out. Men always liked to feel useful. It made them happy if you let them help. It could be pointing out a card to be played, or it could be paying your rent.

"Do you want to play poker or something?" If he suggested strip poker, she would make sure to lose, and that would make things easy. But Tommy was a little bit too much of a gentleman.

"Rummy?"

"Sure," she said. "I'll need you to remind me how to play." That wasn't true, but she knew he'd enjoy showing her.

Sure enough, he grinned and explained in great detail. He really was a sweet guy. Maybe this wasn't going to be a bad idea.

"Do you want to get something to drink?" she suddenly asked. If they had something to drink, it would give her a little excuse for letting things go further than usual.

"We could do that." He put down the cards he'd been shuffling and they went out to his pickup truck and made the quick drive to the grocery store, where he purchased a case of beer, a frozen pizza and some snacks. He didn't ask her to chip in and she didn't offer.

Once back at her place, she turned on her oven and put all but two of the beers into the refrigerator.

"OK, you deal," she said, and cracked open her first beer.

She calculated that she'd want to be plausibly tipsy before he could drink enough to possibly have performance issues. No telling how long that took with Tommy, but at any rate, she was determined to get a couple of beers down before serving the pizza. He needed to believe this was happening naturally, not that she was sleeping with him for calculated reasons.

She finished off the first one before the oven had finished preheating, and she got herself a second beer as she popped the frozen pizza into the oven.

"You want another one?" she called out.

"I'm only halfway through this one," Tommy said. "You must be thirsty tonight."

She ignored that and checked her reflection in the oven door, noting that her hair still looked just right. "So I filled out that application online. You hear anything from your boss?"

"I told him you had applied and he seemed to be pretty on-board. He likes me. I think he'll interview you. That'll be cool to work together again." His eyes never left her as she returned to the coffee table.

"I know. You were fun at the convenience

store." She lifted her beer and guzzled. She didn't really like beer much, but Tommy did. The main thing was to seem just a tiny bit drunk.

The timer on the oven did not work, but she had set the alarm on her phone, and after a couple of games, her alarm went off and she got the pizza and carried it to the coffee table.

"Dinner is served." She got two more beers. It was Tommy's second and her third. She felt so full of beer she wasn't sure she'd be able to eat much pizza. "Be right back."

The problem with this dinky trailer was you could hear everything. She belched as quietly as she could, timing it to line up with the sound of the toilet flush, and then she washed her hands and returned to the living room, where Tommy was wolfing down the pizza.

It was all she could do to finish the one piece of pizza, and she couldn't force down any more beer, either.

"Beer goes straight to my head." She was sitting on the floor, her back to the sofa, and she tilted her head back and rested it against the sofa, aware that this would make her breasts nearly pop out of the scoop-necked blouse she was wearing. And with her head back and eyes closed, she assumed Tommy would be taking advantage of the opportunity to get a really good eyeful. She hoped he was doing so, and held the pose for a while just to give him every chance, before straightening up again.

"You should eat some more pizza," he told her. "Soak up some of the beer."

"I'm so full, though." She was bored with the cards. "Tell me about your house."

"We could go there right now. I haven't even finished my second beer."

She hadn't considered that. If she went to his house, she could check things out as far as a future living situation, and then if he drank more, he'd be unable to drive her home and she could just happen to end up in his bed. She'd know by morning if she wanted to move in.

"Why not? I'll get my stuff." She went into her bedroom and dumped the contents of her cute purse into a big handbag, and stuffed a pair of clean underwear into it. Then she carried it into the bathroom and added her toothbrush, deodorant, makeup bag and a few hair things.

She wanted to seem like she was casually roughing it, but without actually looking rough.

Tommy was eating the last piece of pizza and he considerately placed the pizza pan in the sink before retrieving the rest of the beer from the fridge.

"All right then," she said, and they left.

She'd been there once before. It was just outside of town. It had been more of a country location when it was built, but the town had crept closer to it over the decades. Tommy had mentioned that he'd inherited it from his grandmother.

There was something messy about his family situation, and she struggled to recall the details. Anyway, he'd grown up mostly living with his grandmother, and his mother had lived in a crappy little trailer on the property until some years ago.

The place was pitch black. Country dark. If not for the headlights of the truck, she wouldn't have been able to see a thing. So when he turned them off, the darkness was total. There were enough street lights in the trailer park that it was never truly dark, and she'd forgotten how dark night could get.

"I should have left the porch light on," Tommy said. "Hold on, I'll unlock the door and turn on the light so you don't trip in the dark."

She watched him disappear into the dark, and then he turned on the porch light and she could see enough to make her way over the grass in the side yard and onto the sidewalk that led to a little covered porch. There was an old wooden porch swing that had probably been there since his grandparents had hung it there. And then she was inside the house.

"It's nice," she said. It was a mix of very dated things that had been here forever and newer things Tommy himself had obviously bought. If he let her, she'd get rid of the old stuff and maybe paint the place.

That was if she decided to live here. First she had to sleep with him and see how that went. She was no longer plausibly tipsy, but she didn't need to be if she were spending the night. Sex would happen naturally with a few nudges.

"This is the living room," he announced unnecessarily. "And the dining room." Big wooden pillars and built-in glass-doored bookcases separated the two rooms. "Here's the kitchen," he said. It was about the size of the trailer kitchen. There was no place to sit. You'd have to eat every meal in the dining room, the old-fashioned way. A bathroom and two bedrooms were accessible off a tiny hallway you reached from the dining room.

One of the bedrooms was clearly Tommy's, and had been from the time he was a kid, she surmised. It still looked like a kid's room, except for a few non-kid touches that were layered on top. He'd replaced whatever old bed had been in here with a new-looking queen-size bed.

The other bedroom still looked like a grandma room, with an old and cheap-looking double bed and matching bedside table and dresser. It still had a big polyester floral bedspread on it, too. If she stayed here, she was going to insist on changing some things around. Even if she did move in, she wanted her own bedroom.

"Is there an upstairs?"

"There is, but it's either too hot or too cold most of the year. So I just use it for storage. It's a mess."

"OK." Good to know she'd have plenty of

storage space, though. It wasn't a bad house, all in all. He'd probably let her change things around. She'd ask him early on, when he'd be easier to deal with. Assuming the sex was OK. It was time to give it a try, but she couldn't just propose a sexual tryout. And he seemed to be at a loss, too.

He stood there, in the door to his bedroom, looking like he was trying to do math in his head. Probably doing the same thing she was — trying to figure out a way to move things along. He was trying to figure out how to get laid while still being a gentleman and she was trying to figure out how to let him do it while still being a lady. Or a pretend lady, anyway.

Sometimes the oldest methods were best.

"I know I'm a brat, but you give such good back rubs." She smiled. As if she didn't know backrubs were the most obvious bridge from friendly touch to sexual touch ever invented. "Can I have just a short one?"

She would usually claim at this point to have had a hard day at work, but he already knew she'd been off for a few days, so she dropped the excuse. It didn't matter. He wasn't stupid. He knew what she was doing, and that's why he started smiling.

Kaitlin turned off the light and then stretched herself out on Tommy's bed and lifted her shirt. She didn't take it off; she just lifted it to about bra-strap level. That would allow him easy reach to her entire back, but it still looked like she really just wanted a backrub.

She would take it off later, after he'd made a faint but perceptible move from friendly touch to sexual touch. She wasn't going to do it without the little dance. He would have to do his part here.

Tommy's hands were warm and he really did give a good massage. She allowed herself to make a few more soft moans than usual. "My stupid bra is in the way. Could you unfasten it so you can get those knots in the middle of my back?" As if he were doing her a favor.

Now it was up to Tommy. He could reach her entire back, and there was sideboob available. Sure enough, it wasn't long before his fingers just barely brushed where a friend probably wouldn't touch. She made sure to let out a satisfied sigh. His fingers brushed there again.

"Mmm."

Kaitlin had a theory that guys who were good at massages were also good in bed. In truth, she hadn't really tested this theory out very thoroughly, because she tended to put men into two categories. They were friends or they were men she needed something from. She might get back rubs from the friends, but certainly neither Nathan nor other men she'd dated because of what they could offer her ever gave her a massage or any real affection. Not since high school had she had a boyfriend she'd chosen just because she liked him.

Tommy was in a new category. She liked and trusted him, and she was about to agree to move in for the free rent, but if she actually lived with him, that would be a different kind of situation altogether.

It's not that she had minded having sex with Nathan, but she was always happy when he left and she could clean herself out and go back to sleep. She'd be seeing Tommy all the time.

"I could go to sleep just like this," she said. There was just enough light coming in from the hall for them to see each other. She twisted her head and tried to gauge the expression on his face.

"I can let you go to sleep if you want. I could take the other bed."

"No, stay here with me." She rolled over and held out her arms to Tommy, who didn't hesitate to start kissing her.

It didn't take five seconds for her to know she was moving in.

CHAPTER 44

Darren

The hospital had been bad, but the jail was worse.

He'd had a DUI years before and had barely had his wrist tapped. In the intervening years, the laws had gotten a lot stricter. Angel had seemed to think he'd be home that night, but in fact, he'd been kept two days in the hospital.

Once he understood he'd be going to jail instead of home, he talked up his pain. If he had thought they were sending him home, he'd have downplayed it just to get out.

The pain was real enough, though. It was still bad while he was in jail. They hadn't put him into a pod, luckily. They held him in a sort of sick bay. It was very much like the hospital, actually.

That was one thing to be thankful for, anyway. No matter how boring it was to be lying in a hospital bed in jail, it sure beat the hell out of being on the cellblock. That would have been even worse.

The main difference between the hospital and the jail was that he couldn't even watch TV in jail. It gave him entirely too much time to think about all the ways his life had not gone as he'd hoped.

He didn't particularly like going down memory lane. He'd had plenty of good years when he was earning a solid living all week and getting all the hot sex he could handle on the weekends. But that had been in the very distant past, and he'd had a lot of not-so-happy years since then.

Best to forget most of the last twenty years, but being flat on your back on a hospital bed in jail, in pain, facing legal troubles — all without so much as a TV to occupy your mind — did not tend to make for happy reminiscing.

He finally arranged for bail and got out, taking a cab home because Angel couldn't drive. That had been the whole problem. He would definitely teach her. He wasn't going to be able to get his license sorted for a good long while.

His anger at her had abated as he realized how much he needed her now. It was not just a matter of kinky sex; it was a matter of needing her to drive him around. He'd sign his car over to her as soon as possible to avoid being required to have one of those breathalyzer things installed in his car. He'd known people who had them. You had to blow into a tube just to start your car, and they cost a mint in monthly rental fees. Better not to even own a car than to have to pay for that.

It was good to finally be home. Angel had come right over and cooked him a better meal than usual, and he appreciated it. He'd been eating hospital and jail food for days, and by comparison, Angel's cooking was four-star cuisine. He'd thanked her profusely, and meant it.

"This is really good, Angel. I should have told you before now just how much I appreciate you."

"I'll always take care of you, Darren," she said, and gave him a smile. "In all ways."

Darren groaned. "My back's not ready for what you're talking about. It's getting there, though. Give me a few days."

"I have some really good ideas for once your back is better."

"I bet you do. Now let's have some more of that cake."

He wasn't sure what was going to happen at his next court appearance or how he was going to scrape up all the money for his lawyer, but he was home, he had a damned good dinner and he'd be getting more good sex in a few days.

It wasn't all bad.

CHAPTER 45

Jonesy

He was stuck in every way.

His novel was at a stopping point. He didn't know how to handle the way it had veered off and become a crime novel. It was supposed to be about all the ways new technology was ruining people's lives, and now he had a subplot in which technology was helping to bring a killer to justice. Or something like that. He hadn't written that part yet.

He'd started off with a strong feeling that people needed to understand the importance of living in the moment, not in the past. He felt that people needed to be in the real world, not buried in video games and virtual reality. They should interact face-to-face, not through screens.

The last thing he wanted to write was a whodunit. Yet, he found himself wondering what had happened to Aurelie Laurent. She seemed like a real person, even though he'd come up with her name by searching online for random French given names and surnames. She wasn't real at all.

But when he was sitting in the Loire City Council meeting, he had missed the vote to issue sewer bonds because he was musing about how the mysterious man had captured her and what he had done with her afterward. At the end of the council meeting, he'd had to ask the city clerk to tell him how each council member had voted.

There must be a way to tie in a murder and the central points he was trying to make. He had neatly composed, printed and taped up a reminder of what his central points he hoped to hit:

1. *A lot of human beings suck*
2. *Humans who already suck can suck even worse with the right technology*
3. *People are mostly wasting their lives chasing pleasure*
4. *There's a difference between pleasure and happiness*
5. *Free will is probably an illusion*
6. *The individual has less power over himself than he thinks*
7. *We always blame or reward the person, never the system or culture*
8. *Capitalism assumes everyone is a greedy bastard but that's false*
9. *Socialism assumes everybody has good intentions but that's false*

10. *Nobody has ever figured out how to balance individual rights with the common good*
11. *It's almost impossible to define the difference between fake news and truth*

Under this list, he had handwritten a few more:

12. *Sources of power are government, religion, corporations and social pressure/ culture, and corporations have more and more*
13. *Democracy needs to figure its shit out asap before authoritarianism takes over the world*
14. *Sometimes, people do the right things for the wrong reasons*
15. *Sometimes, people do the wrong things for the right reasons*

He had figured on a length of about 80,000 words, and he was about halfway there but was now off on a murder tangent and he had barely touched on most of his points. There was no good way to work them all in. He thought about copying all the Aurelie Laurent stuff into a different document to make that a separate murder mystery he could write later. But when he tried, there wasn't enough substance to either story to stand alone. He would just have to figure out how to weave the murder story into his larger story.

But the more he went along, the more he

realized he was actually making a separate point altogether: Technology could solve problems that had been previously unsolvable. He was making the exact opposite argument he'd wanted to make. He was arguing against his own position.

He could not even win an argument against himself, even with the ability to create an alternate reality. Jonesy prided himself on being a logical, intelligent, thoughtful man. But now, he had to think about his various relationships and wonder if he'd been the problem all along.

If you hit middle age and still are not successfully coupled up, he'd always privately thought, you might be the problem. He'd considered himself an exception to that rule, though. His issue was his very low pay, he had always believed. Having high intelligence and a solid education but a low-status, low-paying job made it difficult to find a girlfriend.

Highly intelligent, well-educated, well-off women weren't interested in him. He wasn't interested in unintelligent or uneducated women.

The number of women who were smart and educated but happy to commit to a man for whom the rent on a trailer took a big chunk of his pay was a small number indeed; he'd not found one yet. So he was stuck in his personal life, too.

He also was stuck in his moving. He'd packed some things, but he wouldn't be able to actually make the move for another week because the current tenant wasn't officially out yet.

So he couldn't progress with his move, and he'd already had to rip into a box because he'd packed some things and then ended up needing them. His whole trailer was a chaotic mess.

"I can't write like this," he muttered aloud. He was aware that he was looking for excuses, because he still hadn't worked out why anybody would want to kill Aurelie Laurent, and he was still hoping for a way that the murder subplot could be worked out to support his premise about the dehumanizing effect of technology.

Perhaps there was a way he could arrange things so that Killian Pike could, while in Paris for real, save Aurelie Laurent. Perhaps she wasn't dead, just being held somewhere. And perhaps he could manage it in some manner that had nothing to do with technology.

He sighed. Even if he managed it, he'd have to be on guard against his tendency to veer off into a kinky subplot. He didn't want Aurelie Laurent and Killian Pike to end up in bed. He'd put aside enough manuscripts in the past because they'd devolved. This story was going to stay on the straight and narrow.

He put his cigarettes, lighter and phone into the pockets of his old denim jacket and went for a walk through the trailer park. He would smoke and think and come back to the computer with fresh ideas. Walking was a good way to stimulate the brain. He'd written a feature story about that at some point.

Nobody else walked in the trailer park, unless they had no car and thus no choice. You'd see kids out running around in the summer sometimes, but not so many as you'd think, because they tended to stay inside in the air conditioning if they had it. It was cool enough now that just opening the windows made for a pleasant temperature, and soon enough it would be time to turn on the heat.

He was still annoyed that his air conditioning had never been repaired. Of course, Nancy had been incompetent. The new owners might or might not be better, but he wasn't sticking around to find out. He expected things to be better in his new situation, in which he would be literally living in the same house as his landlords. They would be motivated to keep things in good shape, he assumed.

He dropped his first cigarette to the road and ground it under his heel, and almost immediately lit up another one. He never pulled one out of the pack without mildly reproaching himself for doing so. It's not as if he didn't know exactly how harmful they were. It was just that, in a life so devoid of major pleasures, the feeling of a nicotine hit was a little one he could always have. Even as expensive as cigarettes had become in the last decade, they were still cheaper than most other small pleasures.

But he was moving out of the trailer park. Maybe when he moved into an attractive apartment, he could find the motivation to quit. He'd appear about 75 percent less white trashy if he didn't live in a trailer and didn't smoke. He could get better and more frequent haircuts with the money he saved, and maybe even hit 80 percent less trashy.

The remaining 20 percent was out of his hands. He would still be poor and driving a cheap old car. But still. There was that teacher living in the other apartment. They'd run into each other eventually, no doubt. He hadn't met her, but he surmised she was single, since she was living in an apartment.

For all that teachers complained about their pay, he knew he'd have at least doubled his salary if he had become one. Jonesy covered the school board meetings. During every contract negotiation, he'd dutifully quote the president of the union complaining that teachers deserved higher pay.

Jonesy happened to agree with them, but wondered what they'd think if he were to reveal to them that someone teaching for four or five years was likely earning double his own salary. Teachers who had as much experience teaching as Jonesy did reporting made around three or even four times as much as he did, not even considering their benefits.

It had been a goal of his to break $30,000

by his 40th birthday, but he didn't manage it. He counted himself lucky to have managed to hang onto a newspaper job at all, and his current $25,000 salary was as high as he was likely to get. They hadn't given anyone in the newsroom a raise in at least a decade.

Here he was smoking as he contemplated stopping, and ruminating about his shitty wages when he was supposed to be unkinking the twisted plot of his book. He forced himself to concentrate. Wasn't nicotine supposed to help you focus? That was what they said, but he'd seen no evidence of it.

So Killian Pike had a really good description of the suspect, and would recognize Aurelie Laurent anywhere. He could absolutely pull himself together, go to Paris for real, and then investigate the particulars of Aurelie's life. Maybe he could manage to track her down, ideally using old-fashioned techniques, not by using technology.

And then, once he found her, he'd have to either stay in Paris or get Aurelie to come back to the United States with him, because Jonesy knew he couldn't resist having the two fall in love. Maybe they'd settle down happily ever after in the real Loire, France. He'd get a kick out of that.

It wasn't lost on him that while he was writing a story partly set in France, he was living in a crappy small town named after a famous French city. But Loire, Illinois was pronounced in a way that would make a Frenchman choke on his brie and beaujolais.

Illinois was full of city names that the locals had butchered. His favorite was a place named San Jose. The "Jose" rhymed with nose. There was also a Cairo that was pronounced "kay-row." There was also a Versailles, in which the second syllable rhymed with fails.

Putting together the obit page had given him a real education on the number of tiny towns with weird names. There were some with striking Native American names, like Kickapoo. Others were just names reused from larger towns out East. There was Concord (derisively known by some as Corncob) which seemed to take a good thirty seconds to pronounce the way the residents slowly drew out the vowels. It took longer to pronounce the town than it did to drive through it.

Then there was Goofy Ridge. Who the hell would name a town something like that? And Paw Paw. He had eaten a paw paw once, and was not a fan. There was a Wenona and a Wenonah. That had to be a headache for everyone involved, which fortunately was almost nobody, as the populations of both towns together would make a smaller crowd than you might draw to a decent rock concert.

Oblong, Sandwich, Bath, Normal. Jonesy had never lived in any other state, so he wasn't sure whether Illinois had more of its share of strangely named towns than any other state.

Perhaps he could have old Killian track Aurelie down in Loire, France. That would maybe help him sell a few copies here. She could be held at a winery. Jonesy had never been to Loire, but he was confident that by using Google Earth he could get the local color. Then he frowned.

More technology. Damn it.

CHAPTER 46

Nathan

He seemed to have gotten away with it.

He hadn't heard a peep from Little Miss Kaitlin, which surprised him. He'd been prepared to pay her off if necessary. The cops had accepted without question his comment that he was mentoring Jimmy Jackson. If anybody had mentioned to the cops that he'd visited Kaitlin every morning, they hadn't brought it up. It helped that she stayed in her trailer during the whole clusterfuck.

He had continued having mentoring sessions with Jimmy after work once a week. It seemed the least he could do for the man, after he'd whisked him out of a potentially awkward situation.

But he still hadn't been able to figure out why he'd done it. It made no sense. He had already started his internship. Nathan would never have known Jimmy lived in that trailer park, ordinarily. Jimmy obviously recognized Nathan and must have had a pretty good idea of exactly what he had been doing there. So what was his angle? He hadn't asked for a thing.

Nathan knew that Jimmy had lucked into the internship, and had dropped out of college until this opportunity for a free semester's tuition had come along. He'd fully expected Jimmy to ask for money to keep his silence, and he would have paid it, too.

But Jimmy didn't even hint. He had never once made any kind of reference to money, his tuition, Nathan's visits to Kaitlin — nothing. Anybody would think he really did just want mentoring.

Nathan wasn't against it. It made him look good. Progressive, even. Here's the big boss man, taking the underprivileged black man under his wing. And Jimmy really did show promise. It was a shame he might have to drop out of college again with just one semester left.

Amanda still didn't know a thing about any of it. She was a singularly non-curious woman, one of the things he liked best about her. But if she had demanded information on why his car had needed to go to the body shop for a few days, he felt sure that Jimmy would have come in handy. He'd have paid him enough to make it worth his while.

He hadn't replaced Kaitlin yet. He would, but for now he took a breather. By all appearances he'd gotten away with it, but he'd feel better when a little more time had passed. No need to complicate his life until he was good and sure Kaitlin had moved on.

For now, he had started hitting the office earlier than usual to maintain his morning routine. He assumed Amanda's equanimity only went so far. If he'd changed his routine at the same time he repaired the car, would that have been enough to set off her wife radar? How about if his mood had suddenly been just a little too good? Would enjoying a new, hotter, younger woman make a difference in his demeanor?

He wasn't sure. So he resolved to keep his head down and make sure there wasn't going to be any fallout before he added a new complication. On the plus side, he was getting a lot more work done.

But the problem of Jimmy remained. He couldn't decide if he should arrange for him to take another paid internship second semester so he could finish his college degree. He certainly had the authority to arrange such a thing, and he was now known to have taken an interest in Jimmy's career, so it likely wouldn't raise eyebrows.

Heck, he might get some kind of diversity award or something. Or he could slip him the money for the last semester's tuition, which he wouldn't miss, and just hire him after graduation. But he couldn't help but wonder if it wouldn't be better to simply hand him some cash and promise him a rave recommendation for a job outside the area.

What was Jimmy after? And was it better to keep him close or get him out of there?

The man had not ever, in the smallest way, made any hints. He hadn't referred to his financial difficulties, which Nathan was nevertheless privy to, thanks to the big mouth Jimmy's advisor had on him. Jimmy hadn't breathed a word about the accident or Kaitlin or about having had any interaction with him outside the office.

Yet, Nathan understood the power Jimmy held. And he could see that Jimmy was a smart man. He knew it, too.

The semester was drawing to a close, and Nathan had every reason to believe Jimmy was in a bind.

Nathan couldn't imagine what it would be like to be so poor. His own parents had paid his college tuition and topped it off with a generous allowance, freeing him from the need to work even so much as a cushy part-time job at the library.

He'd never had to worry about money in his life. He could only imagine that a man with a wife and two kids, living in a trailer, one semester away from graduation, might be desperate. Yet Jimmy was unfailingly cheerful and professional.

If it ever came out that he owed Jimmy for saving his ass and that Jimmy had something on him, it wouldn't look good that he'd used company resources to reward him. However, if he were to cut Jimmy loose, the man might feel desperate. Desperate men were dangerous men.

The problem went around and around in Nathan's head. Several times, he was tempted just to directly ask Jimmy what it would take to keep him silent, but doing that was as likely to set off the problem as to solve it.

In the meantime, he and Jimmy had what everybody in the office believed to be a completely cordial mentoring relationship. One of the vice presidents had clapped Nathan on the back and told him it was an admirable thing he was doing. Nathan reacted with more humility than was natural for him; if he were really mentoring Jimmy out of purer motives, he'd have bragged about it to the right people. He'd have wanted credit. He'd have seen this as a way to expedite his eventual move to the C-suite.

The answer, he finally saw, came from letting someone else decide what to do with Jimmy. How had he not seen it? That overly friendly V.P., Andy Carls. He could do it. If it didn't come from Nathan, he couldn't be blamed if it all somehow blew up in his face.

Right now, Nathan hadn't done a thing wrong, as far as business ethics went. It wasn't against the law to have a mistress. A lot of executives did, and some were not as discreet as Nathan was. However, nobody needed to give a reason for not promoting you. He didn't want to derail his career for something stupid.

Andy was just the sort to be taken in by a sob story. Nathan would make sure he heard a good one.

This all reminded Nathan of the first big thing he'd ever gotten away with.

When Nathan was 15, he learned his dad was cheating on his mom. It was entirely different from what he had been doing with Kaitlin, of course. He was just having a physical affair, which was not at all the same thing as his dad's cheating. Nathan had found out because his dad wasn't being smart about it.

His dad had been dumb enough to choose a woman from his own social circle. Nathan understood that if he could find out, it was just a matter of time before his mom found out, and that would be a disaster.

The woman was Kris Prentice, Parker's mom. Nathan and Parker attended the same private school and had since third grade. They'd played traveling soccer together. They weren't close friends, but they hung out sometimes. So it didn't seem unusual when Parker asked Nathan to meet him. But then he'd added: "Don't tell anybody anything. Just meet me. It's important." That set off Nathan's curiosity.

Parker confessed he had skipped school that day, expecting to have the house to himself. He'd been in his room, getting high and just generally goofing off, when he heard the garage door open. Parker didn't panic. It was a huge house.

"I figured either Mom or Dad had come home to get some paperwork or something. I'd just be really quiet until they went back to work. All I was thinking about was getting caught." Parker's eyes welled up with tears. They were already red. It looked like he'd been crying all afternoon.

"Yeah, go on." Nathan wasn't sure why Parker thought Nathan gave a crap about him getting busted for skipping school, or why he was crying his eyes out over it.

"Anyway, I just stayed real quiet and listened. It was my mom, but she wasn't alone. It took me a minute to figure out the guy's voice, but it was your dad."

Nathan immediately knew it was true, but he pretended not to believe it. "You can't know it was my dad. You didn't see him, right? You just heard a few words through the door of your room. It could be any guy."

"No. Your dad said he liked the new kitchen. He said something about remembering it was different when he was at our house for the pizza party after we won the soccer tournament."

Nathan remembered that party. Yes, Parker's parents had hosted it, and his parents had attended. That had been maybe six months before.

"My dad wasn't the only dad at that pizza party." He knew his dad was guilty, though. He wasn't the least bit surprised. Parker's mom was pretty hot, for a mom. But it was only right to pretend he thought better of his dad than he did. "And anyway, just talking about your mom's new kitchen doesn't mean anything."

Parker was crying again. "That's not the whole story. I heard a lot more, OK? They went to the guest bedroom and ... I heard stuff."

Nathan didn't want to hear anything more. "OK. What's your plan?"

Parker wiped his eyes. "I guess I tell my dad and you tell your mom, right?"

"No. We don't do that." Nathan had held up his hand. "Let me think for a minute."

"But if my dad ever found out I knew about it and didn't say anything? Or if your mom found out you didn't tell her?"

Nathan stood up and roughly ran his fingers through his hair. "Just hold on. Let me think."

The big danger here was his life falling apart. If his parents got divorced, there was no telling what would happen, but none of it would be good. Even if Parker kept his mouth shut, that was no guarantee that nobody was going to find out. If Parker could find out, anybody could. His dad wasn't being very careful. The whole thing was going to blow up in their faces.

Parker was sniveling and Nathan wanted to smack him. "We aren't going to tell anybody anything. We're just going to make them stop."

"Like how?"

"I have an idea. Give me a minute while I think about it." Young Nathan had begun regarding his brain as a tool, and he liked to think he understood how to use it. At that moment, he closed his eyes and thought about the problem. The goal was to make the affair end before Parker's dad or Nathan's mom found out. If that was the goal, how could they do it?

"We let them know somebody knows," Nathan said. "But we don't want them to figure out it's us. We have to make them think it's somebody else." It had also occurred to him that Parker was a crybaby who was liable to run off and tell his dad everything. The best way to stop that was to compromise Parker.

"I'll send them a letter that will convince them somebody knows. Who would your mom most hate to find out? Besides your dad, I mean."

"I don't know. Grandma. Our minister, maybe."

Nathan smiled. "That's good. Who's your minister?"

"We go to St. Paul's. Episcopal, not Catholic. Rev. Wilhelm."

"We threaten to tell your dad and Rev. Wilhelm."

"Why aren't we threatening your dad?"

"Your mom has more to lose. Your mom only works part-time and needs your dad's money. Anyway, my dad would blow up. He'd probably hire a private detective to figure out who was onto him. I bet your mom doesn't even tell him why she's ending it. It's better this way."

He didn't mention that he intended to ask for money; Parker wouldn't like that. However, it would make things more convincing and if he needed to keep Parker's mouth shut, the money would come in handy. There'd be no way to prove Parker hadn't been in on blackmailing his own mom. Parker would be in too deep to confess. "Leave it to me. I have a plan."

"How are you going to do it? Are you going to disguise your handwriting?"

"I'm not going to write it by hand, you idiot. I'm not going to use the printer at home, either. They can tell that stuff. I'm going to do it at the library. Those printers are used by a million people. Nobody will know it's us. I'll tell them interested parties know what she's doing and they're going to be watching, and that if the affair goes on, they'll share photographic evidence with her husband and Rev. Wilhelm. That should convince your mom."

"How will we get photographic evidence?"

"We don't really have to have it." He'd nearly added, "you dope," but caught himself.

He would also ask for a thousand bucks. That was enough that Parker's mom would take it as a serious blackmailing attempt, but not so much that she couldn't come up with the money on her own fairly easily, he judged.

He'd tell her to put the money in a bag and

leave it somewhere, and he'd threaten that if the affair continued the price for his silence would be $10,000. He'd also say all the usual things about not going to the cops. He had the letter almost written in his head.

"You did the right thing by coming to me," he said, and then he actually gave Parker a hug, just to humor him. "I'll take care of this. But you can never, ever tell anybody what you know. Never. Not if you want your mom and dad to stay together."

Parker had nodded, still sniffling. Nathan's plan had worked. His parents stayed married for another decade, and Parker's were still together last he heard.

Getting the thousand bucks out of the deal was icing on the cake. It was a secret stash he only used for illicit things, like buying pot, because he couldn't be seen to have money he couldn't explain. He and Parker started getting high a lot after school, and only after Parker had smoked up a considerable amount of free pot had Nathan revealed to him where the money for it had come from. "I had to give your mom a plausible reason for some stranger to care that she was banging my dad, right?"

Parker was pretty pissed, but Nathan didn't care. He knew now Parker would never confess. Besides, knowing that Parker's mom had indirectly bought all that pot for them gave Nathan a lot of secret pleasure.

Secret pleasures, he had learned, were the best kind.

CHAPTER 47

Jimmy

"I've missed this."

He put down his fork and leaned back, looking around the steakhouse and at his wife, who was all decked out in a hot dress he hadn't seen her wear since before they were married.

It had been a while since he'd eaten a steak. He couldn't even remember the last time he'd had one. It had also been a good long while since he and his wife had had an evening out without the girls. Janiece's mom had watched the babies a couple of times early on.

But tonight, one of Janiece's friends from school was keeping the girls overnight, and they were splurging on a good dinner, to be followed by some dancing, to be followed by the kind of sex you could not have with lightly sleeping twin toddlers just down the hall.

"I could get used to this," Janiece said. "You see, my advisor was right after all. We just had to think positive, and all our problems are magically fixed."

"Andy Carls magically fixed them." Jimmy took another sip of his wine. He was more of a beer guy, but this was not the kind of meal you had a beer with.

"I never heard you mention Andy Carls before," Janiece said.

"I'm sure Nathan dropped a hint to Andy, but I'm also sure I know exactly why Nathan didn't want his fingerprints on this. He still thinks I might not keep my mouth shut. I'd like to tell him he has no worries there, but just by reassuring him of that, I'd be proving he does. Nope, as far as I'm concerned, Nathan had nothing to do with this. You should have heard the way I made sure everybody knew how grateful I was to Andy. I didn't mention Nathan one time. And you know what? I'd bet money he noticed that. In a good way. Nobody is going to be suspicious about Nathan, ahem, mentoring me. If they remember anything, it will be that Andy Carls came through with an unprecedented internship extension."

Janiece had not been able to finish her steak and had discreetly slipped it onto Jimmy's plate. Now she picked at her rice pilaf, more for something to do than because she really wanted it. "And now you have to decide whether you want to try to stay at LCM after graduation or get the heck out of Dodge. Or Loire. Whatever."

"I think I'll be putting my resume out far and

wide. I expect both Nathan and Andy will make great references. And I don't much care where we live. You can do your last year of school almost anywhere we go. And then you'll be teaching. And we'll pay off all our student loans. And we'll save up a down payment. And we'll buy a house. And then we'll save up enough money that our girls won't ever have to work as hard for their educations as we did for ours."

He held up his wine glass and Janiece lifted hers.

"To the end of the trailer park," Jimmy said, and they took a drink.

"To positive attitudes. That was the only thing missing," Janiece said, and winked broadly. They clinked and drank again.

"To joining the middle fucking class," Jimmy said, and then he had to re-fill their glasses. It wasn't a problem, because he'd already ordered a second bottle of wine. They weren't driving tonight and he intended to make the most of it.

"To sugar daddies and sugar babies," Janiece said, both laughing and whispering.

"To the new apartment," Jimmy said. It wasn't much bigger and it wasn't any nicer, and the girls would still have to share a room, but there was room for the girls to have their own twin beds. And it wasn't a trailer.

"To ... to ..." Janiece giggled.

"To tipsy wives who are gonna have a *good* time tonight." They both drank to that.

"To mentoring! Who knew how useful mentoring could really be!"

"Mrs. Jackson, I think you're drunk. You too drunk to dance?"

"Oh, you are *not* getting out of taking me dancing," she said. "Not after I packed my ass into this tight dress. I thought I'd lost all the baby weight but when I pulled this dress on, I found it. It all went to my ass and stayed there."

"You look better in it now than you did before you had the babies, and you looked pretty damned good in it then."

"Get that waiter's attention, Jimmy. We've got places to go."

CHAPTER 48

Nancy

It broke her heart, but it had to be done: She placed an online ad to sell her furniture.

She still hadn't found a job, and everybody she'd approached about maybe rooming together had turned her down. They either said their landlord wouldn't allow it or claimed they didn't have enough room. And without a job, she had no chance of getting another apartment. The realization had begun to dawn on her that there was a very real chance she'd have to live in her car.

Her mother was out. She couldn't move into her mom's subsidized apartment. Besides, she didn't want her mom to know things had gotten this bad. And you never knew, one of these job applications might pay off. It could still be OK.

At first, she'd applied for management-level jobs, but now fear spurred her into trying for lesser jobs. Gas station attendant. Dollar store cashier. Even fast food. Still, no job. And if she ended up with a minimum wage job, it wasn't going to cover rent anywhere. Not even in the crappiest trailer in the park.

She'd dropped the mobile home schtick. These were trailers, every single one of them, and it looked like they were all going to be out of her price range. She'd even hinted to Kaitlin about moving in with her. It was her most desperate moment, but Kaitlin had always been friendly and she thought it might be fun to room with her. And you never knew, Kaitlin might have a guy friend who'd be interested. Maybe she'd meet someone and end up moving in with him in a few months.

But Kaitlin had not reacted the way she'd hoped. It was as if Kaitlin had forgotten they'd ever been friends.

"I already started moving my stuff into my boyfriend's house. I'm not staying here," she'd said. "Oh, that's right. You wouldn't know that now, would you? Because they fired you."

Nancy had gone home and cried after that. She didn't know where she was going to move once her lease was up. She didn't know if she was going to have any money once her unemployment ran out. Thank God she owned her car. If she'd gone ahead and bought a new car, as she'd been planning to do, it would have been repossessed and she wouldn't even have that to fall back on.

The awful truth was that she was going to

have to drop the price on her furniture pretty soon. She had assumed she'd get full price or close to it, because she'd kept it in perfect condition. Her sofa was absolutely pristine, because she kept a sheet over it to protect it. The living room set had been expensive — $139.99 per month for 24 months. That came to more than $3,000, and she had already discounted it to $2,799. It was a deal! But she'd gotten no calls.

It was the same with her bedroom suite. Not a nibble. Worst of all was her dream kitchen. It had cost her $129.99 for 24 months, and she loved it so much. It had been the last furniture she'd bought. She'd needed the bed first of all, and then had bought the living room set, making do without a kitchen table until she'd paid off the rest of her furniture. She had eaten her supper at the coffee table for a long time.

The day the rental place had delivered her kitchen table and chairs had been so exciting. If anybody had come over and had seen she didn't have a kitchen table, she'd have been embarrassed, so she didn't invite anybody over. She'd known exactly which set she was going to buy. It was the top-of-the line six-piece dining collection. Some of it was solid oak.

Very likely, it was even nicer than the stuff Shirley had had in her miniature mansion she was always going on about. Yet nobody had called about it. She was going to have to drop the price of everything down, probably by a lot.

She'd never had nice things before. It had been just her and her mom, and they'd moved around a lot. Most of their furniture had come from thrift shops or they'd plucked it from the sidewalk on trash pick-up day.

Nancy had never had a new piece of furniture until she got the trailer park job. When she thought about how much she'd bragged to her mother about her great job and nice home full of new furniture, she wanted to cry. And while she'd been excited to show people her perfect place, she hadn't yet had anyone to show it to at all.

She went online and looked at her furniture ads. She dropped all of them down by a hundred bucks, and then, thinking about it some more, dropped them all down by yet another hundred. That was $600 out the window, right now. Gone.

But maybe it was good that nobody had bought them yet. If she managed to get a job and an apartment, she'd still have her nice furniture.

Shirley was sitting outside smoking and Kaitlin wasn't with her, so Nancy decided to do something she'd never done before: She made herself a cup of coffee, adding a liberal slug of her fancy French vanilla creamer, and walked over to Shirley's place.

Up to now, it had not seemed wise, because she had felt she needed some professional distance from the tenants and herself. That was pointless now. But after Kaitlin's rudeness, she only wanted to see Shirley if Kaitlin wasn't around, and she wasn't right now. Probably with the new boyfriend. Kaitlin had bragged that she was moving in with her new boyfriend who owned his own house. Big deal. Lots of people owned houses. He had inherited it from his grandma; he hadn't done anything special to earn the house. Nobody had given Nancy a house. She'd had to work hard for everything she had.

The tar and gravel road could be a little smoother, Nancy thought, as she walked the short distance to Shirley's trailer, holding her cup carefully.

"How are you, Shirley?"

Shirley looked a little too surprised. After the rude way Kaitlin had blown her off, Nancy felt nervous suddenly that Shirley might not really like her, either. But to her huge relief, Shirley was still nice.

"Have a seat, Nancy. How have you been?"

Nancy sat down. The furniture wasn't that comfortable, she immediately noted. It certainly wasn't what she'd choose if she were buying patio furniture.

"Not the best, Shirley. Not the best. I still haven't found a new job, and without a job, I can't get a new apartment. So I'm trying to sell my new furniture."

Shirley made sorrowful little clucking noises and shook her head. "You have not been treated fairly. Not at all. They ought to be ashamed of themselves."

Nancy brightened at this; here was her first opportunity to unburden herself. She should have visited Shirley long ago. If she was going to have to listen to Shirley talk about her old house, so be it. It would be worth it.

"You had to give up a lot of things when you moved here, I know. Maybe you have some advice."

Shirley pounced right on this, just as Nancy had expected.

"It was a terrible time. John had died — my husband, John." Nancy nodded. She knew this story but was prepared to listen to it all over again in order to be able to tell her own story. "It's bad enough to lose your husband, but then to lose your house and most of your nice things. It wasn't easy. But you have an advantage I didn't have, Nancy. You see, I had never paid a bill in my life. I went straight from being taken care of by my parents to being taken care of by my husband. I didn't know a thing. I didn't know how to check an account balance, even. I never had to! John had done everything."

Nancy nodded and took a sip of her rapidly cooling coffee.

Shirley paused to light another cigarette.

"I thought we were set. I didn't know John wasn't as good at taking care of money as he had been at earning it. So you can imagine, when I found out our money was nearly gone, I had to learn about how to deal with financial things when I was still grieving. Part of me was angry with John. We'd always talked about getting a little condo in Florida for the winters. I never thought I'd be a widow so young and I never thought I'd have to live in a trailer."

Nancy didn't point out that Shirley wasn't young, and she didn't point out it might be a little rude to complain about living in a trailer when everybody here lived in one. She just nodded. Her coffee was cold and nearly gone, but she took tiny sips just to have something to do. For the first time, she understood what people got out of smoking.

Now that she'd done Shirley the courtesy of listening to her, she felt it was her turn.

"I worked really hard to get my associate's degree in business and to run this park. And it took me a long time to pay for my furniture. It's really nice. I don't want to sell it, but I have to. It doesn't seem fair that I might lose everything I've worked hard for just because one company decided to sell to another company. I did a good job. I worked hard."

Shirley was standing up. "Do you want a refill?" Her hand stretched out and Nancy handed over her cup. "Do you take cream and sugar?"

"Yes, thanks," Nancy said, handing over her cup. She didn't tell Shirley she liked French vanilla. She'd settle for whatever Shirley used. It was only polite.

Shirley was gone a little longer than Nancy thought she should be. It occurred to her that Shirley thought the life she was living was a diminished life, because she'd lost her big house and a lot of her fancy stuff. But it looked pretty darned fulfilling to Nancy. If she had everything Shirley had, she wouldn't complain at all.

Nancy wasn't greedy. She didn't expect to have a giant house all to herself. She didn't expect to have a second place in Florida for winter. She didn't expect to have a Lincoln. Not even an old one. All she'd wanted was a nice trailer and some new furniture, and it appeared she was not going to get to keep even that. She never got to keep anything.

Suddenly, she felt anger. Who did Shirley think she was, anyway? She hadn't offered even a tiny bit of sympathy. She'd just gone for more coffee.

Shirley came back, walking down the steps very carefully so she wouldn't spill the two cups of coffee. Probably afraid of falling and breaking her hip. Why did this old bitch think this place was so bad? If she didn't have any kind words, Nancy was going to tell her off.

"Thanks," she said as she took the coffee and gave it a sip. It was good, but it wasn't French vanilla good.

"What kind of work did you do, Shirley?" She already knew the answer to this.

“I was a housewife. I raised two boys. That was what a lot of us did then.”

“What was your degree in?”

“I got married right out of high school. That was common back then. We didn’t have the same kinds of opportunities you girls have now. It was a different world.”

Nancy put her coffee down. Her hands were starting to shake. “I don’t see that we have a lot more opportunities. I see that we have a lot more work. I had to go to college, well, community college. I had to manage this whole park. I don’t see why we changed everything. You had a nice big house and you’ve never had to work. You had an easy life and you still have a really nice trailer. Maybe not as nice as your house was, but still. Don’t you think you’re lucky?”

Shirley looked hurt. “I guess I never looked at it that way. It didn’t feel easy. I always felt busy. There was cooking and cleaning. There were always social obligations. I volunteered at the school a lot. I was never paid for any of it. It all depended on what man you married. You had to marry a man you could trust. That was how the world worked. It wasn’t like now. You couldn’t do whatever you felt like. Mothers explained the rules to their daughters, and most of us followed them.”

“I don’t think it’s fair that some people get to have so much without working and other people can have everything taken away from them no matter how hard they work."

Shirly looked at her for a long time. It was like she didn't know what to say, Nancy thought. "You're so young. You might get married, you might get an even better job. You might get both."

Nancy could see that Shirley wasn't going to give her any sympathy. She'd never understand because she'd never had to worry about a thing. "I guess so. Well, anyway, I'm going to go put in some more applications. You have a nice day, Shirley."

When she got back to her trailer, she microwaved her coffee and added a dollop of her French vanilla creamer before she started scrolling through jobs. There wasn't anything new to apply for, other than a shitty telemarketing job. But the coffee, doctored up with Shirley's cream and sugar and now a dose of her own French vanilla stuff, was as sweet as a cookie, and Nancy relished it.

At least she still had a few small pleasures in life. Soon, she might not.

CHAPTER 49

Angel

Driving wasn't so hard.

She'd actually taken drivers ed in high school, but hadn't followed through. With her old high school transcript, her birth certificate and some other paperwork, it was a fairly uncomplicated process. Darren gave her a refresher driving course and her mom agreed to drive her in to take her test. She even let her borrow her car for it. Darren had said he'd sign over his car to her as soon as she got her license.

Her mom had been her usual very negative self.

"With a car, you'll be able to get a job."

"You know how I feel about that. Maya needs a full-time mother." Her mother really had a way of ruining a good day. It felt strange to be driving her mother somewhere. Her mom had always driven her around.

"Maya is a teenager now. You could at least get something part-time during the day."

Angel just stared at her mother before remembering to return her attention to the road. "Do you know how much trouble a teenager can get into if they're left unsupervised? Maya doesn't drink or smoke or do drugs or mess with boys. I want to keep it that way."

Her mom didn't come in. Angel didn't care. She was just glad her mom had agreed to give her a ride to the driver's license place. Now that she had a license, Darren was giving her the car. It would be half hers anyway once they were married, but a man didn't give you a car every day. It was thrilling.

It wasn't much of a car, she thought as she crossed the street. But it ran just fine. This would make grocery shopping so much easier.

Normally she didn't come over this early, but she wanted to show him her new license. Well, she didn't want him to look at it too closely, because the camera they used added around 50 pounds. But still, she was glad to have her license.

"Good job," Darren said. "We'll go in tomorrow and transfer the title."

Things were coming together. Now they just had to get married. His back was still hurting him, though. They'd had sex a few times, but he didn't want to play his usual games. His back still wasn't 100 percent. That meant she hadn't put her plan into effect yet.

She needed his back to be in perfect shape to

nudge him into marriage.

CHAPTER 50

Janiece

This would be the last hard year.

Next year, the girls would start all-day preschool and she could go back to school. She and Jimmy had talked and had agreed that they'd figure out a way to get some kind of car for her so she could drive to her student teaching. If he got hired as a mechanical engineer, that shouldn't be very hard.

And then, she'd be teaching and the girls would be in kindergarten and they'd have two paychecks coming in. She thought of little else these days. The girls were more than ready for school; she'd taught them everything they needed. They knew their colors and numbers and the alphabet. They did some kind of art project almost every single day. She read multiple books to them every evening.

Her kids were not going to struggle like she had. How many generations of her family had made that vow? Her own mother had had high goals, but none of them had been realized. Still, she'd managed to instill ambition in her own daughter.

When Janiece had told her mother she and Jimmy were having a baby and were going to get married, she'd watched a light dim in her mother's eyes. It was as if she'd known all along that something was going to go wrong to derail the dream. Her mother had wanted to be a teacher but while she was still in high school she had gotten pregnant with Janiece, and here history was repeating itself.

Her mother loved the babies, of course. You can't help but love babies instantly. Her mother had visited them in the NICU every day, but she wasn't allowed to hold them for a couple of weeks. After that, the NICU staff let her come in and hold first Jordynn and then, a couple of days later, Jazzmynn. Her mother had cried, cradling her tiny granddaughters, and Janiece knew those tears expressed a mix of joy, fear and sadness.

Things would be different for Jordynn and Jazzmynn, though. For one thing, she wasn't going to harp on them day and night about the importance of not having sex, as her mother had done. She realized her mother was only doing what she thought was best by trying to prevent Janiece from making the same mistake she'd made. But a trip to the doctor for birth control would have been a better idea.

The misguided emphasis on virginity before

marriage was a crock. Even in the olden days, plenty of young brides went to the altar already pregnant with their first child. There's a biological drive to have sex, and it's going to happen no matter how many rules you make. People will break any taboo to have it. When society and biology disagree, biology usually wins.

Janiece had thought about this a lot. Did it really matter so much if you got pregnant as a teenager if you were equipped to deal with it? A teenage girl hundreds of years ago already knew all the things she needed to know: how to cook and clean, care for children, maybe make clothing. There was little point in putting off marriage until she was 25. She was perfectly ready at some point in her teen years.

The difference now was that women did need to wait. They needed to complete their education. They couldn't just know how to run a household. They needed some kind of job training. It took many years to learn everything they needed to know to navigate a complicated world.

It was the same with men; young men in pre-modern times developed the basic survival skills they would need early. They didn't have to wait until they were 30 and had completed a doctorate in wildebeest hunting or advanced hut construction.

But people today still had the same instincts

and urges their ancestors from thousands of years ago had, so something had to give.

We could have chosen to make early marriage easier to navigate.

We could have decided to make sure free daycare existed so young mothers could finish their education, and we could have decided to normalize young couples living with one set of parents the first few years.

We could have normalized the idea of everybody having access to good contraception from puberty on.

Instead, we'd decided to shame young people for having sex before they were married, while also tacitly acknowledging that almost everyone was going to do it anyway, and we made access to sex education and birth control political.

That sure had worked out great, Janiece thought.

Janiece couldn't change society and she couldn't change biology, but her girls were for damned sure going to get an IUD or something before they needed it. If despite everything, one or both of the girls got pregnant before they meant to, they wouldn't have to deal with it alone, regardless of what any boyfriend did or didn't do.

Her girls would know she had their back, and if they had to live at home for a while, so be it. She and Jimmy would be in decent financial shape by then. They'd be able to help their children, and there'd be no shame.

Janiece and Jimmy should have kept living with one of their parents. They'd both be done with their degrees by now if that had been the main goal.

Instead, they both felt obligated to try to prove something. What had they proved? That it was hard as hell to finish college while taking care of babies? That daycare and a second car and college tuition could not be covered with a $13.50 per hour job, even though he usually got some overtime?

Not to mention, a good number of young people were trying to get by on the starvation wages of a fast food job and maybe some government benefits. She shuddered, knowing how lucky they were that things weren't quite that bad for them.

She would like to have another baby, but first they wanted to catch up to where they needed to be in their lives, and she would prefer to take off at least a year to care for the new baby. So they probably wouldn't. If she'd gotten pregnant just one year later, everything would have been entirely different.

It was crazy what a big difference the timing of a pregnancy could make in your life. It had meant her mother had never gone to college at all, and for her, it had delayed completing her education and starting her career.

The several years of lost wages she and Jimmy

had experienced amounted to about the cost of a starter house, all because they were in love and doing what every young couple in love from the beginning of time did.

They had been using condoms. She had been waiting for her appointment at the college health service so she could get on the pill. They required her to make an appointment for an exam first, and it had taken a month to get in, and that was the month she got pregnant. The if-onlys used to hit her hard.

The joys of motherhood helped a lot. But still. She could have had the joys of motherhood a year later.

CHAPTER 51

Kaitlin

Apparently, shit was going to work out.

She still had some time left on her lease, but almost all her stuff was moved into Tommy's house, and she'd texted Naomi — with great pleasure — that she was quitting.

Tommy had agreed to everything she asked, so they'd painted his grandma's room and put the old furniture upstairs — it was super messy up there, all right — and they'd moved in her bedroom furniture from her trailer. So she had her own little retreat, even though she slept in Tommy's room.

The job at the laundry wasn't as bad as she'd feared. The work was hot and sticky, but there were several young people who worked there, and they all had fun together. For the first time in her life, she actually had health insurance and dental, too.

All her life, she'd avoided the trap of a full-time job, but it turned out it really wasn't that bad. She and Tommy went to work and came home together, so she didn't have to worry about having enough discipline to organize her days. Most of the time, they ordered takeout or drove through for fast food on the way home, which was good, because Kaitlin had never learned to cook.

She usually took a shower and then retreated to her room for a while every night after work to play on her phone, but then she'd come out and be ready to hang out with Tommy.

He was the easiest guy she'd ever known. He didn't have any rules she had to follow. She could smoke when she wanted and eat what she wanted. He didn't complain if she had garlic breath or if she left some dishes out overnight.

He hadn't even asked for her to pay anything, but when she got her first paycheck, she'd asked him how much he wanted her to contribute, and they'd agreed she'd pay half the utilities. She still had lots of money left. Not strip club money, but still, more than she needed.

There was just one thing missing.

"Is it weird that I kind of miss Shirley?" she asked Tommy one night as he gave her a backrub. He never asked for one in return and she idly wondered whether she ought to offer.

"That's the old lady with the Lincoln you lived next to?"

"Yeah." She could feel where he was going with this backrub, but she honestly didn't mind. He always made things worth her while.

"She's staying put?"

"Yeah. She owns her trailer, so she said she didn't want to go to all the trouble and expense of moving it and then maybe end up with her lot rent at the new place increasing anyway. It costs a mint to move a trailer." She paused. "Can you do that little spot on my lower back? Yeah. There." He really did give a great massage.

"Why doesn't she just move it here? All the stuff is still in place from when my mom's trailer was parked here."

There was an old concrete pad not far from the house. Tommy had sort of lived with his mom and sort of lived with his grandma for a good bit of his childhood.

From the stories he'd told, his grandma was the stable influence, with his mom having her good periods and her not-so-good periods as she flitted from man to man and from job to job.

Kaitlin felt a familiarity in his stories about his mother's rough life; she was reminded of some of her own mother's rockier stages — and of her own. Her mother was presently living four hours away with a man Kaitlin could not stand. It had already become clear to her that moving in with a nice guy and getting a full-time job had changed her life in ways she hadn't expected. Everything felt different now.

"You would just let Shirley move her trailer and live here for free? Just because I miss her?"

She twisted her body around and looked at Tommy.

He looked like he didn't understand the question. "It wouldn't be free. She'd have a water and power bill. She just wouldn't have any lot rent."

"You'd do that for me?"

"I'd do anything to make you happy, Kaitlin." He started kissing her, and the backrub led to exactly what it usually led to.

And that's when Kaitlin knew.

CHAPTER 52

Shirley

Kaitlin's new young man was a very good influence on her.

He'd helped her get a full-time job and he gave her a place to stay. That was nice of him, although she suspected he had ulterior motives, and she hoped Kaitlin understood what she was getting herself into.

It was going to be tough to get him to propose after just moving right in with him like that. That would have been a very big no-no in her day. Still, times had changed.

But when Kaitlin and Tommy had come to pick up the last of Kaitlin's stuff from her trailer and had loaded it up into Tommy's truck, they'd come over to visit Shirley and, she thought, to say goodbye. The thought of not having Kaitlin's pleasant chatter to look forward to anymore gave her more of a pang than she'd expected.

When they'd proposed she move her trailer to his property, she had put down her cup of coffee and found she didn't have a thing to say.

"You should just come out and see," Kaitlin said.

Shirley didn't want to squish into the pickup truck, so she followed them out to Tommy's house. It wasn't very long before Tommy pulled into a long driveway that led up to an old farmhouse; the sort of simple old house you always passed by without noticing when driving from one rural town to another. It was a white bungalow with a porch out front. Nothing fancy, but solid.

Across the yard was a concrete pad. By the looks of things, somebody had just cut a lot of tall vegetation that must have been growing freely around it. The cut weeds made a thick pile just to the side of the pad. Somebody had then hosed off the pad, which must have been an unpleasant job now that the weather was getting colder. A small sidewalk led from the concrete pad to the graveled driveway. There was more separation here than there was in the trailer park. She'd need a little spot for her patio furniture. But there'd be room for her to plant flowers like she'd had at her house; the area might look quite nice next summer.

"Your mother's trailer was here? All the hook-ups are in order?"

"Yes ma'am," Tommy said. That was one of the things she liked about Tommy. He had manners, probably thanks to his grandmother.

"We could have our little talks on my days off," Kaitlin said. "Or after work. We go in early and we get off early." Kaitlin's childlike enthusiasm was what convinced Shirley.

She had no other friends in the trailer park, and here she'd have free lot rent. It would probably take at least a year of free lot rent to make up for the cost of moving the trailer and having all the wiring and piping and whatnot unhooked there and redone here, and she wasn't sure she could end her lease, but eventually her living expenses would be practically nothing. Just power and water and cable. It was hard to think of a good reason to say no.

At first she'd wondered what would happen to her if Tommy and Kaitlin had a falling out, but one look at their faces was enough to dismiss that fear. That boy was smitten, and Kaitlin wasn't stupid.

"I'll find out who moves trailers and what it costs," she finally said, and Kaitlin actually took her hand and squealed.

It took several weeks and many irritating phone calls to get it all arranged, but one Friday morning the moving company came by and transported her trailer from the Loire Mobile Home Park to Tommy's side yard. Shirley didn't do a thing; she paid extra so they'd handle every detail. The actual transporting of the trailer didn't take more than 15 minutes. But all the prep work and set up at the new place took hours.

Once they had it in place, they had to tie it down, replace the skirting and do whatever they did to the roof where one piece connected to the other.

Plus, while she had thought the furniture would come along during the ride, it didn't. Turns out you had to take out all your furniture, move it separately, and move it back in afterward. That was much more trouble than she'd expected, but by dinnertime, she was back in her home, and if she didn't open the curtains it felt exactly the same. It was an odd feeling to open the door and see a house there instead of Jonesy's trailer.

Kaitlin had begged to have the patio furniture placed on the front porch, near the porch swing, and Shirley had agreed. Now they could smoke and have coffee even in the rain. Shirley had ordered pizza for dinner, something she hadn't done in years, at Kaitlin's suggestion, and they'd had it right in her trailer. It was the least she could do to thank them.

"I'm the first one on the street to move, but I won't be the last," Shirley noted as she nibbled on a piece of pepperoni pizza. She had never quite understood what the appeal of pizza was, other than the fact that it was handy to order when you didn't have an opportunity to cook.

"Jonesy is leaving," Katilin said. "I heard the black family is leaving. They're still there right now as far as I know. Nancy will definitely leave. I don't know about Darren or that new woman."

"Angel." Shirley rolled her eyes.

"Yes. Angel. She's a strange one. And that daughter of hers is one weird kid. I almost think she's got some kind of problem maybe."

"The only thing wrong with that child is that her mother is a psycho." Shirley was done. Two pieces of pizza were enough, and she frankly did not care if she didn't have another piece for a year. Kaitlin seemed to like it; how she stayed so thin if she often ate this much pizza was a wonder. Of course young men could eat all they wanted and seldom needed to worry about it. Kaitlin must have a job feeding this one.

She noticed Tommy found every opportunity to touch Kaitlin, his fingertips reaching toward her as he handed her a piece of pizza and putting his hand on her shoulder as he spoke to her. Kaitlin wasn't necessarily touching back, but she smiled each time he touched her. Yes, these two were going to do just fine.

She'd not asked about the old boyfriend, the one who had the weird work schedule. They'd clearly had some kind of falling out. She had the tact not to bring up the fact that it was Kaitiln's ex-boyfriend who had rammed into her car, injuring her head and damaging her car.

Kaitlin probably felt bad enough about it already, so they'd never spoken of it. But it was clear that this boy was better suited to Kaitlin anyway. She talked about Tommy non-stop, but she never had a thing to say about the old boyfriend. Best not to bring it up.

It was getting late now.

"I had forgotten how dark it gets out in the country," she said.

"I know! I noticed the same thing," Kaitlin said. "If we forget to turn the porch light on before we leave, we come home and can't see a thing.

"I don't need to see," Tommy said. "I could walk right to anything I want with my eyes closed."

"Well I can't. I need the porch light. Or the light on my phone if we forget. But yeah, keep your porch light on, Shirley. We don't want you falling down out here." After pizza, Shirley suggested they play cards, and it turned out Tommy was keen, Kaitlin maybe not as much. Kaitlin said she really only knew how to play rummy, while Shirley knew lots of games.

"What I used to play, back in the day, was bridge. But we need four players. Oh, the girls and I used to play that every week. We'd take turns at each other's houses. I miss those days."

"Why did you stop then?" Kaitlin was shuffling, and she wasn't great at it. Shirley's hands itched to take over, and a glance at Tommy told her he felt the same. Their smiles met over Kaitlin's head.

"Oh, once my husband died and I moved into a trailer, it just wasn't the same. I didn't have a house to invite everyone to. Plus, some of the girls had moved away. Two of them passed. I doubt any of the group still plays. I used to really look forward to the weekly bridge games, though. Back in the day, I'd get my hair done that morning. We'd dress up to play cards! Can you imagine?"

Kaitlin had at last completed her shuffle, and she doled out the cards. You could tell a lot about a person by how they played cards, Shirley had often thought. Some people were just there to have fun, but others approached it quite seriously and were determined to win. Plus, some people frankly couldn't be trusted. She'd seen more than one friend take advantage of someone's absentmindedness to get a good look at their hand. Shirley wouldn't think of doing such a thing.

Tommy won the first hand and Shirley suspected he was letting Kaitlin win the second hand, so she held back as well. Kaitlin's childlike delight when she won made it worth it.

"I'm an old lady and I've had a long day," Shirley announced. "I think I'm going to go to bed early." She scooped up the cards and Kaitlin and Tommy said goodnight and left.

She had the strangest feeling that when she got up in the morning, she'd be back in the trailer park.

CHAPTER 53

Jonesy

It felt a bit like starting fresh at a new school.

Moving from a trailer park into a huge old Queen Anne mansion — well, into a little section of one — made him feel like he was starting new. Nobody here knew Old Jonesy; it was a chance to become New Jonesy.

Old Jonesey had smoked. New Jonesy didn't. He hoped he could make that stick. He'd carefully doled out his last pack of cigarettes, counting them on the last day. One when he woke up. Others at prescribed intervals. When he moved out the last few things, including his cleaning supplies, he'd stuffed everything into his car — what he thought would fit easily almost didn't, because he had more odds and ends than he thought — and sat on the steps to smoke for the last time.

This wasn't exactly his happy place, yet he took a mental snapshot as if he were making an optimized memory like the characters in his book did. Just sitting on the steps, smoking, looking out over the street. Kaitlin and Shirley were both gone. Kaitlin's empty trailer looked the same, but Shirley's lot was empty now.

Cigarettes always went fast, and this one was over before he'd expected. He took one deep, final drag, dropped it to the ground and stepped on it. "That's that," he said out loud, then drove to the shuttered office to push his keys into the dropbox. They made a satisfying clink when they landed inside. Then he made the short drive to his considerably nicer new digs.

He'd gotten a haircut the previous day, choosing a slightly more fashionable cut that he knew would require more frequent visits to the barber to keep up, but this was New Jonesy. New Jonesy didn't wait for a job interview to clean himself up.

It was a drag carrying everything up the exterior staircase, but his scant furniture was already in place, including the new-to-him desk he'd splurged on. Now he only had to putter around unpacking boxes and putting things away as he listened to his music over the bluetooth speakers he'd already set up.

It was pleasant work, figuring out where everything would go. Some of his stuff looked a lot tackier here than it had in his trailer, and his living room was mostly empty because he'd given his sofa, coffee table and recliner to the young reporter who had helped him move the heavy stuff last weekend. It was more suitable for a cheap first apartment than it was for this place.

He could finance better furniture and more frequent haircuts, he'd figured, with what he would save by not buying cigarettes. Decent second-hand furniture could be found online for a steal, especially because he was going to go for something with a vintage look. Almost nobody wanted Grandma's old furniture anymore, but he did.

He was pleased with the appearance of his bedroom, because he was still using the same old bedroom set that his grandparents had given him years ago when they'd bought brand new furniture for themselves. The antique finish was a little scuffed up in places, but more appropriate to this house than to anyplace else he'd ever lived. It fit right in, and he'd chosen the desk to coordinate. This was where he'd spend most of his time, so he didn't really care about the living room being empty for a while.

Two or three months without purchasing cigarettes would probably cover the cost of the kind of second-hand furniture he wanted to get.

Health reasons hadn't ever been enough to motivate him to quit smoking, but maybe the prospect of nice furniture would be. It was more than better furniture, though. This felt like his last chance to reinvent himself.

But already, he had that strange feeling that

can't be explained to those who have never felt it. That vague feeling of needing to do something. Kind of like an itch. Kind of like being hungry. Kind of like being horny. Kind of like being bored. Kind of like a lot of things, but not like them, either. It would go away instantly, but temporarily, if he lit a cigarette.

He closed his eyes and tried out his new technique of pretending he'd had his smoking memory optimized. He visualized a little implant in his hippocampus, home to countless real smoking memories. Still, even after lighting thousands of cigarettes, he'd never paid close attention to the process until he decided to make a memory.

The rounded lighter fit perfectly inside his curled fingers. His thumb found its place over the rough ridges of the spark wheel and moved down in one quick motion to depress the small ignition button, which he held down as he sucked firmly at the cigarette in his mouth. The raspy sound of the rough spark wheel turning and the little pop of the flame contrasted with the barely perceptible sound of the thin paper catching fire.

The way his mouth felt when he sealed his lips around the filter. The way the warm smoke tasted on his tongue. The way his chest rose as he filled his lungs.

It sounded almost sexual when you described it, but wasn't it? It fulfilled some kind of lusty need. That was why so many smokers gained weight when they stopped smoking. They had to have some kind of oral satisfaction. He'd seen other smokers turn to chewing straws or toothpicks or just chomping aggressively at gum. He hoped to avoid all these.

Nicotine addiction withdrawal symptoms were the worst on the third day, according to his research, so he had arranged a week off to move. He associated working with smoking and wanted to be out of the office until the worst cravings were over. But he knew it was about more than the nicotine. It was the smoking rituals he'd miss most. He hoped keeping his fingers busy on the keyboard would distract him from his lost routines.

His computer was already set up, and he sat down to figure out what in the hell had happened to Aurelie Laurent, and to try to get back to making his point about the shortfalls of modern society.

CHAPTER 54

Darren

Holy fucking shit!

Angel just kept surprising him. Now that his back was more or less recovered, they were back to their usual fun and games. She had kept hinting that she had something big planned, and tonight was going to be the night.

The woman had actually fried up a whole chicken. He could not remember the last time he'd had homemade fried chicken, but it sure smelled good. There would also be mashed potatoes, homemade gravy and a can of green beans, and he was looking forward to everything but the beans.

Angel had done some different things to herself, too. She had a new haircut and a new outfit and was wearing more makeup than usual. The woman was no beauty, but he appreciated the effort.

Now that she could drive his car, she was driving everywhere. Just today, she'd gone after groceries, had her hair done and bought the outfit she was wearing. It was maybe not the most flattering dress — it was more like a big pink bag. But hey, she was trying. She had a big package that she said was for a surprise later and God only knew what kind of kinky thing she had in there.

He'd been under the impression at first that she wasn't much of a cook, but when she had dinner ready, he had to revise that belief.

"Angel, if this isn't the best damned chicken I've ever had in my life, I don't know what was. It's delicious."

She beamed. "I believe in a woman taking care of her man. I'm glad you like it. I've got ice cream for dessert."

"Not sure I'll have room for it." He wiped his hands on a paper towel before taking a bite of the potatoes, which were also first-rate. The green beans? They seemed to be more for decoration than anything. He took a bite and found they tasted the same way canned green beans always tasted. No matter. The rest was delicious.

"If you don't want the ice cream, I have a different dessert in mind. I'll be serving it after dinner in the bedroom."

"I always have room for that!" He laughed.

He was in a good mood. He'd seen his attorney and while the news wasn't great, it seemed very unlikely he'd do any more jail time. His license was toast, but Angel would drive him anywhere he needed to go.

All in all, it could have been worse. So why had he avoided commitment all this time? He just needed the right kind of woman. Angel was willing to come over, feed him, do any damned kinky thing he wanted, and then go home. Plus, she'd run any errand he needed. He was one lucky son of a bitch.

He did have room for the ice cream, after all. She'd even bought some whipped topping and a jar of hot fudge, which she microwaved and then poured over the ice cream. Hot damn.

And there was still some kind of kinky stuff to come. He could not believe his luck. How much longer was this ride going to last? He already knew that even after it ended, his nights with Angel would be his go-to memories he'd jack off to if he wasn't looking at porn.

Up to now, it had been a woman named Barb, who was better looking but not as kinky. He hadn't jacked to thoughts of Barb since he met Angel. The Angel memories were definitely going to be hot enough to last him the rest of his life.

After dinner, Angel led him back to the bedroom.

"I went to the store to get something so we could play a new little game," she said, bringing out some light ropes. "Here's how it goes. You tie me up, and then I try to get away. I brought different clothes you can rip off me after you tie me up. I'll be begging you to stop, but don't you stop for anything."

"Same deal as before," he said. "You say the word 'spaghetti' if you do want me to stop."

"Darren, you're the man. I'd never ask you to stop. You know you're in charge."

That was all it took for him to get an instant erection.

"Change your clothes. I'll be right back." He left the room while she changed into a different outfit she didn't mind him ripping to pieces. It helped preserve the fantasy.

When he could hear her lie down on the bed, he re-entered the bedroom. She was pretending to be asleep, although she had a big smile on her face.

Breathing hard, Darren attached each of the four ropes to the frame of his bed and tied her arms and legs down, being careful not to make them so tight that they'd hurt her, but tight enough that she really couldn't get away. He wanted her to be able to struggle realistically without accidentally slipping out. He was so damned excited.

This was something he had always wanted to do. He'd tied a couple of women down with silk scarves, but it was understood that it was all play and there were strict limits.

But Angel didn't do these things by half measures. They'd played the fake-rape game enough that he knew he could be surprisingly rough and she wouldn't flinch. With the ropes holding her down, it was going to be even better.

He stripped off his clothes and then grasped both sides of her button-down shirt and yanked hard so all the buttons flew off and he could see her new bra. He wouldn't rip that, he'd just scooch it up so he could get to those big titties.

Angel pretended to wake up. "Oh, no! What's happening? I was asleep!"

He roughly grabbed the light cotton lounge pants she had put on. Jeans were too hard to rip off, and she'd thought ahead. He ripped them easily and laughed with delight.

"Girl, I'm going to rape the shit out of you."

CHAPTER 55

Nancy

She was saved.

Telemarketing wasn't exactly what she'd hoped for, but she couldn't be picky. Time was running out, and if she wanted to get a new apartment, she had to be able to prove she had a job. Now she did.

The base pay was very low, but there were all kinds of bonuses available, and as long as she managed to get some of them, she'd manage OK, she thought. She'd work very hard and would impress them with all the siding sales she was going to make.

An hour into the new job she felt despair. The computer was relentless. As soon as she hung up from one call — or, as was much more frequent, as soon as the caller hung up on her — it auto-dialed and she was speaking to another person.

Everybody rolled their eyes at how annoying telemarketers were, but what was worse than getting telemarketing calls was having to make them. Most of the time, she didn't get even one sentence into the prepared spiel before the person hung up on her.

It took three long hours before she had any success. Finally, a person agreed to have one of the installers come by and give her an estimate for new siding. Nancy was jubilant. If she could make two more appointments today, she'd get a $50 bonus.

But by the end of the day, she'd not managed to make even one more appointment, and she didn't get any the second day.

"Are you smiling?" her supervisor had asked. "People can hear if you're smiling!"

Nancy had smiled.

She was desperate for this to work out, and started reading every free online sales tip she could. Her supervisor had been right; lots of people advised smiling. But also, if you wanted to be a successful salesperson, you needed to solve a problem the person had. She remembered some of this from her community college courses, but maybe she needed a refresher, so she kept doing online searches for things like "how to make more telemarketing sales."

She learned it was not enough to smile. You also needed to be sitting up straight. You needed to maintain a natural tone of voice. People could tell if your heart wasn't in it. She studied the company's brochures and websites so she could speak with authority. Even with all this, she was averaging only about one appointment a day.

Across the room, a guy named Bob slouched and didn't smile at all, yet he regularly made the desired three appointments per day. He sounded lazy and relaxed, but he somehow did very well. Nancy could not figure out how he did it.

After her first paycheck, she realized she was not going to be able to make it on this salary. She got a call back from a janitorial service and she nervously asked them what her hours would be. As it turned out, she could clean office buildings part-time in the evenings and that, together with the telemarketing, would be enough to pay her expenses.

Now she just needed to find an apartment. She was going to stay in her trailer until the very last day they allowed it, and in the meantime she scrounged every dollar so she would have enough for first month's rent, last month's rent and deposit. After she started the second job, she was confident she'd have it, and that was a huge load off her shoulders.

But it wasn't easy. It wasn't easy at all. The day job ran from 8 a.m. to 5 p.m., and the office cleaning job started at 7 and went until 11 p.m. They couldn't start earlier because the office people didn't want to see the cleaning crew if at all possible.

So now she wasn't fit to be seen by professional people. Even though she used to manage an entire trailer park. Even though she had, at the moment, a beautiful home. Even though she had an associate's degree.

It wasn't fair. Half the people working in the office building she cleaned probably were not as serious about business as she was.

She was tired. As soon as she finished the office cleaning job, she fell into bed so she could get enough sleep to wake up at 7 so she could be at the first job at 8. Her only free time was the weekend and the two-hour period in between jobs, and in that time she had to change clothes, eat and drive.

You could forget making special casseroles when you worked that many hours. She ended up driving through and eating fast food a lot of nights, and sometimes she just ate peanut butter sandwiches.

She used her weekends mostly to catch up on sleep and laundry and to clean her own place, which was often a mess now. She put so much energy into cleaning other places that she couldn't clean her own. It would be great if she could find a better job, but when was she going to find time to search and apply for anything else? She didn't have the energy for it.

But at least she still had her nice furniture, and she wasn't going to have to live in her car.

CHAPTER 56

Jimmy

The new apartment was ugly as sin.

It was a squat brick building that obviously had been built as cheaply as possible. There were four apartments on the ground floor, each with a small concrete pad where one could place a grill or a couple of lawn chairs if desired, and another four apartments above, each with a small balcony.

Their apartment was at the end of the first floor. It had a second bedroom just big enough to hold two twin beds and a dresser, and that was good enough. It was carpeted with that cheap tan stuff you only saw in apartments, and while the landlord claimed it had just been cleaned, they doubted that was true.

There was not one attractive thing you could point to in the entire place.

Didn't matter. This was a one-year arrangement. They'd get the hell out just as soon as Jimmy had another job, but for now they'd very happily signed a one-year lease. It was even cheaper than their trailer rent had been, and $300 less than what their new trailer rent would have been if they'd stayed. They'd already moved over a few boxes of things and would do the big move next weekend.

For now, things were going great at LCM. He was already putting in applications at other firms, and he hoped he'd have a solid offer by the time he got his degree.

He and Janiece had debated. Stay at LCM, or go elsewhere?

It came down to Nathan. Jimmy didn't trust him. Nathan had just gotten a promotion, and had dropped the supposed mentoring he'd been doing, to Jimmy's relief and, he assumed, to Nathan's. If anybody had been listening in, they'd never have heard either of them say one thing to imply there was any issue at all. Every single conversation they'd had was friendly.

"But Nathan knows that I know. And that's gotta be eating at him. He must be thinking that sooner or later I'm going to be trouble for him. He's got more power than ever now. Best I go somewhere else."

"You're probably right. And you know, if we leave the area, I can finish college almost anywhere. I might have to repeat a class or two, but so be it. Or maybe the new job will be within driving distance. Just try to keep it in Illinois if you can. Different states have different teaching requirements."

Jimmy had identified half a dozen Illinois firms likely to hire a newly graduated mechanical engineer, and now he waited. In the meantime, he helped Janiece pack and he looked forward to getting the hell out of this shitty trailer park and into their even shittier apartment. It was only for a year. Maybe less.

The next day at work, Jimmy had asked Nathan if they could talk, noting the quick look that crossed Nathan's face, just briefly. It was some mix of fear and concern, but before Jimmy could even identify it, Nathan had it under control and smiled.

"Of course. Let's go to my office."

Nathan had a heck of a nice new office that Jimmy hadn't seen yet. He was impressed and took one of the two black leather chairs that faced Nathan's heavy glass desk. This wasn't a desk where one did real work. This was an impressive desk across which one had important conversations. As far as Jimmy was concerned, this was one of the more important ones.

"What can I do for you?"

"Well, Mr. Clark, I want to first say how much I've appreciated the mentoring you've given me. I hope you won't be too disappointed to learn my wife and I are interested in relocating closer to where our families live after graduation." He and Janiece had agreed that sounded plausible, and Nathan wasn't going to know or care whether he actually took a job close to family — or just far from Nathan.

"I was wondering if you'd be willing to write me a letter of recommendation I could submit to potential employers." His eyes locked with Nathan's. "Only if you think my performance here warrants it."

He didn't think he was imagining the look of relief in Nathan's eyes.

"Of course, Jimmy. I'll work on that tonight and have it for you tomorrow morning. I'm extremely pleased with your performance here. In every way. I think you'll find that with the letter I write, some doors will open for you. And please, use me as a reference. I'll do all I can to help you find a new position."

Jimmy stood up. "Thank you kindly, Mr. Clark. I sure do appreciate it."

And then he got the hell out of there.

CHAPTER 57

Nathan

He'd be relieved when Jimmy was gone.

Whatever small chance there was of the man trying to cash in on his knowledge of Kaitlin would soon be gone. Just because Jimmy hadn't made any effort to cash in so far didn't mean he wouldn't later.

That was one thing he was glad to get sorted. The other was settling on a new sugar baby. He'd made multiple trips to the strip club, chatting up the girls, and he had narrowed it down to two candidates.

He had specific requirements in mind. Naturally, she had to be young and hot. Secondly, he did not want one of the girls who would perform sex acts in the VIP room. He'd ruled out several possibilities when they'd readily given him blowjobs back there. He enjoyed them, but marked them off his list. Another even offered full sex. He'd accepted a blowjob instead, and had eliminated her as a possible sugar baby.

Those girls lacked standards. When he'd chosen Kaitlin, it was because even after he plied her with a lot of money in the back room, she'd been very clear about what lines she would and would not cross.

Keeping certain lines uncrossed was important to him. There were rules to breaking the rules. For other people, anyway.

One girl used the name Stephanie. She was 21 and very thin with creamy pale skin and delicate-looking features. Her glossy black hair hung halfway down her back and she danced so gracefully he wouldn't be surprised to learn she'd taken classical dance classes.

Stephanie was a perfect beauty, and she'd declined to suck him off in the back room. He liked that in a woman. However, her breasts were quite small.

The other one he liked was called Eden. She was just 18 and had short spiky red hair and was as voluptuous as a girl could be without actually being fat. She was more cute than beautiful, but her tits were absolutely perfect. They'd start sagging in a few years, but he'd be long gone by then. She had the puffy pink nipples only young girls had, and he always liked that.

Eden laughed a lot and seemed to enjoy her work. Stephanie had a shy smile and was more of a mystery. He'd had repeated lap dances from both of them, and he was sure he'd enjoy sex with them. He wondered what their real names were.

He needed to set something up soon. He was having sex with his wife daily and jacking off every time he took a shower, but it just was not enough. He was prepared to pay more than he had given Kaitlin. She'd been a steal at $800 per month. Whoever he chose would have to give up stripping, and he'd make up for that. He could easily afford to pay top dollar now.

Classically beautiful, quiet Stephanie or cute little firecracker Eden? Or were there better possibilities? He avoided the blondes; he had one of those at home and he liked variety.

Amanda was a sensible woman who didn't raise an eyebrow at her husband visiting a strip club. She liked that when he came home from a night out, he was always hot to have her. Either she didn't realize he was fully capable of ejaculating into a stripper's mouth and then coming home and wanting her an hour later, or she didn't care. It was even possible that she had her suspicions about him having sugar babies.

There were some things it was best not to speak of openly. It was enough that she never hassled him about visiting strip clubs. It was one of the reasons he never complained about how much she charged on her credit cards.

He returned to the club again and again, drawing Stephanie and Eden into conversation as much as he could, and sometimes getting blowjobs in the back from girls he'd already marked off his list.

Did he really have to choose between Eden and Stephanie, or could he manage to keep both girls? He was so tempted. His sexual needs raged like a wildfire.

He needed to make a decision. He was an alpha male, and alpha males never limited themselves to one woman.

That was how the world had always worked, and he liked it that way.

CHAPTER 58

Kaitlin

Living with Tommy had taught her a lot.

Her original assumption was that Tommy would provide the house and she would provide the sex. But he always made sure she was satisfied before he'd let himself finish. So what kind of a deal was this, anyway? She was getting more out of the arrangement than he was, and at first this concerned her. What if he decided she wasn't pulling her weight?

So when Shirley offered to teach her how to cook, Kaitlin felt it would be wise to take her up on it. Her own mother had scarcely ever cooked, and Kaitlin knew very little about meal preparation.

But Shirley knew everything. Together, they made a little feast almost every night. Roast chicken and mashed potatoes. Spaghetti and garlic bread. Meatloaf and scalloped potatoes. Lasagna and green salad. Roast with carrots and potatoes. Chicken noodle soup that didn't come out of a can. Even cakes and cookies.

"You can't just drive through or order pizza every night," Shirley had gently scolded. "There are two things every man wants. You know the one thing. This is the other one."

She'd offered Shirley money in return for the cooking lessons, assuming that was the polite thing to do, but Shirley had been hurt and Kaitlin, a little confused, had apologized.

She was also learning to play bridge. One of Shirley's old friends — emphasis on the old — came over and the two older ladies taught the young couple how to play. It seemed needlessly complicated to Kaitlin but Tommy was mad for it and wanted to make the games a weekly thing, even though Shirley and Linda badly beat them. Sometimes she felt like a housewife from the old TV shows.

But had those old arrangements really been so bad? She'd had worse ones, after all.

Not everything is a deal, she was surprised to learn. Some people do things without expecting anything back.

CHAPTER 59

Maya

Maya finally had a friend besides the TV.

At home, she continued watching her shows and had just started a second TV notebook. The cop shows were her favorite, but she liked the funny shows, too. Sometimes she watched old sitcoms. She'd watched so many different ones now that she had to really look to find good new ones, and she felt proud that she'd finished so many.

At school, Emma and Krystal had more than enough venom after attacking Aaliyah to make Maya miserable as well.

But then one day, something new happened: While Maya was eating her lunch alone as usual, she looked up to see Aaliyah standing there with her tray.

"Can I sit here?"

Maya said yes, just because nobody else had ever asked her before, and she had never dared ask anybody if she could sit with them. Her mother wouldn't approve, of course, but she would never know if Maya talked to a black girl. Maya had prayed every night for a friend, and finally He had answered her.

Aaliyah said she liked to draw and showed Maya her notebook, which was full of sketches of her family's two dogs. "What do you like to do?"

"I like TV," Maya said. "Cop shows mostly. I can fit in a whole season in a day on the weekends. Or in the summer."

"That sounds nice. My parents only let me watch one hour of TV a day," Aaliyah said.

"Why?" Maya could not understand the purpose of such a rule.

"I don't know. I guess because there isn't time for more."

"I have plenty of time. My mom goes to her boyfriend's house every night so I can watch as much as I want."

Aaliyah had two brothers and two dogs. Her parents both had jobs. She went to camp every summer and had chosen drawing camp last year, but wanted to ride horses this summer.

"We should go to the same camp next year."

"I don't know," Maya said. "I might be busy babysitting." She didn't know why she said that, but she somehow knew there was no way her mother would ever send her to camp.

But that night, she asked her mother about it.

"Can I go to camp this summer? There are camps where you can ride horses."

"You're not riding a horse. You could be killed! No, you can forget that." Her mother was folding a basket of laundry. She'd bought herself a few new outfits, but nothing for Maya.

"What about a camp where they teach you to draw?" She reached into the basket and pulled out one of her shirts and folded it. It might help if she could demonstrate how responsible she was.

"We'll see," her mother had said, finishing the basket and carrying it into the back of the trailer to put everything away. Maya knew what that meant and picked up the remote.

"I'm just going to go visit Darren. There's peanut butter and jelly in there if you want it. Or soup." She left. Like she left every night.

Maya put down the remote and went into the kitchen to figure out what she wanted to eat. She was sick to death of soup and didn't want peanut butter, either. Nothing looked good. There were a couple of carrots in the crisper, but they were covered with gross little white hairs. There were some eggs, but she'd never cooked eggs. There was some sliced cheese. She could make a cheese sandwich.

Except the bread was moldy. Ugh. She brought down a box of cereal and poured it into a bowl. She could at least have a bowl of cereal. But there was no milk.

Whatever. She plopped onto the sofa with her bowl of cereal and picked up the remote.

Something was wrong with the cable. There

was a blue background that said to call for service. She had no shows and she didn't have a good dinner and every single day she went to school with her ankles showing. Aaliyah probably never had to eat plain cereal for dinner, and her jeans fit and she at least got to watch an hour of good TV every day.

Eggs could not be that hard to make. She got out the carton of eggs and a skillet and put the skillet on the stove. She'd never been allowed to turn it on before, but it was pretty obvious how it worked.

She turned the burner all the way on and broke two eggs into the skillet. Bits of shell had gotten into the second one, and she picked them out as best she could. The raw egg was slippery, though, and it was hard to grasp the tiny shell fragments. The yolk got broken and she hated broken yolks, but she pressed on.

You had to flip the egg at some point, she knew, and found the flipper thing. But the egg was stuck onto the bottom of the skillet, and her attempts to scrape it didn't work very well. No matter, now she had scrambled eggs. Those were still good. She would eat them right out of the skillet so she wouldn't have to wash a plate.

They weren't very good, honestly, but she ate them. A good amount of the eggs was still stuck firmly to the bottom, though, and she was still hungry. She picked at the thin, crunchy brown edges but found they tasted bad. The bowl of dry cereal just didn't look appealing.

She gazed into the refrigerator again. There was nothing else there she knew how to cook, so she pulled out a slice of cheese, unwrapped it, and ate it plain. It tasted OK.

But plain eggs, some dry cereal and a slice of cheese still weren't enough. There was still plenty of soup but the very thought turned her stomach. However, she found some raisins and ate a handful of those.

Now her stomach felt a little off, and she went to the bathroom. Her mom had just bought new hair stuff. She sprayed some of it on her hair and combed it again. It looked the same as it ever did, though.

All the lights were on in Darren's trailer, she noticed. Not just in the kitchen and living room. All of them. It wasn't allowed to leave the lights on if you weren't in the room. That was her mom's rule. She said electricity was expensive.

When her mom had first started cooking dinner for Darren every night, she had said Maya could come have dinner with them. Maya had hated that idea.

But now she wondered what her mother had cooked tonight. It could be something good like spaghetti, which Maya had not eaten for a long time. Or maybe it was something like mackerel patties, which she hated. You never knew.

But whatever there was, it was certain to be better than what she'd had. And besides, she had to tell her mom the cable wasn't working so she could do something about it.

She tried the remote again. There was still no cable, just the message to call for service. That did it. She walked over to Darren's trailer, but before she could knock on the door, she heard terrifying noises.

"No, Darren, don't! Please let me go, you're hurting me!" Her mother was shrieking. But Darren just laughed at her mother's distress.

She knew what she had to do. She ran back home as fast as she could. If they had a phone she could call the police, but she didn't. Her mom had one, but she had it with her. Nobody else was around, she didn't think, except the black people, and she knew her mom would not want her to go to them.

It was up to her to save her mom.

The gun was on top of the Bible, and after she snatched up the gun, she pressed the palm of her hand against the Bible.

"Help me, God," she whispered. The smell of burnt eggs filled the trailer and her stomach felt funny. None of this seemed real. And then she ran back to Darren's trailer and carefully opened the door.

They weren't in the living room or kitchen so she crept down the hallway to the bedroom at the end of the trailer. She knew what he was doing; she'd seen this on TV a million times.

But it was worse than she'd thought it would

be. Her mother lay tied up on the bed, her clothing torn away, and Darren was naked and hurting her. Neither of them noticed her until she fired the gun.

The first shot went into the ceiling and she tried it again. She had to get closer, she knew, even though it might mean he would hurt her, too. He had already turned around, looking shocked, and she knew he would hurt her if he could get to her. She squeezed the trigger again and this time it hit him in the belly.

"Mommy!" she heard herself scream.

Her mother was screaming, too. "Stop! Stop!" Her mother was struggling to get away from Darren, but she could barely move. Darren was screaming too, now. He'd fallen back against the bed and some blood was coming out of his stomach. She remembered now that you needed to shoot as many times as the gun would let you, and she emptied the gun as fast as she could. She only hit Darren once more, but it was in the neck, and a lot of blood was coming out. So she knew her mother was now safe.

But her mother would not stop screaming.

CHAPTER 60

Janiece

It was amazing just how much stuff they'd accumulated, even though she liked to think she never bought anything.

Sorting through the baby clothes was hard. She probably ought to donate most of them, but it was hard to let go. Maybe they'd be able to afford to have another child eventually after all.

In the end, she decided to go ahead and take all the baby stuff with them. Same with the toys. The girls had outgrown so much. But she could not part with any of it.

Jimmy would be home in a little while, and she had a pot of potato soup waiting on the stove. After they ate, they'd drive over a carload of stuff to the new place. It would be nice to have as much done as possible before moving day. Jonesy had a co-worker with a truck who had helped him move, and the same guy had jumped at the chance to make a few bucks helping them, too.

Jazzmynn started whining. "Hungies!"

"We'll have some soup in a little while," she told her. "Daddy's almost home." She pulled her phone out of her back pocket and glanced at the time. Jimmy would be another half an hour. Maybe she should go ahead and feed the girls now if they were hungry. Nothing was worse than a hangry toddler, except two hangry toddlers.

"Do you girls want to eat right now?"

Before either child could answer, Janiece heard what sounded like a gunshot, and then, seconds later, several more, and loud screaming that went on and on. She didn't hesitate; she scooped up both girls and ran into the bathroom and popped them into the bathtub. They were protesting, but she got them in and harshly whispered for them to hold still.

Only then did she realize the bathtub was fiberglass and likely of no use. A cast iron bathtub would protect you from gunshots. Not these cheap tubs. But still, she didn't know what else to do. She lay on the edge of the tub to turn her body into an extra layer of protection, and tried to force both girls' heads down. They didn't like it.

"Hush! Lie still!" She realized she should call the police, and she used one hand to pull out her phone and call 911.

"There's gunshots and screaming in Loire Mobile Home Park. On Cardinal Court. I think probably in the first trailer." She had to speak loudly to be heard over her children's crying.

Every street in the park was named for a bird. The next street over was Robin Way. It was stupid, the way most of the things in this damned park were stupid. Both girls were crying now and the dispatcher wanted to know where they were.

"I'm calling from No. 2 Cardinal Court. We're fine. The babies are just scared. It's just myself and two children here. My husband isn't home yet." The dispatcher wanted her to stay on the line so she did.

She couldn't hold the phone, balance her body on the edge of the tub and hold both girls' heads down. They'd knocked all the shampoo bottles over onto themselves, but the caps were screwed on tight. She wasn't worried about that right now. She visualized the order of the trailers on the street. "I think the shots were probably in No. 7 Cardinal Drive. I'm not sure, but I think so."

Her front door was locked, but if anybody wanted to get in, it wouldn't be hard. She wished they'd already moved. The new place was at least more secure than this flimsy piece-of-shit trailer. The dispatcher was telling her to stay calm. The dispatcher was asking her if she heard anything else.

"I heard several gunshots and the screams, but I haven't heard anything else since," she said. "There are only a few of us living on this street right now. There's a woman named Angel and her teenage daughter next door, in what would be No. 1. Then there's us. The next trailer is empty. There's a woman at the end of the cul de sac, but she's probably at work. Then there's an empty lot, and then there's an empty trailer. The man at the end is named Darren. No, I don't know his last name. He lives by himself, but the woman across the street from him visits him a lot. She might be there now. She has a teenage daughter living with her who is probably still in No. 1."

Finally, she heard sirens approaching, and the dispatcher confirmed it was the police on their way. Her whole body was drenched in sweat and she had some soapy residue on her hand from where she'd kept grasping the edge of the tub to keep her balance. She wiped it on her jeans.

At least the girls weren't crying now. They had pulled down the plastic basket full of bathtub toys that had been attached to the shower wall with suction cups. They were playing much the same way they would if they were taking a bath.

Janiece stayed on the line, neither she nor the dispatcher talking much. At least two police cars had arrived, by the sound of things, and she stayed right where she was. But after a minute, it was starting to hurt her hip and she wanted to see what was going on.

"The police are here now," she said, unnecessarily. "I'm going to hang up."

"You stay right here and play," she told the

girls, and she crawled into her bedroom to look out the window.

The action was all at Darren's trailer so far. Then an ambulance and more police arrived. That wasn't a good sign. This was the second time an ambulance had been to Darren's trailer in a few weeks.

Where was Jimmy? But when she looked at her phone, she saw it had been less than five minutes since she'd called 911. It felt like hours.

She called Jimmy but he didn't answer. He was probably driving home right now. She sent him a text, telling him they were safe but there'd been gunshots and cops were at the neighbor's trailer.

A cop was going door to door. Well, nobody lived at several of them. When he got to her door, she answered it and told him she was the one who'd called. She answered all his questions but he wouldn't answer any of hers. But he did say it was fine to let the girls out to have dinner, so as soon as he was gone, she dished up soup for both of them.

She dished up some for herself, but it was just for show. She knew her stomach would reject anything she ate tonight.

CHAPTER 61

Jonesy

Jonesy was hot for teacher.

He was about halfway infatuated just with the idea of her before he'd even seen her, so when he finally met her a couple of days after he moved in, he was smitten right away.

He introduced himself and learned her name was Lori, which he found amusing. "Or should I call you *Loire*?" he'd joked, pronouncing it properly, and he was relieved when she laughed.

"Only if you want me to call you *Jonas*," she'd said, nailing the French accent surprisingly well.

They'd proceeded to have an entire conversation with exaggeratedly bad French accents.

"I am, how you say, new here, Mademoiselle Loire." He swept an imaginary hat from his head and bowed to her.

She was a tiny thing with an elvish look about her, with delicate features and short brown hair. She'd fit right in as an extra in *Lord of the Rings,* he thought, but kept that impression to himself. She probably wouldn't see that as a compliment, even though he meant it that way.

"Bonjour, Monsieur Jonas. Je suis … a teacher. And how do you, uh, earn les francs?"

"Je suis journaliste, Mademoiselle."

"At the newspaper? Sorry, I can't think of that word."

"We have reached the limits of my French as well. Yes, I work for the paper. I was so happy when I interviewed here that I'd had a year of conversational French and knew how to pronounce the name of the town, only to be shot down."

She taught American history at the high school, as it turns out, and they fell easily into the kind of conversation he'd been missing for a long time.

"You want to come up to my place? I'm just doing cheese omelets for dinner, but I could open a bottle of wine."

"That sounds great," he said. And then the phone in his pocket buzzed. It was a text from Carl.

"Oh, no," he said. "It's my editor. There's been a shooting. I gotta go, but can I get a raincheck?"

"Oui. Au revoir, Jonas."

CHAPTER 62

Maya

Some things were better and some things were worse.

Her other grandma did not allow her to watch as much TV as she wanted, but she had bought her three new pairs of jeans and she allowed Aaliyah to come over to play. She said she might be able to go to the horse camp this summer with Aaliyah, too. So it wasn't all bad.

The kids at school all knew who she was now. Some of them had said she was brave for saving her mom. Some of them were still mean and held up their hands like guns and pretended they were shooting at her as she walked by. Krystal and Emma had backed off, at least for now.

Her mom had said she would just stay with her dad and other grandma for a while, but Maya thought it was looking like she might be living here for good now.

Her mom didn't seem happy that she'd saved her from Darren. In fact, she'd seemed sad and mad. This made Maya feel disappointed and miserable; she thought she had been a hero.

The policeman had said things that made her feel good, and so did her dad and other grandma. The only people who didn't were her mom and her regular grandma she used to live with.

It was probably because her mom was having another baby. Her dad and other grandma said her mom just needed some time to think.

Her other grandma cooked dinner every night, and it was delicious. When they asked her what she wanted to eat the first night, she said anything but a cold can of soup, and her dad and other grandma had looked surprised and asked her if that's how she'd been eating it.

"It's really good that way, but I'm tired of it because I ate it almost every night for a long time." They looked at each other funny when she said that.

But when she got sad, and every night before she went to sleep, she got out her special copy of the newspaper article. It didn't mention her name, but everyone knew it was about her. She kept it carefully folded away inside her best TV notebook.

She liked to close her eyes and remember exactly what it felt like when the cops told her she was a brave little hero who had probably saved her mom's life.

It was her favorite memory ever.

CHAPTER 63

Nancy

The whole place had fallen apart without her in charge.

That was Nancy's take on the shooting. She'd seen Janiece cleaning out her trailer and had come over to hear whatever she knew about the story, but if Janiece knew anything, she was keeping it to herself. Also, Jonesy had written a newspaper article about it. It didn't even mention Nancy, even though for now she was still living on this street. You'd think that would have merited a mention.

"You see, everybody is fleeing now that the new owners have taken over. Nobody new has even moved in. If they had kept me, I'd have lined up new tenants by now."

She took a bitter satisfaction in knowing exactly how much money the new company was out every single month just on her own street. There had only been two tenants left who had intended to stay on this street, and now one of them had killed the other one.

Angel had moved back in with her mother, so now Nancy was the last one here. She could see that a similar pattern was taking place over the rest of the park, except none of the others had shot each other. Still, occupancy was way down. Stupid new company.

"When are you moving?" Janiece hadn't said much. She was on her hands and knees, scrubbing out the inside of the kitchen cabinets. That seemed a little excessive, even to Nancy. It had never even occurred to her to check if that had been done.

If she were still working here, she'd have had a hard time finding a reason not to return their security deposit. However, you could always find something. You just had to look harder sometimes.

"This is my last month here. I'm looking for a really good place. I have such nice furniture, it would be a shame to settle for an ugly apartment." Janiece had told her what apartment building they'd moved into. Nancy knew the one. It wasn't very nice. Nancy's would be better.

"Good for you." Janiece stood up, emptied her bucket into the sink and refilled it with fresh soapy water and started in on the upper cabinets, while Nancy leaned against the wall by the door.

"I'm glad I have my degree. All that business knowledge has really helped me. There are so many things you need to know to succeed. I've got a new profile on LinkedIn. If you want to, you can follow me there. In case you ever decide to get a job. It's not what you know, it's who you know."

"Thanks, Nancy, but I'm going to finish my degree next year and will probably look for a teaching job outside the area. It'll be wherever Jimmy gets an engineering job."

People moving from a trailer to one of the crappiest apartment buildings in town probably shouldn't turn down an offer for help. Especially as nice as she'd always been to these people.

"The good thing about working in sales is you don't have any discipline issues and you are the one in control of your income. If you hit your sales goals, you get bonuses. And you don't have to deal with any kids."

Janiece didn't even turn around to answer her. "I love children, so I expect to be very satisfied with my career choice."

Nancy couldn't think of anything else to say. There was a reason she'd never tried to make friends with these people. Janiece was rude and didn't show a bit of interest in Nancy's new job. She hadn't told her she had two of them now. She preferred to say she worked in sales, not cleaning.

"Well, I hope it goes well for you. I've gotta run. Lots to do today." She waited for Janiece to say something back.

All the woman said was, "Bye!"

So Nancy left.

CHAPTER 64

Jonesy

It beat the hell out of his story about the new Chinese buffet that was coming to town.

Local Teen A Hero, Police Say

By Gilbert Jones
Loire Daily Register

Police are crediting a 13-year-old girl's bravery and quick thinking with possibly saving her mother's life.

Police responded to a report of multiple gunshots and screams at the Loire Mobile Home Park at about 5:45 p.m. Wednesday night, where they found the teen and her mother in the bedroom of No. 7 Cardinal Court, the home of Darren Lewis, 52, who had been shot twice. Coroner Robert Hutchinson declared Lewis dead at the scene.

"The young lady had come to the residence to get her mother and heard sounds of an attack underway," said Loire Police Chief Timothy Sanders. "She ran home and retrieved her

mother's .38 caliber handgun and shot the man as he was in the act of sexually assaulting her mother."

The names of the mother and daughter are being withheld. The Loire Daily Register has a policy against naming rape victims and minors.

Hutchinson said the victim was bound to the bed and there were clear signs of a sexual assault.

The victim did not have a valid FOI card, but Sanders said under the circumstances there were no plans to charge her. The handgun had belonged to her father, who is deceased.

Lewis had recently been arrested for a DUI after a minor accident just outside his home and was convicted of another DUI in 1998. He had no other police record.

That had been the first story he wrote, but he was working on a follow-up piece. The mother had agreed to be interviewed, and he still hoped to talk to the daughter. There was a good story there, and it would touch on a lot of big themes — poverty, single motherhood, sexual abuse. It was going to be a good one.

This was why he had become a reporter.

CHAPTER 65

Angel

Well, what was she supposed to do? Admit the truth?

It wouldn't bring Darren back. It would just shame her. And she'd get in trouble for having her dad's old gun. They might have charged Maya with murder, even. Everybody was quick to blame Darren, so she went along with it. She liked to think he would have understood.

The reporter who had lived down the street had not interviewed her for the first story, but he'd talked to her afterward and said he wanted to do a much longer story.

She liked that idea. She told him about all the struggles she and Maya had gone through. He said it was very possible the newspaper would set up a fund to collect donations for them, so she decided to go ahead and reveal to him that she was having Darren's baby. She was just betting that would bring in more donations. Who wouldn't feel sorry for her then?

God was in control. Maya had told her that

when she'd picked up the gun, she had asked Him for help. So this was all a part of God's plan.

It was also proof that sex before marriage was wrong. Except with Jeff, every single time she'd had sex, somebody had died. So while this was all in God's plan, it was also a sign of her sin. She could see that now. But she'd only been trying to get a stepfather for Maya, and she knew God understood that. She was just being a good mother.

The cops had made a big deal of Maya, but she couldn't stand to look at her. When the cops had asked if there was somebody they could call to look after her daughter while they took her to the hospital to be checked out, she'd given them Jeff's number. Let him be a father for once. It was time for him to live up to his responsibilities.

When they did the exam in the ER, they figured out right away that she was pregnant, and she pretended to be surprised. They called in a different doctor who said she was about four months along. They'd all been very sympathetic, and then they'd actually asked her if she wanted to continue the pregnancy! She told them if God wanted this baby to be born, it would be, and it wasn't up to any of them. That had shut them up.

Then they asked her about prenatal care and she told them she didn't think she could afford any, so they'd brought down a lady who had set everything up. Now she didn't need to worry about all that. She owned Darren's car now.

It was lucky he'd already put the title in her name before he died, because she couldn't imagine how she'd ever be able to afford a car otherwise. Now she could drive to her first prenatal appointment next week.

Plus, her mom was being nicer to her than she had been in years. She said she should come back home for a while, and hadn't said a word about Angel getting a job.

Except for Darren being dead, everything really had worked out for the best.

CHAPTER 66

Jonesy

Jonesy had convinced Angel, who had a hell of a story to tell, to let him do a full interview. She was going to allow him to interview her daughter, too. It was likely to be the best story he'd ever written. It might even get him some much-needed professional attention.

That would be good, because he hadn't figured out how to get out of the morass that was *The Happy Place*.

Lori had some great ideas, and when he went to her place to make dinner with her, they had discussed the themes in the book.

It was a stroke of luck, meeting Lori. She hated smoking, as it turns out, so he decided not to bring up the fact that he had only just quit. He let her assume he'd quit ages ago, as just about every other middle- or upper-class ex-smoker had.

He was not middle class, of course, but he was doing a passable imitation of it. She'd seen his place and its empty living room and he had merely said his old set hadn't fit in and he was looking for the right pieces to go with the room. He didn't admit he was still saving up for them.

She was fortunately very impressed by his hundreds of books. The quality of his personal library had finally gotten him laid.

All in all, he felt like he was living a completely different life now. He looked better. He no longer lived in gloomy surroundings. He was eating better. He had met someone who seemed to like both talking to him and having sex with him, and he wasn't sure which he was enjoying more.

The positivists, as he thought of them, would have told him it had all been in his power to improve his life all along, but he wasn't so sure. There are so many forces in the world. In a different era, with the exact personality and talents he had now, he would have made a decent living as a journalist. He might have married and had kids.

There are infinite choices everyone makes, every day. Nobody gets to go back and see how things would have worked out if they'd made different ones. Even if things turn out to be a disaster, you don't know if they might have been an even bigger disaster if you'd done something else.

He envied Lori her faith; even as a history teacher, she still believed a better world was possible. He remembered when he'd felt that way. But as a journalist; he'd lost his faith in people and everything else a long time ago.

"The system wasn't really designed for people like you and me," Lori said, as she chopped an onion. "It works great for people who really want to make a lot of money. It doesn't work for people who are motivated by other things. I can tell you," she said with a laugh, "I didn't choose teaching for the money."

He laughed, too, but for a different reason. She seemed to assume they were more or less in the same financial boat. He didn't want to admit how close he was to sinking.

"Aren't you worried about turning the masses into lazy freeloaders living off breadlines?" He picked up a baguette and pointed at her with it. The bread and the bottle of wine had been his contribution to tonight's dinner. It was more than he'd usually spend on dinner, but he reasoned that he could tap what would have been his smoking fund.

"Not at all. Lots of people work hard without being paid all the time. My mother worked her tail off raising six kids and keeping a big garden. Mom was even less motivated by money than I am." She tipped the chopped onion into a skillet shimmering with hot olive oil and began stirring.

He suspected she'd never known anybody living in real poverty before, except maybe for him. He loved the idea of a system in which everybody worked hard for all the right reasons;

it was how he'd always operated.

But he knew the world would always have to contend with people like Angel. So he said nothing. The water in the stock pot had started to boil, so he added a sheaf of pasta, then busied himself poking at it with a fork until all the pieces were submerged.

"I don't have the answer," he finally said.

"Sometimes I think we will eventually need to have some kind of revolution."

He briefly thought about asking her if she'd read Camus, but then he decided to let her keep her faith — and to preserve his chance of being invited to spend the night. So instead, he picked up the white dish towel lying on the counter and waved it at her. "Vive la France!"

They smiled across the kitchen island that held her cooktop. Her apartment was bigger and no doubt more expensive than his. She had an extra bedroom she used as an office and an absolutely stunning fireplace in her living room that he coveted.

They'd built a fire in it the night before, and had had sex right there in front of it. He'd always wanted to do that, although he figured out pretty quickly that doing it on a rug by the hearth made a better fantasy than reality. Sex on a mattress is a lot more comfortable.

She finished making the pasta sauce while the spaghetti boiled, and he sliced the bread and poured the wine. He reminded himself to use his very best table manners; she talked a good poverty game, but the tablecloth, candles and nice tableware told him her idea of poor and his were two very different things.

He guided the conversation back to *The Happy Place*.

"I don't think Aurelie is dead," Lori said. "I think she moved to get away from her abusive boyfriend. Killian Pike has been blowing all his time worrying about other people when he should have just gotten on with his life."

She tested and drained the pasta, poured it into a serving bowl and carried it to the table. He carried everything else. Personally, he'd have poured the sauce into the stock pot full of drained pasta and simply filled the plates at the stove, but that was not her style. "Your message should be to stop living in the past. He's been obsessing for no reason, and he should move on."

The way she said it made him think for a moment that she was hinting about his own life, but she couldn't yet know how stuck he was. He looked at her face, and was relieved to see that she really was talking about his character, not him.

"So if you could have a memory optimized, what would you pick?"

She sat down and took a sip of her wine before she answered.

"Wouldn't that mean you'd given up on life? That you thought there was nothing better coming? I think that would be really sad."

He'd been hoping she would say she would choose her memory of their lovemaking in front of the fire. Maybe he needed to up his game.

CHAPTER 67

Jimmy

His wife thought she was right again.

A month ago, she had helped him make a list of potential employers. "Don't just apply for jobs that are advertised. Get on everybody's radar." So he had. The letter from Nathan was impressive as hell, and Andy Carls had come through with a glowing recommendation, too.

He already had two interviews set up. There was an excellent chance he'd have a job lined up by the time he graduated, and it wasn't going to be at LCM. He hated to think where they'd have been if his wife hadn't nudged him into calling his advisor when he did. He'd still be working on the factory floor, pissed that he couldn't afford to finish school.

"As soon as we know where we're moving, I'll get the girls enrolled and I'll get myself enrolled, and we'll be on our way. See, I told you it would all work out."

"I give all the credit to Nathan's shenanigans

with Kaitlin," he joked. "If that man hadn't been at the wrong place at the wrong time ...."

"It wouldn't have mattered. That's not how you got the internship."

He raised his eyebrows and looked at her in a pointed way. "But that's how I got the *second* internship."

"You might as well say it was because Darren had a drug problem."

He shook his head. "That's a sad situation all around. That poor little girl. I hope she's going to be OK."

"I'm glad we got the hell out of there."

He knew she would have said "heck" if the girls were awake, but they were sleeping peacefully in their room. Now that they had their own beds, bedtime was easier. Everything was easier.

"You know how it seemed like we just could not catch a break? Everything was going against us, no matter how we tried?"

"I'm aware," she said flatly.

"But now, it seems like everything is working out. It's not because we weren't trying and now we are. It all just happened one way, and now it's all just happening another way. Most of it was out of our hands."

"Not all of it. We kept trying. We watched for opportunities." She took his hands and looked intently into his eyes. "We made this happen. You and me."

He didn't argue with her. This was something his wife needed to believe or she couldn't be happy.

But for once, he thought, she was wrong.

CHAPTER 68

Jonesy

He felt like a million bucks.

After an early morning interview with Angel, Jonesy strode into the office smiling. The interview had gone great. He had the story half written in his mind already, and it was going to be good. He could feel it.

"Jonesy." It was Carl, and he was standing by Jonesy's desk. He did not look happy.

"Carl, I know I owe you two tweets and a video, but you're gonna forgive me when you see what I'm bringing back."

"Dani is in the conference room waiting for us."

Jonesy groaned and looked around, and then dropped his voice. "God, not her, not today." He rolled his eyes. "Well, let's get it over with." He felt more contempt for Dani than almost anybody else he'd ever met, and he'd interviewed two serial killers.

She was sitting in what was usually Carl's

seat at the end of the table, looking like a kid playing grown up with her bouncy little brown ponytail and bangs and little-girl-size business suit. "Good morning, Gilbert. I've been waiting here for a while. I expected to see you here at 8."

"Appointments are always a good idea, Dani. I'm a reporter. I'm often out reporting. What brings you to Loire today?"

"We're laying you off."

That took the wind out of him.

"You're laying me off. You. *You* are laying *me* off?" All the contempt he'd bitten back for the last few years came oozing out, thick and bitter.

She slid a packet across the table and began explaining the unemployment process.

"Skip it, Dani. I'm a professional. I've been reporting since you were in grade school. You? You're not qualified to talk to me. You are ignorant, unintelligent, empty-headed, unsophisticated, simple-minded, unread, unworldly, untrained, unqualified, bumbling, bungling and unprofessional." He paused. "Did I mention incompetent? That should have been the first one."

She wasn't looking so perky now. Her face was red and she had at last lost that self-satisfied little smirk he hated. "Are you done, Gilbert?"

"I'm not sure." He turned to Carl. "Did I leave out unfit?"

"You did." Carl hadn't lost his composure at all. He sat back looking like a man who could use a bag of popcorn.

Jonesy turned to Dani again and pointed his finger toward her. "Unfit."

And then he wheeled around and walked straight to his desk. He dumped an overflowing box of used-up reporters notebooks onto the floor, where they made a small blue and white pile, and began tossing in his personal belongings. His copy of the AP Stylebook. His Strunk and White. His grammar books. His collection of thank-you notes and cards from people both famous and unknown. His most recent Illinois Press Association awards plaques. An old pica pole and proportion wheel that he kept for sentimental reasons.

"Security is on its way to walk you out," Dani said.

He ignored her, but in response he picked up a folder that contained every newsroom password and dropped it into the box. Carl was a solid journalist but as disorganized as a toddler and anytime he needed a password, he'd ask Jonesy. Jonesy was the unofficial keeper of all the usernames and passwords they needed to sign into all the hundreds of websites the paper depended on.

Without that folder, good luck figuring out how to access the horoscope or advice column, the online courthouse records, the wire services or countless other things. If Dani hadn't been such a bitch, he'd have left the folder behind.

He picked up the box and walked right by her as if she were a ghost. She was dead to him.

"Carl, it's been a pleasure," he said as he walked by him.

"Likewise." Then, in a lower voice, "I'll be in touch."

Carl had called him later — after Dani left, of course — and told him the company had also laid off the obit clerk, the sports editor and the woman who had been their last remaining photographer. Everyone older than 40 was gone now, except Carl.

"I'll be me next time," Carl said.

"I hope you practice your speech ahead of time. She took me by surprise. I've thought of a lot more adjectives now. I should have been better prepared."

That night, Lori said maybe it was for the best. "You work such weird hours. Haven't you ever thought about teaching? The money's crap, but the hours are better."

"What's the current pay for subs?"

"I think like only $125 a day. I know, not a lot. But if you like it, there are ways to pick up your teaching certificate and then you'd stand a good chance of getting hired."

She couldn't know it, but that pay didn't sound half bad to him. Of course, it wasn't a long-term fix, because substitutes didn't get paid for summers and school holidays the way regular teachers did. But she was right, it was a good way to try it out and maybe get his foot in the door.

"I'll call the district tomorrow. Thanks."

And then, without him knowing he was going to do it, he started crying in the way older men who had never cried before cry at their father's funeral. It was a harsh, dry cry. His body did not know how to do it.

He cried because he knew he would never work for another newspaper. He would never win that Pulitzer, never work for the *New York Times,* never uncover a Watergate. He wasn't even going to get to write the story about Angel and Darren. He'd given journalism his life and his soul and in return, journalism had unceremoniously sent an incompetent bitch-child to tell him his life and soul were no longer wanted.

Lori put her arms around him. "I'm sorry. I can see you loved it. I'm so sorry. You have to let it go." She comforted him as if he'd lost the love of his life.

He had.

CHAPTER 69

Shirley

She'd been reading the paper every day, and still, there wasn't a word about Charles Darby being arrested for arson, even though she'd told Jonesy she was sure Charles had done it.

Finally, she came right out and asked Linda. They were sitting on Shirley's patio furniture on Tommy's porch while the kids were at work.

"Do you think your ex burned down the bowling alley?"

Linda had stopped smoking two decades ago, but now she reached for Shirley's pack of Winstons and helped herself to a smoke.

"I know he did." She drew in a tentative lungful and coughed.

"How do you know that?"

"Well, technically I don't. We don't exactly have a cordial relationship these days. But you saw what that building looked like. He hadn't kept it up. It needed a lot of work. I doubt he could have gotten much if he sold it, so he burned it down for the insurance money, same as he did that apartment building. I've been keeping that secret for 17 years."

Shirley leaned forward in her seat. "Really?"

"He never keeps anything up. The apartment building had gone to pot. The tenants were all assholes and felons he wanted to evict, and we didn't have as much money as I thought we did. "

Shirley made a gruff little noise in her throat that could almost pass for a laugh. "I know that one."

"Well, in his case, it's because he's an alcoholic and a compulsive gambler. I couldn't keep him off the damned riverboat. And when he runs out of money, he either sells something or burns something."

Linda and her cigarette were two old friends, reunited. She smoked as casually as if she had last lit up only half an hour ago. Shirley realized Linda had always been one to talk with her hands, and the cigarette helped. She wielded it like a conductor's baton. How had Linda ever managed to communicate without a cigarette?

"It's not so easy to evict tenants, but if you have a safety hazard, that's different. So he invented a safety hazard. He pretended he was working on the empty unit and caused a bunch of power outages to the place. That was convincing enough to force them all out of there. He rewired some of it with old aluminum wiring that he knew was the wrong kind. The smartest thing he did was get a written estimate from a real electrician on the cost of rewiring the whole building. This was in the winter. Then he set up a space heater in one of the rooms with the new bad wiring and cranked it up. And then he waited for the inevitable, which took a couple days, but sure enough, the thing burned."

Linda finished her cigarette and immediately helped herself to another one. She probably needed it to tell her story. "It was genius that he had the electrician out there right before to establish the wiring was known to be bad. All very convincing, yes?"

Shirley wanted to ask if she'd been in on it, but asking would be rude, so she just nodded her head slowly and waited for Linda to keep talking.

"I didn't know it at the time. I was suspicious because the timing was too good. It saved our tushies financially. But Charles was drinking so much the last few years we were married. One night he couldn't resist telling me he could get away with anything he wanted to, and he confessed the whole thing. I took it as a threat. The next day he didn't remember telling me anything, but I knew it was time to get out. You'll never convince me that bowling alley just burnt itself down."

After Linda left, Shirley called the paper and asked for Jonesy. Now he'd have to do the story. But the girl who answered said he was no longer with the paper and asked if she wanted to talk to anyone else.

"Never mind," Shirley said, and hung up.

CHAPTER 70

Jonesy

Jonesy was done trying to force *The Happy Place* to make sense. It was a mess: part dystopian nightmare, part crime thriller, part political commentary. When elements of a love story started creeping in, it was just too much.

Anyway, he had a better idea. Unemployment gave him a little bit of a breather, so he spent just about every waking moment at the computer in his bedroom, and in three weeks he'd cranked out the first draft of a roman à clef he tentatively called *Night Falls in the Trailer Park* under the pen name Killian Pike.

He invented a small trailer park and gave it a cast of interesting characters, all much more colorful and criminal than his former neighbors. They included a prostitute, a meth dealer, an opioid addict and an arsonist.

He took what he'd learned about the probable arson of the bowling alley and made it about a bar. The story of Angel and Darren turned into a tale of a prostitute being abused by her strung-out pimp, who owned the bar where she worked. He included the shooting, but in his version, the shooter was the meth dealer and he shot several people at once in a drug-fueled rage.

About half of his characters did not survive the book and those who did went on to live new but still broken lives in other places.

There was no underlying message in the new book. It didn't try to explain human behavior. It did supply fast action, some gratuitous sex and a car chase. It had been much more fun to write than *The Happy Place.*

Finishing the book helped make up for his disappointment that he never got to write the story of Angel and Darren.

One minor character came out of *Night Falls in the Trailer Park* alive and better off — a handsome science fiction novelist named Burt Jonas who went on to write a bestselling novel called *The Happy Place*.

Burt Jonas' book was much like Gilbert Jones' original concept for the novel; Jonesy found it was much easier to describe that plot than to actually write it. His favorite novelist, Kurt Vonnegut, had pulled a similar stunt, Jonesy thought, so why shouldn't he?

Vonnegut's literary alter ego was a writer named Kilgore Trout. Any time a novel idea struck Vonnegut's fancy but he didn't want to go to the trouble of writing the whole book, he'd simply describe the plot and attribute the book to Trout. Jonesy thought that a neat trick. Thus, Killian Pike.

He wondered if anybody would notice what he'd done.

He sent the manuscript off to a dozen agents and hoped for the best. Then he called the school district and applied to become a substitute teacher.

Now he waited to see what would happen.

He was doing everything he could. From here, it mostly wasn't up to him and he knew it. Either some luck would come his way to activate his hard work or it wouldn't.

He'd be damned if he was going to blame himself for all the things that were out of his control.

Believing you're the master of your own fate is validating for the wealthy but demoralizing for the poor.

EPILOGUE

Michelle

The book had not turned out as it had in her head.

She had tried to make some points about how society was much less of a meritocracy than people thought. She had hoped to illustrate that people are poor for all kinds of reasons, and not all of them have to do with factors within individual control.

She wanted to talk about income inequality, about the lies we tell the masses to get them to work harder, and maybe even make some points about racial injustice. She did that by making the black couple among the most sympathetic characters in the book, while hoping that nobody would think her black characters were tokens. How could she, a white woman, write authoritatively about the black experience?

She couldn't, obviously. The black couple weren't affected by blatant racism so much as simple working class issues. Some of the couple's struggles had been very similar to her own, and she was white as hell.

Halfway through the book, she realized that a lot of the characters were just based on parts of her own past. Then she nearly deleted that sentence for fear someone might think she'd been a stripper or lived on welfare. She had done neither. Not that there was any judgment for those who had.

Also, she had never drawn disability or played in a band. She had, however, grown up in a trailer and worked at a newspaper, and Jonesy's struggles at his newspaper were very much like her own.

She feared she had not even made her central point, which was that the world is full of rules. Some of them were written down. The Golden Rule. The Ten Commandments. The Society of Professional Journalists Code of Ethics.

Others were not written down, but everyone knew them and they were stringently enforced. Still others existed and were followed but were seldom recognized.

Unwritten rules can outrank the written rules. Think of all the men who lost their positions for raping or sexually harrassing women. It had always been illegal to rape, but it was OK for wealthy and powerful men, if they chose the right victims and raped them in the right way.

The unwritten rule was that if the victim

needed something from you, like a job or a movie role, you could do what you wanted as long as you arranged a plausible suggestion of reciprocity. Then that unwritten rule changed rather suddenly and caught lots of rapists with their pants down. (Sometimes literally.)

Sometimes things come up and it's hard to determine the correct behavior. Should you follow the letter of the law? The spirit of the law? An unwritten law? The most expedient thing? Your professional ethics? The commandments of your religion?

You very often must choose, because different rules systems sometimes dictate widely different actions. That is why two fairly decent people who mean well can take actions they both believe to be right and harshly judge the other's actions. It's as if one of them is following the rules from Monopoly and the other Risk, but neither understands they're playing different games.

In the end, she decided to steal two of Kurt Vonnegut's ideas. She wrote herself into the end of the book and turned one of her characters into a sci-fi author. If it was good enough for Vonnegut, it was good enough for her.

One of Vonnegut's genius moves was to invent a guy named Kilgore Trout who performed the useful chore of writing sci-fi stories. By attributing the ideas to Kilgore Trout, Vonnegut was able to describe the barebones outline of interesting plots without the tedium of writing the entire book, and Michelle decided to outright steal this plot device.

It amused her, after naming a character Killian Pike as an homage to Kilgore Trout, to learn that renowned science fiction writer Philip Jose Farmer had written a book called *Venus on the Half-Shell* that he pretended was written by Kilgore Trout.

Reportedly (meaning according to Wikipedia) he did this with Vonnegut's permission, but Vonnegut later regretted giving it.

Michelle actually met Farmer once at some event in a hotel ballroom, while she was working as a newspaper society editor. She'd never heard of him at the time, and all she can remember about him now was how uncooperative he was when she was trying to take his photo.

She was well aware that including this epilogue broke a number of literary rules, but decided it would also help clarify what the book was supposed to do.

And anyway, if Vonnegut and Charlie Kaufman (and Gilbert Jones) can get away with such shenanigans, why shouldn't she?

Literary rules are made to be broken.

ABOUT THE AUTHOR

Michelle Teheux

Former newspaper editor Michelle Teheux is a writer on Medium.com and publishes a newsletter on Substack.com about income inequality called Untrickled. She has two children and two grandchildren. She and her husband, Harrie, live in a small town not unlike Loire, Ill.

Printed in Great Britain
by Amazon

43598865R00214